Nancy
Marble
Rm. 418

Harlequin Presents...

Other titles by

ANNE MATHER
IN HARLEQUIN PRESENTS

ANNE MATHER

valley deep, mountain high

Harlequin Books

TORONTO • LONDON • NEW YORK • AMSTERDAM • SYDNEY • WINNIPEG

Harlequin Presents edition published January, 1977
ISBN 0-373-70673-1

Original hardcover edition published in 1976
by Mills & Boon Limited

Printed in U.S.A.

CHAPTER ONE

ANDREA CONNOLLY stood at the sitting-room window of the hotel suite staring out without pleasure. She saw nothing appealing in the gaily painted hotels and restaurants that thronged the main street of Grossfeld, or in the snow-clad slopes that stretched high above the roofs of the little town, dwarfing it by their magnificence. She had seen it all before. This was not her first visit to Austria, and the reason she was here now brought a mutinous crease of anger between her wide set green eyes. That her father should have done this, packed her off like an unwanted baggage, just because he did not approve of her friends! For once she wished she had a mother to appeal to.

Her lips pursed rebelliously. What did he hope to achieve by sending her here? How was he to know she would not make equally unsuitable acquaintances at this well-known skiing resort? He didn't, of course. But he had sent Janet along to keep an eye on her, and no doubt she would deter the most ardent suitor.

Glancing round at her cousin supervising the luggage, Andrea felt a fleeting sense of shame. That wasn't fair. Janet was a nice girl, an attractive girl; it wasn't her fault that she had no dress sense or that Aunt Lavinia should resent her husband's brother's success to the extent that she was continually finding reasons to find fault with Andrea's way of living. One could almost say that Lavinia was responsible for Andrea being in Grossfeld at this moment, and a less charitable person might find Lavinia's reasons for having her own daughter accompany such a supposedly irresponsible member of society rather strange.

But Patrick Connolly, Andrea's father, did not look for ulterior motives, not when Andrea herself admitted that she was having second thoughts about her university entrance next year. He put it all down to the group of young people she was running around with, a mixture of students, artists and drop-outs from society, to whom money was a dirty word.

His sister-in-law was only too eager to agree with him. For a long time she had disliked Andrea and the opportunities which had come her way so easily, when her own daughter, Janet, had had to struggle to reach 'O' level status. Patrick would have paid for Janet to have the same kind of education that his own daughter had had, but his brother, Joe, wouldn't have it. Consequently, Lavinia had had to divert her ambitions in other directions. The girls were eighteen now, and although Janet had left school and seemed to be enjoying her work in a travel agency, Andrea, having gained three 'A' levels, was awaiting entrance to university. This had infuriated Lavinia, Andrea knew, but her father didn't see it that way. So far as he was concerned, Lavinia was his brother's wife and therefore could only have the best interests of the family at heart.

Now Andrea heard the door close and turned to face her cousin. They were not at all alike. Janet was of medium height, inclined to plumpness like her mother, with the dark eyes of her Celtic ancestry. Her hair was mid-brown, but she had blonde streaks put into it, and it had a natural curl which was attractive.

Andrea on the other hand had an almost Latin darkness, apart from the brilliant green eyes. She was tall, too, remarkably slender considering the amount of food she could put away, with very straight dark hair which her father said affectionately looked like rats' tails. In fact, her hair was one of the most attractive things about her, and the sheen on it owed nothing to artifice. In addition to which Andrea almost always dressed in jeans and shirts, much to her father's disgust, whereas Janet, influenced by her mother, chose the most unsuitable full skirts and fussy blouses. Andrea longed to see her cousin in well-cut pants and masculine plain shirts, and she had long wished to extricate her from her mother's suppressive influence. Perhaps this was the opportunity. It might provide a diversion in this dull place.

Janet was opening the bedroom doors, exploring the rooms which were to be their home for the next four weeks.

'Which bedroom do you want, Andrea?' she asked, in her cultivated little-girl voice. 'They're both super!'

Andrea threw off the sheepskin coat she had been wearing, and lounged into one of the striped satin armchairs, one denim-clad leg draped carelessly over the arm. 'You choose,' she replied, without enthusiasm. 'I don't care, so long as it has a bed.'

'Oh, Andrea!' Janet giggled, and went into one of the rooms. She emerged a few moments later, her eyes wide. 'I say, we each have our own bathroom. Isn't that marvellous! I mean – two bathrooms for two of us!'

'We can hardly both use the same bathroom at the same time,' remarked Andrea dryly, and then felt a twinge of selfishness as Janet's face drooped. Just because she hadn't wanted to come here it did not mean she had to make it miserable for Janet as well. And after all, Janet was used to a house with only one bathroom. Forcing a mocking grimace of self-derision, she added: 'Besides, I don't think your mama would approve of you using the same bathroom as me. You might become contaminated by my reckless character!'

'Oh, Andrea!'

Janet said these words a lot, and Andrea hoped they would not always jar on her as they did at this moment. She flicked back her cuff and consulted the masculine watch on her slim wrist.

'Well, it's one o'clock. What say we go and find some lunch before tackling the cases?'

Janet nodded excitedly. 'Oh, yes, let's. I'm dying to see some more of the hotel. It's a super place, isn't it?'

Andrea was about to say: 'It's all right' when her conscience stopped her. 'Super,' she agreed goodhumouredly, getting to her feet with a lazy grace that accompanied everything she did. 'Come on.'

The Hotel Kützbuhl was really a very comfortable hostelry, with every modern convenience for its guests' enjoyment, including a sauna and indoor swimming pool in the basement. The public rooms were on the ground floor – a large lounge overlooking the ski slopes at the back of the hotel; two bars, one of which was large enough to accommodate the *après-ski* entertainment for which the hotel was famous; and a well-lit restaurant that faced the busy street outside.

Andrea accepted it all with the ease born of long use, but Janet kept emitting little gasps of excitement at each new discovery, and even Andrea was touched by her enthusiasm.

'You're going to have a marvellous time,' she assured her, across their table in the wide window bay of the restaurant,

The restaurant was not crowded at this time of day, lots of the guests spending the whole day out on the ski-slopes.

Janet, sampling *Schnitzel* for the first time, looked up at her cousin doubtfully. 'You're going to enjoy it, too, aren't you, Andrea? I mean, I know you've been skiing before, lots of times, but Uncle Pat said you'd never been to Grossfeld before.'

'I haven't,' admitted Andrea, holding up her glass and studying the pale wine within. 'But one ski resort is pretty much the same as another.'

'What do you mean?'

Andrea sighed, glancing round the restaurant thoughtfully. 'Well, let me see. The people are the same, for one thing.' She paused reflectively. 'There are only two kinds of people here, you know. Those who have money, and those who'd like to have it.'

'That's a very cynical thing to say.' Janet was shocked. She, too, glanced surreptitiously round the room. 'They all look very nice people to me.'

'Oh, they will be, to you.' Andrea's lips twisted.

'What does that mean?'

'Janet, I may not be any older than you are, but I have had a little more experience, I think. A girl alone in a place like Grossfeld is fair game for every fortune-hunter prowling the slopes from here to the Italian Alps. You'll see. Oh, there'll be nice young men with Daddy's money, of course,' she grimaced, 'but the really attractive men never have a cent and consequently you're aware that they're only dating you for *your* money.'

'Chance would be a fine thing,' remarked Janet wryly, and Andrea had to smile.

'You say that, Jan, but honestly, it's much better to know you're liked for yourelf. That's why I run around with the crowd I do back home. At least they're real people, not *papier-maché* facsimiles of each other.'

Janet wrinkled her nose. 'I don't believe that all the wealthy young men who come to Grossfeld are unattractive. They may not be hairy swingers, but at least they live ordinary decent lives.'

Andrea rubbed her nose. 'You sound exactly like Aunt Lavinia, do you know that?'

Janet flushed. 'Well, what's wrong with that?'

'Nothing, nothing.' Andrea spread her hands apologetically. Then she applied herself to the wine bottle. 'Will you have some more wine?'

Janet hesitated. 'I'm not used to drinking wine at lunchtime.'

'And Mummy wouldn't like it?' Andrea mocked her.

'I didn't say that.' Janet sniffed. 'All right, I'll have some more, thank you.'

As Andrea filled her cousin's glass her spasm of derision left her and she felt slightly ashamed. 'I'm sorry, Janet,' she said. 'I'm not very good company right at this moment. I'll improve – I promise.'

Janet sipped her wine. 'I don't understand you, Andrea, I don't honestly. You've got everything – looks, money, sex appeal! If I had any one of those three, I'd be happy.'

'Would you?' Andrea looked bored for a moment. Then: 'Oh, Jan, don't be a fool! You're a very attractive girl – or you would be if you wore the right clothes.'

'What's wrong with my clothes?'

'Surely you don't need me to tell you that!'

Janet's plump face turned pink. 'You're also very unkind, Andrea! I don't criticize the way you dress, so why should you pick on me?'

Andrea lay back in her seat. 'What can you say about my clothes? They're clean, and they're cheap. That's about all.'

'You look like – like one of those students you see on television, going in for sit-ins and that sort of thing.'

'So what? They cover me, don't they? I'm not indecent or anything, am I?'

'That depends. You wear your jeans very tight.'

'Oh, really?'

'In any case, I don't go in for that hippy kind of gear. I'm choosy about where I buy my things.'

'Where do you buy them? Oxfam?'

Janet's face was beetroot red. 'Andrea! Oh, you – you *cat*!'

With her handkerchief pressed to her lips, she got up from her chair and rushed across the room to the double doors just as a man and a woman were entering the restaurant. Janet collided with the man, and he brought his hands quickly up to her shoulders to prevent her from losing her balance altogether. He was a tall man, around six feet, Andrea estimated, with a lean muscular physique and silvery fair hair which brushed his collar at the back. Janet glanced up at him tearfully, mumbled an apology, and then fled over the hall and disappeared up the stairs.

Andrea had watched this little tableau with an irritating renewal of the guilt she had experienced earlier. It wasn't fair to make her cousin the scapegoat for her father's misdoings, but Janet was so pathetically easy to hurt.

The man and woman who had entered the restaurant at Janet's moment of departure were moving across to a secluded table set in one corner of the room, and Andrea's eyes followed them almost absently. She was thinking that the woman was several years older than her escort, when the man turned and looked her way and their eyes met. It was a shattering experience for Andrea, particularly as those cool grey eyes conveyed in no uncertain terms that their owner knew she was responsible for the other girl's distress.

Andrea dragged her gaze away and stared down mutinously at the food on her plate. The veal had gone cold and was congealing unappetizingly on her plate. But, she decided, she would not give *him* or Janet the satisfaction of knowing they had upset her. With a determination her father would have admired, she forced herself to clear the plate, and when the waiter came to ask whether she wanted a dessert, she ordered fruit and honey-filled pastries and managed to eat two of them. Black coffee completed the meal, and it was fully half an hour later before she pushed back her chair and left the restaurant. Even so, she felt sure those cool grey eyes followed her progress between the tables, and curiosity made her glance backward over her shoulder. The man appeared to be deep in conversation with his companion and didn't even look up. Andrea tightened her lips and went out into the hall.

'*Andrea!*'

The eager greeting in some part soothed her ruffled composure. She turned slowly to confront the girl who, together with a group of young men and girls, had just entered the hotel. Dressed in parkas, vorlagers and woolly hats, they had obviously just come off the ski-slopes, and their faces gleamed with good health. Most of the male eyes turned in Andrea's direction, and she could sense the kindling of their interest. But this was nothing new to her. She was not a vain girl, but it would have been impossible for her to live eighteen years without becoming aware of the effect she had on the opposite sex.

'Hello, Susie,' she responded, to the girl who had first spoken, and they all crowded around.

'What are you doing here?' continued the girl called Susie. 'I thought you didn't dig these places.'

There were several sarcastic comments at Susie's rather unnecessary question, but ignoring them, Andrea replied: 'I'm here with my cousin. She's never been skiing before.'

'Oh,' Susie nodded. 'Did you just arrive?'

'A couple of hours ago. How about you?'

'Oh, I came with Mummy and Daddy and met up with the gang,' replied Susie with a grin.

'Are you staying long, Andrea?' This question came from a young man standing near her, a dark-haired handsome youth with amorous brown eyes.

Andrea smiled. 'We're here for a month,' she told him, and he looked considerably pleased with himself.

'Where's your cousin?' Susie was asking now. 'Do I know her?'

'I don't think so.' Andrea shook her head. She and Susie had been at boarding school together. 'And she's upstairs right now. I expect you'll meet her later.'

'And will we meet you later?' asked the dark-haired boy, and a girl standing beside him nudged him in the ribs with her elbow.

'Mind your own business, Roy,' she muttered angrily. 'You'll not be here later. You promised to take me to the *Mühlrad*, remember?'

Andrea looked away from Roy's unmistakably inviting expression and Susie said: 'Let me introduce the gang . . .' She reeled off a string of names, but the only one Andrea really registered was Roy Stevens.

'I'd better go,' she said, when she began to be aware that the girls in the group were not half so friendly as their escorts. 'Janet will be wondering where I am.'

'Janet?' Susie frowned. 'Oh, is that your cousin?' Andrea nodded, and Susie added: 'Well, most of us will be in the Tyrolean Bar later. We'll probably meet up again.'

'Probably,' agreed Andrea, and with an apologetic smile, excused herself.

Janet was not in the sitting-room when she entered the suite and, sighing, she crossed the soft apricot carpet to open the first bedroom door. Her cousin was lying on her back on the bed, and her eyes were puffy from weeping.

Andrea leaned against the door jamb and regarded her resignedly. 'Honestly, Jan, can't you take a joke?'

'It wasn't a joke!' retorted Janet at once. 'You meant it, you know you did. Oh, I wish I'd never come on this holiday!'

'No, you don't.' Andrea straightened and walked into the room her thumbs looped into the low belt of her jeans. 'All right, I'm sorry. I apologize. I didn't mean to hurt you.'

'Yes, you did.'

Janet was not to be so easily placated, and on impulse Andrea sat down on the side of the other girl's bed and regarded her appealingly. 'Jan, listen to me! All right, maybe I was – unkind. But I meant well.' She paused. 'Your clothes are dated! No, please – listen,' this as Janet uttered a fresh sob. 'I just want you to realize your potential, that's all. In the right clothes, with the right make-up, you could be quite something, believe me!'

Janet looked suspiciously at her. 'You're poking fun at me again.'

'No, I'm not.' Andrea stood up. 'Look, how about going shopping this afternoon? Daddy's given me more money than I'll ever need for this holiday, and there are usually some excellent stores in these resorts.'

Janet sniffed and propped herself up on her elbows. 'What would we be shopping for?'

Andrea sighed. 'What would you like?'

'Me?'

'Yes, you!' Andrea swung away from the bed and walked towards the windows. 'I'll treat you to a new wardrobe.'

Janet gasped. 'You can't do that!'

'Why not?' Andrea glanced back at her. 'I can afford it.' Her tone was laconic. 'I might even enjoy it.'

Janet sat upright now, her tears disappearing altogether. 'But – Mummy – Daddy wouldn't like it.'

'Daddy won't know. At least, not until the holiday's over, and by then it'll be a bit late to object, won't it?'

Janet swung her feet to the floor. 'I don't know, Andrea . . .'

Andrea turned to face her. 'Let me see,' she mused, as if her cousin had not voiced any objections, 'some pants, and shirts, a couple of dresses for the evening. That should do to be going on with.'

'I can't wear trousers!' exclaimed Janet in dismay. 'At least, I have some *vorlagers* . . .'

'I know. I've seen them.' Andrea's tone conveyed her opinion of Janet's skiing clothes. Then she brightened. 'Anyway, you don't know what you can wear until you try.'

'But the suitcases . . .'

'We can unpack later. We'll have heaps of time. Right, are you ready?'

Janet got to her feet, feeling her hot eyelids. 'I must wash my face and try to disguise this.'

'I shouldn't worry overmuch,' Andrea replied consolingly. 'Everyone will think the cold air has burned them.' She walked to the door of the sitting-room. 'I'll wait in here.'

Outside the hotel, the air was indeed freezing, and Andrea snuggled her ears inside the fur collar of her sheepskin coat, her hands thrust deep into the pockets. Janet wore the tweed coat she had worn to travel in and its thickness did nothing for her ample figure. Nevertheless, she looked much brighter, and Andrea was relieved.

The busy main street of Grossfeld was thronged with cars and buses and horse-drawn vehicles. But somehow everyone seemed to get by in spite of the confusion. There was much shouting and laughter and honking of car horns, a thing which seemed peculiarly continental. Andrea pointed out the gaily painted inns with their overhanging eaves and balconies decorated with curly wrought iron; the coffee houses, whose windows were an insistent invitation to sample the delicious cakes and pastries they served; and the parish church of St. Michael, with its rococo scrollwork and a tower which dated from the sixteenth century.

'Are you sure you haven't been here before?' exclaimed Janet, when her cousin suggested they went into a store displaying all manner of sporting equipment in the window alongside lurex-threaded sweaters for *après-ski* wear.

Andrea smiled. 'As I told you, one ski resort is much like another. And these small towns were here long before the tourists discovered them.'

Stripped down to her slip, Janet looked ridiculously vulnerable, and Andrea felt that now familiar twinge of doubt as to the integrity of her motives. But a little while later, seeing her cousin emerge as she had known she could in slimming trousers and military style shirts, she felt she was

13

justified. Without fussy frills or thick materials which could add inches to her bust and hips, Janet looked well rounded, but not fat.

An apricot crêpe silk dress, which brushed Janet's ankles, gave her height, and a caftan made of some soft jersey material hinted at the contours beneath with only gentle emphasis. The sales assistant was most helpful, and most complimentary, although Andrea thought cynically as she wrote out the cheque that she could afford to be in the circumstances.

As they walked back to the hotel, each armed with boxes, Janet was chattering enthusiastically to her cousin. 'Mummy always said that I'd got too short legs for trousers, and that in any case, they weren't feminine.' She chuckled. 'But they are, aren't they? I never realized it before.'

'You're feminine,' returned Andrea dryly. 'Not the clothes you wear. And if you're feminine enough, you can wear the most masculine gear possible, and still look attractive.'

Janet nodded. 'Oh, but those dresses are dreamy! They quite make my hostess gowns look frumpy. Do you think I should wear one this evening?'

'I should hope so,' Andrea declared fervently, leading the way into the hotel, and then stopping short at the sight of a man leaning negligently against the reception desk talking to the girl on duty. It was the man from the restaurant, the man Janet had collided with on her way out, the man who had given Andrea such a cool, denigrating appraisal. In a dark brown corded jacket and pants which drew attention to the powerful muscles of his legs, he moved with a lean pantherlike grace, turning to rest his elbows on the desk, surveying them intently.

Janet, close behind Andrea when she entered the hotel, had drawn abreast, her mouth opening to question Andrea's sudden cessation of movement, when she too recognized the man by the reception desk. Her cheeks turned pink and she smiled, and Andrea, who would have gone on, was forced to witness the man straightening and affording Janet a slight bow. She guessed the gesture to be typically Germanic in origin, and when he moved a trifle reluctantly, she felt, towards them, and bowed again, her suspicions were confirmed.

'*Guten Tag, Fraülein. Wie geht es Ihnen?*'

He had addressed himself to Janet, and Andrea shifted impatiently, but her cousin was brimming with excitement at this unexpected encounter.

'I am afraid I do not understand,' Janet articulated carefully, speaking in a slightly louder voice than was necessary, as if he were deaf and not simply of another nationality.

'You are English, of course.' The man spoke their language with only a faint guttural accent. 'I should have guessed.'

Janet bloomed attractively. 'Well, it was very kind of you to remember.'

'*Bitte schön.* Not at all.' His smile was only faintly mocking, but it irritated Andrea. 'It is not every day that a beautiful young English girl throws herself into my arms.'

'Oh!' Janet giggled, obviously delighted. 'How gallant!'

He shook his head, looking at the parcels she was carrying. 'And now, may I help you with these, *nein*? You are — how do you say? — overladen?'

'We can manage, thanks.'

Andrea replied before Janet could accept his offer, and his eyes shifted to her face, still tanned from a holiday in Bermuda with her father in November. 'As you wish, *Fräulein*,' he said, his thin lips curling slightly. He bowed once more, this time to both of them. '*Auf Wiedersehen.*'

Casting a rather annoyed look at Andrea, Janet responded with: '*Auf Wiedersehen*,' and then, with great daring, she added: 'Are you staying at this hotel, Herr — Herr—?'

'Von Mahlstrom, *Fräulein*,' he told her politely, very stiff and correct suddenly. 'Baron Axel von Mahlstrom, at your service, *Fräulein. Und nein*, I am not staying at the hotel, I regret.'

Janet's lips formed the word *Baron*, but she didn't repeat it aloud. She merely managed a rather inane smile, and then hastened after Andrea who was waiting impatiently at the foot of the stairs.

As they went up together, Janet stared wide-eyed at her cousin. 'Did you hear that?' she demanded, in an awed tone. 'He's a baron, Andrea. A real live *baron*! Austrian, do you think?'

'Austrian, German — what's the difference?' Andrea was unimpressed. Extracting the key of their suite from the bag she wore over her shoulder, she opened the door and went in, switching on the lamps against the darkening gloom of the day. 'The title means nothing these days.'

'What do you mean?'

Janet came into the room after her, backed against the door to close it, and dropped her parcels on to the couch with evident relief. Andrea had already unloaded hers, and she flopped down into an armchair and sighed.

'Janet, do you remember what we were talking about earlier? About fortune-hunters?' she prompted.

Janet gasped. 'You're not suggesting that – that Baron von Mahlstrom is a fortune-hunter!'

Andrea shrugged. 'I'd say it was highly likely.'

'Why?'

'Oh, Jan, be your age! Didn't you see the way he was looking at us, assessing us, deciding which of us was worth cultivating?'

'Andrea, that's a dreadful thing to say!'

'As I said before, Jan, give me credit for having a little more experience.'

'But he was so nice – so friendly . . .'

'They always are. So attractive, too,' Andrea added dryly.

'Oh, yes!' Janet clasped her hands together, staring dreamily into space. 'He was gorgeous, wasn't he? The sort of man you never ever expect to meet. He reminded me of Steve McQueen, all sort of lean and craggy-looking.'

Andrea raised her eyes heavenward. 'Honestly, Jan, it's just as well your father isn't a wealthy man. You'd be fair game for every handsome Casanova who made a play for you.'

Janet unbuttoned her coat. 'So what! I'd have fun, too, wouldn't I?' She shrugged out of the heavy tweed garment. 'I mean, I wouldn't care if it was my money they were after, just so long as I got to be with them.'

'Oh, Janet! If Mummy could hear you now!' Andrea mocked.

Janet flushed. 'Well,' she said defensively, 'it's all right for you. You can joke on about these things, but I can't. This may be my only opportunity to meet a man like – like that.'

Andrea considered her cousin's petulant face thoughtfully, the stirring of an idea beginning to emerge in her mind. The memory of the Baron von Mahlstrom's sardonic face was strongly imprinted there and the possibility of thwarting any plans he might have and in so doing giving Janet a taste of the life she craved was a tantalizing temptation. Whether the Baron was staying at the hotel or not was unimportant. They had seen him here twice in one day, which meant that he was not an infrequent visitor. It was not beyond the realms of possibility that he actually worked at the hotel although she doubted Janet would believe such a thing.

Nevertheless, Janet was attracted to him, so why shouldn't she be given every opportunity to attract him? Andrea decided cynically that she was imagining herself as the fairy godmother who waved her magic wand and produced a prince for the serving girl, but she couldn't deny that there would be a certain satisfaction to be gained from watching the Baron make a fool of himself. Of course, he might not rise to the bait, and if he didn't there was no harm done. But if he did ... She chewed at her lower lip. Any sense of conscience she might be troubled with could be quickly dispersed by the knowledge that he was as guilty as she was. More so, in fact. And it might enliven what promised to be a terribly dull four weeks.

'Jan,' she said, getting up from her chair and unfastening her sheepskin coat. 'Jan, I've been thinking . . .'

'Yes?'

Janet's round face was suddenly expectant, and as suddenly Andrea couldn't go through with it. What a bitch she was, she thought, pretending she wanted to help Janet when all she really wanted to do was score against that arrogant so-and-so downstairs!

'Oh – er—' Now she sought desperately for something to say. 'I just thought – we might get up early in the morning, and go for a swim in the pool before breakfast.'

Janet's expression lost its animation. She bent to pick up one of the boxes which had fallen off the couch, and nodded. 'Well, all right, I'll come for a dip in the pool. But I don't swim, you know.'

'Don't you?' Andrea was surprised. Then she smiled. 'I'll teach you.'

'Will you?' Janet smiled in return. 'My father used to say that, but he didn't achieve his objective.'

Andrea shrugged, and picking up her cases walked

towards the opposite bedroom from that which Janet had already occupied. 'Well, I think I'll go and unpack and take a bath before dinner.'

Janet nodded. 'I'm going to hang these things up first, and then I'll do the same. Which dress should I wear, do you think? The apricot one or the caftan?'

Andrea paused. 'The caftan, I should think. Keep the silk dress for a special occasion?'

'What kind of special occasion?'

'Dinner with the Baron?' suggested Andrea mockingly, and Janet sighed ecstatically.

'Do you think he might ask me?'

Andrea hesitated, dreadfully tempted to relate her idea. But then she shook her head, and opened her bedroom door. 'How should I know?' she said. 'Stranger things have happened.'

CHAPTER TWO

ANDREA lay on her back in bed, her arms linked behind her head, staring at the ceiling. A dull light was filtering through the curtains she had drawn the night before, and a glance at her watch a little while ago had told her it was a few minutes after seven. There had been no sound as yet from Janet's room, but Andrea didn't find this surprising. They had been quite late to bed the night before, and this, combined with their journey from England, had tired the other girl out.

The evening had started quietly enough in the restaurant. But after dinner they had joined Susie Nichols and her crowd in the *après-ski* bar, and things had become progressively more hectic. Susie's friends were, in the main, a friendly crowd, and once the girls had assured themselves that Andrea was not interested in their boy-friends, they became very much friendlier. Janet fitted in quite well. As Andrea's cousin, she was accepted, and Andrea could see the other girl gaining in confidence. She was glad. For too long Aunt Lavinia had kept Janet very firmly under supervision.

The hotel had its own band of musicians, which Susie said were often supplemented by a group of folk singers and dancers who yodelled and taught the guests their kind of dancing. Andrea had experienced that kind of thing before, but it was all new to Janet, and she was having a marvellous time. Her mother did not approve of modern dances, but apart from an occasional waltz that was the only kind of dancing available, and in no time at all Janet was gyrating with the rest of them.

There was no sign of the attractive Baron this evening, Andrea had noticed with relief, although she had sensed that Janet was disappointed for the same reasons. Her cousin's eyes had darted revealingly round the bar when they had first entered, but eventually she had had to accept that this evening the Baron Axel von Mahlstrom had more important things to do.

In spite of protestations from the others, Andrea did not do a lot of dancing. Slim and indolently elegant in purple velvet pants and a matching wild silk shirt, she was quite content to sit and watch the dancing, curled in her corner by the huge log fire which occupied one end of the bar, sipping her own particular blend of vodka and fruit juice. In the smoky overheated atmosphere, it was impossible to believe that outside the temperature was well below zero, and if there was one thing about this holiday which Andrea was looking forward to, it was the prospect of getting out into that cold air and climbing high into the mountains.

The evening had proved uneventful until around eleven when the young man Susie had introduced as Roy Stevens, and his girl-friend, had returned from wherever they had been. They came into the bar searching for their friends, their faces glowing from the cold, making a beeline for the crackling logs of the fire.

Then Roy saw Andrea, and pushing past Susie and her boy-friend, Paul, he inched his way on to the wooden seat beside her. Ignoring the furious stare he was getting from the girl he had come in with, he put his arm along the back of Andrea's seat and turning successfully hid her from the others.

'Hi,' he said, and his face was very close to hers. 'Did you miss me?'

Andrea half smiled. 'Should I have done?'

'Of course. But you heard Ruth say that we were going to the *Mühlrad*, didn't you?'

'Ruth? That's your – girl-friend?'

'She's a girl, and she's a friend, yes,' he agreed wickedly. 'Are you my friend, Andrea?'

'I'm friendly with everyone.'

'That's not what I meant.'

Andrea wriggled round in her seat a little and glimpsed Ruth's angry face. 'Your – girl-friend won't like this.'

'Won't like what?'

Andrea made a face at him. 'Don't play the innocent! From your – behaviour, I would guess this isn't the first time you've done this sort of thing.'

He assumed a wounded air. 'How unkind! Do you think I'm in the habit of going around chatting up every bird that takes my eye?'

'Yes.' Andrea looked at him steadily. 'And I'm sorry for Ruth.'

'Why?'

'I wouldn't put up with it.'

His expression sobered for a moment. 'You wouldn't have to. Perhaps if Ruth was more like you, she wouldn't have to either.'

'That's no excuse.'

'It's not meant to be.' Roy tugged gently at a strand of her silky dark hair. 'Come and dance with me.'

'Dance with Ruth.'

'I don't want to dance with Ruth. If you won't dance with me, I'll find someone else who will.'

Andrea believed him, and she shook her head. He was very persuasive, and she hadn't done much dancing this evening. 'All right,' she agreed at last. 'Just because I feel you'll be safer with me than with someone else.'

'Don't you believe it,' he grinned, and taking her hand he drew her after him on to the floor.

As Andrea went into his arms, she saw Janet's worried face. No doubt she, like some of the others, would consider her behaviour outrageous. But after all, she hadn't invited this, and Ruth should have had more sense than to get involved with someone like Roy.

Roy danced in a very seductive way, his arms looped around her waist, hands resting on her hips. He rested his cheek against her hair, and when she tried to draw back, said: 'Relax and enjoy it. You know you want to.'

Andrea stroked one finger down the open vee of his shirt, feeling the tensing of his muscles as she did so. 'You think you're so irresistible, don't you?' she parried.

'No,' he replied, his lips against her hair. 'I think you are.'

'Nice try,' murmured Andrea mockingly, and he sighed impatiently.

'I mean it. You're beautiful,' he told her without emphasis. 'Why are you being so aggressive? What's Ruth to you?'

'What's she to you?'

'My stepsister.'

'Oh!' Andrea's lips formed the circle.

'Does that explain the situation?'

'Mmm, a lot.' She looked up at him. 'It explains how you're so sure of yourself.'

'What do you mean?'

She smiled. 'All that hero-worship! It would take a better

man than you are to cope with it.'

'Thanks very much!' He sounded put out.

Andrea chuckled. 'No, really – she really digs you, doesn't she? And after living with you for – how long?'

'Fifteen years.'

'Fifteen years!' Andrea shook her head. 'Crazy girl!'

He stared at her quizzically. 'Are you sending me up?'

'Does it sound as though I am?'

'Yes.'

'Well – perhaps just a little bit,' she conceded laughingly. 'Oh, Roy, don't look so offended. Just when I was beginning to like you.'

Roy breathed deeply into her ear. 'What are you doing tomorrow?'

'I don't know. That depends on Janet.'

'Janet? Oh, the cousin you mentioned.' He grimaced, lifting his head to stare across at the group gathered round the table near the fire. 'I imagine that's Janet – in the long dress? She's not at all like you, is she?'

'Don't you think so?' Andrea glanced round too. Then she looked quickly away again, digging her fingers into Roy's arms. 'Are you aware that your stepsister is watching our every move? She looks livid!'

He smiled down at her. 'Tomorrow,' he said, ignoring her protest. 'Come skiing with me. You do ski, don't you? You're not just learning?'

'I might be,' she countered. 'In any case, as I told you, I shall be spending the day with Janet.'

Roy sighed again. 'Tomorrow night, then. Let me take you out for dinner.'

Andrea shook her head. 'I can't make plans until I see what Jan wants to do.'

'I'll get Susie to fix Janet up.'

'No. No, don't bother. We'll probably see you in here again tomorrow evening.'

And with that he had to be content, and not even Ruth could fault Andrea's behaviour for the rest of the evening. Roy did his best to stay near her, but Andrea chose to join in the dancing with the others, and she noticed that Ruth went to occupy the place beside Roy as soon as she was able. Andrea felt sorry for her, but she did throw herself at him and he was the type of man who enjoyed a chase.

Later, in their suite, Janet had tried to bring the subject

up, but in this instance Andrea was adamant. She was tired, she said, and she had no intention of discussing her affairs with her cousin at this time of night.

But now it was morning and Andrea conceded that Janet was almost bound to find some way of turning the conversation in Roy Stevens' direction. She stretched lazily. Oh, well! Maybe this holiday Janet would learn that everything was not simply black or white, but several shades of grey as well.

She was surprised therefore when the door of her bedroom opened very quietly and her cousin put her head round, eyes widening in surprise when she saw Andrea was awake.

'I thought I might wake you,' she said, coming into the room in an unbecoming pink quilted housecoat. 'It's nearly half past seven. Are you going down to the pool?'

'Why not?' Andrea kicked back the covers and then uttered an impatient exclamation as Janet quickly averted her eyes. 'We are both female, Jan!' she said, reaching for her white silk wrapper.

'I know, but—' Janet looked up warily, and then looked relieved to find Andrea fastening the cord of her gown about her. 'I mean – sleeping like that! How can you, Andrea?'

'Why shouldn't I?'

'I – well, aren't you cold?'

'No more than you, I shouldn't suppose.' Andrea flicked a finger at Janet's brushed nylon nightdress, showing at the cuffs of her housecoat. 'Don't you know that without stimulus, the body loses its ability to generate heat?'

'But – but naked . . .'

'Nude,' amended Andrea mockingly. 'Oh, what's wrong, Jan? Has Aunt Lavinia made you ashamed of your own body, as well?'

'No. Not ashamed. But . . .'

'Honey, Daddy and I used to swim in the sea near our villa in Bermuda without worrying too much about anything except sharks,' remarked Andrea laughingly. 'Don't you know it's the only way to get an all-over tan?'

Janet looked shocked to the core of her being. 'You mean – you and Uncle Pat—'

'Mmm.' Andrea was fast becoming bored with this conversation. She padded across to the windows and drawing back the curtain, peered out. 'Brr, it looks jolly cold out there!' Then she looked back at her cousin and sighed. 'Come on, Jan! Grow up. Surely the adult human form holds no secrets from you!'

Janet's plump cheeks turned red. 'Well, I – I've never seen a man without – without any clothes.'

Andrea chuckled. 'There's a treat in store!' Then at Janet's continued look of disapproval: 'Jan, there's no shame in anyone seeing your body. Oh, I'm not suggesting you should go topless on the beach, or strip off in front of a crowd of rugby enthusiasts, but just – being without clothes is a natural experience.' She paused. 'Anyway, forget it. Go and put your bathing suit on, and we'll go down to the pool and warm ourselves up in the water.'

Janet hesitated. 'Do you think anyone will be there?'

'Now who do you mean? Some of Susie's crowd? Or the bold bad Baron?'

'Oh, Andrea!' Janet turned away for a moment, but then she looked back. 'Do you think he might be there?'

'Who? The Baron? I don't know, do I? In any case, he'll probably have some female in tow. His type usually do. Like that middle-aged dame he was escorting yesterday.'

'She wasn't middle-aged, Andrea. She was only in her – well, thirties!'

'And the rest. Oh, go on, Jan. You're wasting time.'

'Are – are you seeing that boy today?'

'If you mean Roy, why don't you say so? You know his name as well as I do. And yes, I expect so. I don't see how I could avoid it, seeing that they're staying at the same hotel we are.'

'You know what I mean, Andrea.' Janet paused. 'Ruth was terribly upset last night, you know.'

Andrea thrust her hands into the pockets of her gown. 'Was she?' she asked quietly, her fists clenched.

'Yes. Don't you think it was rather mean of you to encourage him?'

'I didn't encourage him! At least – not much. Oh, Jan, you don't understand. If I hadn't danced with him, he'd have found someone else. At least with me he was reasonably safe.'

'Well, Ruth didn't know that, did she?'

'Ruth should have more sense.'

'Oh, Andrea, don't be so heartless! She's crazy about him.'

'I should imagine no one has been left in any doubt as to that, including Roy! Jan, you don't do that sort of thing — hang on to a man as if he was your lifeline!'

'She loves him, Andrea. What else could she do?'

'She could find someone else and try making him jealous for a change, if that's possible.'

'But they're married, Andrea—'

'*Married?*' A wave of unease swept over her. 'You're not serious!'

'I am, too. Her name's Ruth Stevens!'

Andrea breathed again. 'Oh — oh, I see!' She almost laughed. 'Jan, she's his stepsister. I imagine her mother, or his, changed their names when they got married again.'

'His stepsister? Gosh!' Janet bit her lip. 'Oh, that's different. She was talking about where they lived, about their home! I naturally assumed . . .'

Andrea nodded patiently. 'I know. Now — will you go and get changed?'

'Yes, of course.' Janet smiled apologetically. 'See you in a few minutes.'

Andrea nodded, closing the door behind her and leaning back against it. Suddenly she didn't want to go down to the pool after all. What if the Baron was there? What if he made a play for Janet? How would she handle it when she could get so upset over someone else's affairs?

When Andrea and Janet stepped out of the lift at the basement level, it was to find that only three other people were using the pool at that moment, and none of them was familiar. The pool itself was large and heated, and the atmosphere was intensely humid. Pale green tiles shimmered beneath the water, giving it a tropical appearance, while the surround was a stone mosaic in shades of blue and green. It was a most attractive setting and Janet became quite enthusiastic, in spite of her initial disappointment at the nonappearance of the Baron.

They left their towelling jackets in one of the cubicles provided, and while Janet was tugging a rubber cap over her hair, Andrea dived cleanly into the water. Of the two of them, Janet's swimsuit should have appeared the most daring, being in two pieces that left her midriff bare. Andrea's suit was black, one-piece, and clung to her skin like sealskin, moulding her breasts and hips, and succeeding where too much exposure failed.

Andrea swam the length of the pool at an easy crawl, and then came back to where Janet was now sitting on the side, dangling her toes in the water. Shaking back her shiny rope of black hair, Andrea tugged mischievously at her cousin's feet.

'Come on in,' she exclaimed. 'It's beautiful!'

Janet glanced nervously about her. 'Is anyone looking?'

'Of course not. And even if they were, what of it? You're on holiday, Jan. Don't let anyone else spoil it for you.'

'Oh – all right.' Janet slid slowly down into the water, and squealed as its momentary chill caught her unawares. 'Ooh – Andrea! It's freezing!'

Andrea sighed. 'No, it's not. You'll soon get used to it. It's your body that's overheated, that's all. See, it feels better already, doesn't it?'

Janet nodded, bouncing about in the water and causing little waves to spread across the pool. 'It's quite nice really, isn't it? No, don't take me out of my depth. Let me get used to it.'

Andrea splashed around patiently while Janet accustomed herself to the feel of the water, and then she said: 'How about a lesson, hmm?'

Janet looked doubtful. 'But I'm enjoying just playing about, Andrea. Couldn't I just enjoy it this morning and start lessons tomorrow?'

Andrea's mouth turned down at the corners. 'Oh, Jan, you'll never learn if you don't make the effort.'

Janet pursed her lips. 'Well, I don't see why I have to. Make the effort, I mean. I'm quite happy in the shallows.'

Andrea uttered an exasperated exclamation, and rolling on to her stomach swam away, up to the deepest part of the pool. She found it difficult to understand Janet's reasoning. She would have far more fun if she could swim, instead of wading about in breast-high water, incapable of doing anything but jump up and down. Besides, it was safer if one could save oneself in an emergency.

She was floating idly on her back, staring up at the domed ceiling, when someone dived into the water close beside her, and sent a wave of choking water into her mouth and nostrils. Grimacing, she struggled upright, coughing and sneezing and feeling an intense annoyance towards the person responsible. She rubbed the water from her eyes, slicked back her hair, and glared round angrily, straight into the mocking eyes of Baron Axel von Mahlstrom.

'*Guten Morgen, Fraülein,*' he greeted her, with a bow of his head, and an intense anger seized her.

'Are you responsible for almost drowning me?' she demanded furiously.

He trod water, regarding her with mild amusement. '*Nein.*'

'What do you mean – *nein*?'

'*Verzeihen Sie*, no.'

'I understood what *nein* meant, Herr Baron.'

'You did?' He inclined his head again. 'Then what do you mean?'

'You know you just dived in beside me!' she declared hotly.

He nodded. 'I am not denying it.'

'You are! When I asked you—'

'You asked me whether I was responsible for almost drowning you. I denied it. I have been watching you, Miss Connolly, and I am quite sure an unexpected ducking came nowhere near to drowning you.'

Andrea made a rather schoolgirlish face at him, and turned away, but he swam alongside her and turning on to his back, said: 'I give you permission to – how do you say? – get your own back, *ja*?'

Andrea looked down at his lean, muscular body. Like herself, he had an even tan, and with that intensely light hair, it was startling. Not that his hair was particularly light at the moment – the water had artificially darkened it, and it clung smoothly to his head and neck. Sideburns grew down his face almost to his jawline, and his nose and chin were firmly defined. His mouth was thin and sardonic, vaguely cruel-looking, and Andrea recognized the determination and strength of purpose, allied to a certain cynicism, which hardened the steely greyness of his eyes. He also possessed a strong sensuality, and she was not unaware of it.

The temptation to push his mocking face under the water was too powerful to resist, and reaching towards him, she pressed her hands hard down on his shoulders. To her dismay, he laughed, and grasping her arms pulled her down with him. For a moment she was on top of him under the water, her legs tangling with his, her breasts hurting against the hardness of his chest. Then he thrust her deliberately away from him, and she surfaced, spluttering.

The Baron came up a few feet away, seemingly un-abashed by her attempt to duck him, and she rubbed her eyes angrily, annoyed at the way her pulses had raced at the feel of those hard hands holding her against him. 'You rotten pig!' she declared furiously, relieving a little of her frustration at least, and he laughed again.

Then he swam back to her, and looking across at her said quietly: 'You are all right, are you not?'

The unexpected concern in his voice momentarily disarmed her, and she looked up at him curiously. 'What are you doing in this pool anyway?' she demanded. 'You said you weren't staying at the hotel.'

'I am not.' Thick lashes narrowed his eyes. 'I live not far from here. But Nicolas Leiber is a friend of mine, and he allows me to use the pool.'

'Nicolas Leiber?' Andrea frowned. 'Oh – Herr Leiber, the proprietor!'

'*Ja*, that is correct.'

'And – do you own a hotel, Herr Baron?' She was probing but she couldn't help it.

He shook his head. 'Unfortunately, no, *Fraülein*.'

Andrea hesitated. 'You – don't have an – occupation?'

His smile was vaguely self derisory. 'Ah, *ja*, *Fraülein*. I am not the – how you say? – *dilettante*? I am a ski-instructor, *ja*?'

A ski-instructor!

Andrea should have been prepared for it, but somehow she wasn't, and the knowledge infuriated her afresh. A ski-instructor! She should have known! Particularly after all she had said to Janet!

And then something else struck her, too. Something equally significant. In the beginning he had called her by her name, *Miss Connolly*! How did he know her name, unless he had been making inquiries? Neither she nor Janet had introduced themselves.

With what she hoped was casual interest, she said: 'You used my name just now.'

He nodded. 'But of course. I met your father once, many years ago. At the home of a Swiss banking friend of mine, Herr Steiner.'

Fritz Steiner!

The name trembled on Andrea's lips, but she didn't say it. A surge of contempt was sweeping over her, and it was all

28

she could do not to tell this arrogant brute exactly what she thought of his methods. So – he had learned who she was, and no doubt who Janet was, too. And that accounted for the fact that he had chosen to dive into the water next to her instead of joining Janet in the shallows.

Andrea felt more angry than she had ever felt before. The gall of the beast, she thought, clenching and unclenching her fingers. Did he imagine she would succumb as swiftly to his charms as her cousin had done? Oh, if only there was some way she could cut him down to size!

There was!

The recollection of her thoughts the night before overcame discretion, and a faint smile touched her lips as she said recklessly: 'I'm afraid you've made a mistake, Herr Baron. I believe you're talking about Patrick Connolly, aren't you? But he's my cousin's father, and my uncle!'

The Baron's brows drew together in a scowl. *'Ist das so? Entschuldigen Sie.* I must be mistaken.' With what to Andrea appeared to be a great effort, he forced a smile. *'Es tut mir sehr leid*, I am sorry.'

Andrea trod water lazily. 'It's not important, is it?'

He hesitated, and then shook his head. 'Not at all.'

Andrea glanced towards the shallow end of the pool and saw that Janet was now watching them with evident irritation. 'There she is,' she indicated to her companion. 'My cousin, Janet. You met her yesterday, remember?'

'Of course.' His smile was a little tight now, and bringing his arm out of the water, he consulted the watch on his wrist. 'And now, you must forgive me if I leave you. I am, as I have said, a working man, *Fraülein—*'

'Oh, call me Andrea, please,' she exclaimed, half mockingly delighted with the evident disconcertion she had caused. 'I – er – I expect we'll see you again, won't we?'

For a moment his grey eyes bored into hers, and what she saw in their depths brought a shiver of apprehension to her spine. 'Without a doubt, *Fraülein*,' he responded, his politeness belying the expression in his eyes. 'Be so good as to convey my regards to your cousin. *Auf Wiedersehen.'*

He swam smoothly and expertly to the side and swung his muscular length out of the water. Watching him, Andrea saw that he was wearing brief navy shorts which, clinging wetly to his body as they did, left no doubt as to his gender. She shivered again, half wishing she had been wrong about him, and then chided herself for doing so. The most attractive men were always either married or poverty-stricken, and for all she knew he could be both.

He strode away towards the changing cubicles without so much as casting a glance in Janet's direction, and remembering what she had done, Andrea swam slowly back to the shallow end of the pool.

'*Well!*' Janet glared at her, red-faced. 'That was a rotten trick, wasn't it?'

'What?' Andrea feigned ignorance.

'Keeping him all to yourself! The Baron! Don't pretend. I saw you, Andrea. It was deliberate, wasn't it?'

Andrea summoned all her patience. 'Did you see everything that happened, Janet?' she asked quietly.

'Of course I did.'

'Then you must have seen him dive in beside me.'

Janet shrugged. 'What of it?'

'Why do you think he did that?'

'I don't know. Coincidence . . .'

'Oh, Janet!' Andrea shook her head. 'It was no coincidence. I've learned a little more about our friend, the Baron. Like for instance, he's a ski-instructor.'

'A ski-instructor?' Janet was nonplussed.

'Yes, a ski-instructor. Who just happens to be a friend of the proprietor of this hotel and is allowed to use its amenities because of it. In addition to which, he knew my name. Or at least, he thought he did.'

'What do you mean?'

Janet was beginning to shiver, and Andrea nodded towards some steps leading out of the pool. 'Let's get out of here. You're getting cold, and it's time we were getting dressed for breakfast.'

'But what about the Baron?' wailed Janet.

'Later. In our rooms. Come on.'

Towelling herself dry in the comfort of her own bathroom, Andrea was not surprised when Janet appeared after only a few minutes, fully dressed.

'Didn't you take a shower?' she asked, and Janet shook her head.

'I'll have one later. Go on about the Baron. You can't keep me in suspense any longer.'

Andrea cast the towel aside and began putting on her underwear. 'Well . . .' she paused significantly, wondering how Janet would react when she told her what she had done, 'he did know *my* name. He said he had met Daddy once at Fritz Steiner's house in Berne. I suppose he'd found out our names from the receptionist we saw him talking to yester-day.'

'Well?' Janet still looked put out.

'Well? Isn't it obvious?'

'Isn't what obvious?'

'Janet, the reason he was sociable to me this morning is because he believes I'm Patrick Connolly's daughter.'

'You are.'

'I know. But I told him *you* were!'

'You did what?'

Andrea pulled on warm trousers, and fastened the waistband. 'I told him you were me. Oh, Jan, don't look like that! You should be pleased. You're going to get your dearest wish. The Baron will begin paying attention to you.'

Janet's plump face showed her confusion. 'How on earth can you know that? Did he tell you—?'

'Oh, no! Don't be silly, Jan. Look . . .' Andrea pulled a scarlet sweater over her head, scooping out the coil of damp hair that clung to her neck, 'the reason our friend the Baron paid attention to me this morning instead of you was because he thought I was the most interesting proposition – financially.'

'That's a foul suggestion to make!'

'But unfortunately true. Jan, when I told him I wasn't Pat's daughter, that you were, he couldn't get away from me fast enough.'

Janet was beginning to look doubtful. 'You're not serious, Andrea . . .'

'Why not? He hasn't paid any attention to me up until now, has he?'

'He hasn't really paid any attention to either of us.'

'Of course he has. He offered to carry your parcels, didn't he?' Andrea began to brush her hair. 'It's obvious, he thought you were the one with the money. I must say, you look the part better than I do.'

'But imagine telling him that I was you!' Janet's expression was almost ludicrous. 'Andrea, why did you do it?'

Andrea turned away, unable to sustain her cousin's candid stare. 'Why do you think? So you could have the fun you said you wanted.'

'We'd never get away with it!'

'Why not?'

Janet sought for words. 'Susie knows you — all her crowd know you!'

'Susie knows me, admittedly. But she won't say anything if I ask her not to. So far as the rest of them are concerned, we're cousins, our surnames are the same. Either one of us could be Patrick Connolly's daughter.'

'I don't know.' Janet twisted her hands together, but Andrea could tell from the faintly speculative look in her eyes that she was weakening. 'What if he finds out?'

'Who?' Andrea grimaced. 'My father — or the Baron?'

'Why, the Baron, of course.'

'I should worry more about what my father will say if he finds out rather than the Baron,' retorted Andrea wryly. 'So far as Axel von Mahlstrom is concerned, he's hardly in a position to complain, is he?'

Janet's lips twitched. 'Oh, if only we could ...' she breathed.

'We can. We already have. Or at least, I have.'

Janet bit her lower lip. 'I suppose we might get away with it.'

'Have courage!' Andrea was in no small way relieved that Janet was seemingly no longer angry. 'It will help to relieve the boredom. And I always found the idea of being plain Andrea Connolly and not just Patrick Connolly's daughter appealing.'

CHAPTER THREE

A FEW days later, Andrea stood at the head of the Feldberg ski slope, gazing down broodingly into the valley below. Grossfeld nestled at the foot of the glacier, its roofs and spire dwarfed from this height, but sharply defined in the clear morning air. She stared around her at the pine-clad slopes that fell away below the tree line, she could hear the ring of metal as the ski lift brought more climbers up the mountain, and she could smell the coffee from the small cafeteria that invited enthusiasts to take something hot before braving the chills and thrills of the downward slope.

For once she was free of Janet's company, and while her cousin's presence did not jar on her as much as it had done at the beginning of the holiday, it was nevertheless pleasant to be on her own for a while.

Since their agreement to change identities, there had been no sign of the attractive Baron, and Andrea couldn't help but wonder whether he had decided to give both of them the cold shoulder. After all, there were plenty of other girls in Grossfeld, and she didn't suppose that the Kutzbuhl was the only hotel he frequented.

Janet took her disappointment at his non-appearance heavily, and Andrea's own guilt at her part in the scheme of things had forced her to the conclusion that she was no better than he was. In consequence, she had done everything possible to interest her cousin in other things and other people, and at last Janet seemed to be getting over it. Today, for instance, she had accepted an invitation to join Susie Nichols and her parents on a trip to Innsbruck. Both girls had been invited to go, but Andrea was glad of the opportunity to do some serious skiing at last. There was a ski school near the hotel and Janet was a pupil there. But in the circumstances, Andrea had felt obliged to stay near her, and watching the other girl scramble up and down the nursery slopes was no substitute for the real thing.

Succumbing to the tempting aroma of the coffee, Andrea unfastened her skis and draping them over one shoulder made her way into the brightly painted chalet which was the small cafeteria. The warmth inside misted her dark glasses, and she put them into the top pocket of the thick parka she was wearing. Stowing her skis, she made her way to the counter.

A few minutes later she was seated at a small table by the window, a mug of steaming coffee in front of her, munching her way through a wedge of new bread filled with salty German sausage.

'I thought you lived on Energen rolls and lettuce leaves,' remarked a vaguely familiar voice, and Andrea looked up to find Roy Stevens standing looking down at her.

Wiping her mouth with the back of her hand, she said: 'I suppose you're about to tell me that this is a coincidence!'

For the past five days Roy had turned up with infuriating regularity in many of the places she and Janet had frequented, but always Andrea had refused to have anything to do with him. But then she had always had Janet with her.

Now Roy hooked out the chair opposite with his foot and straddled it lazily. 'I wouldn't insult your undoubted intelligence,' he replied, with a smile. 'I admit – I followed you. Who wouldn't, when the bodyguard is no longer in evidence.'

'Janet is not my bodyguard,' retorted Andrea, taking a drink of her coffee.

'You could have fooled me.'

'Perhaps you're easier to fool than you think.'

Roy sighed, 'Hey, stop getting at me.' He glanced round the busy room and then looked at her again. 'Aren't you at all glad to see me?' He flicked his thumb expressively. 'You're being very thoroughly appraised by those two creeps in the corner. Doesn't it worry you to come skiing up here, alone, when you might land in trouble with only God and providence to help you?'

Andrea permitted herself a quick look in the direction he had indicated. Two bearded characters were sharing a table, but they didn't look up, and her lips curved laughingly.

'Perhaps it's you they fancy,' she teased him. 'They don't seem particularly interested in me.'

Roy sighed again. 'So what's wrong with me? Why won't you even give me the time of day?'

Andrea finished munching another mouthful of her roll and shrugged. 'We're talking now, aren't we?'

Roy studied her impatiently. 'That's not what I mean,

34

and you know it. What is it? Is it Ruth? Has she been saying anything?'

'I doubt if Ruth would say anything to me,' remarked Andrea dryly. She finished her roll and cupped the mug of coffee in both hands elbows resting on the table. 'Don't you want anything to eat or drink?'

Roy hunched his shoulders. 'No.'

Andrea swallowed the remainder of her coffee with her eyes on his bent head, and then she said: 'All right. Shall we go?'

Roy looked up. 'You mean – together?'

'Isn't that what you came for?'

'Why – yes. Yes.' He grinned, his confidence returning. 'Sure. Let's go.'

In spite of still having some misgivings about encouraging Roy, Andrea enjoyed the day. It was exhilarating out on the slopes, and as Roy was easily as proficient as she was there was no restraint placed on either of them. They soon grew tired of using the conventional slopes and devised races, using the trees as obstacles. There was danger in this practice, but it added to the excitement, and they drove each other to the limits of their ability. Scything down into the valley, crouched against the icy onslaught of the wind, her skis seeming to find the smoothest course without effort, Andrea was filled with wellbeing, and when the light began to fail she was almost sorry they had to go back to the hotel.

'You were great!' exclaimed Roy enthusiastically, as they walked down the road towards the Kutzbuhl. 'I've never met a girl who could really compete before.'

Andrea gave him a sideways glance. 'Oh no? Isn't that a rather brash statement?'

Roy had the grace to look slightly shamefaced. With her, he had lost a lot of that unattractive over-confidence. 'You know what I mean. You are good. You must have had a good teacher.'

'My fath – er's brother,' replied Andrea, only just remembering to conceal her identity. 'Er – Uncle Patrick.'

Roy seemed to have noticed nothing amiss but merely nodded, and then they had reached the hotel and Andrea went ahead of him up the steps. In the reception area, the lights from the small bar gleamed invitingly, and from within came the sound of voices and laughter.

'I think the Nichols' have returned,' remarked Roy, rather gloomily. 'I gather that means you'll have your cousin in tow again tonight.'

Andrea smiled up at him. 'Well, we have had a marvellous day, haven't we?'

He nodded, his eyes holding hers. 'Marvellous!' he agreed softly. 'What about tomorrow?'

Andrea was about to make some vague reference to waiting and seeing what happened, when two people emerged from the bar, and one of them, recognizing Andrea, called her name. It was Janet – but such a Janet as Andrea had never seen before, flushed and animated, almost beautiful in her excitement about the man who was accompanying her. Andrea hardly had to move her gaze to be aware that it was the Baron.

'Andrea!' Janet was saying, scarcely granting Roy more than a perfunctory glance. 'Guess who we met in Innsbruck today!'

As the Baron was standing silently behind her showing a polite interest in what was going on, Andrea felt the question was unnecessary to say the least.

'Did you have a nice time?' she asked, refusing to make some inane reply.

'Oh, yes,' Janet nodded vigorously. 'We went to the Hofburg, and we saw the tomb of the Emperor Maximilian, and we went shopping along the Maria-Theresien-Strasse . . . I bought Mummy the most gorgeous carving of a mountain chalet, and when you lift the roof there's a musical box inside.' She glanced round at the Baron. 'I – Axel knows Innsbruck very well, don't you, Axel?'

Andrea should not have been surprised, but she was. It was what she had expected, and yet . . . She felt an intense anger towards the man standing so stiffly behind her cousin. To think she had felt guilty about this! She had actually considered herself no better than he was. But she was. And she despised him, utterly.

Janet was introducing Roy, rather belatedly, to her escort. There was pride in every word she uttered, and even Roy seemed somewhat disconcerted by the other man's undoubted air of hauteur. This infuriated Andrea anew, and with uncharacteristic malice, she said:

'The Herr Baron is a ski-instructor, Roy. Perhaps we should ask him to give us some lessons, hmm?'

Only by the faint tightening of his lips did the Baron display any reaction to this statement, and after a moment's surprise, Roy shared her amusement. But Janet was far from amused, and her good humour disappeared as she turned to Andrea.

'The Baron has asked me to have dinner with him this evening,' she told her shortly. 'At the Gasthof.' She mentioned the name of a rather expensive eating house in the town. 'You don't mind eating alone for once, do you?'

'Naturally your cousin is free to join us, should she wish to do so, Janet,' interposed Axel von Mahlstrom politely, and Andrea half wished she dared accept. She would have enjoyed baiting him some more, but Janet's expression did not encourage this idea.

'I – er – I'm hoping Andrea will dine with me,' put in Roy slyly, delighted at this opportunity, and Andrea had to give in.

'Yes,' she said, avoiding the Baron's cool grey eyes, 'I think that would be best, but thank you anyway.'

Axel von Mahlstrom bowed, and then turned to Janet. 'And now I think I must go. I will call for you at eight o'clock, *ja?*'

Janet's smile blossomed anew. 'Lovely,' she agreed, allowing him to take her hand and raise it almost to his lips. '*Auf – wiedersehen*, Axel.'

'*Auf wiedersehen.*'

The Baron's words encompassed all of them, and with another bow he left them.

After he had gone Andrea breathed an exaggerated sigh of relief. 'Such exalted company!' she commented mockingly, and Janet turned on her angrily.

'I don't know what he must have thought of your rudeness!' she exclaimed. 'Couldn't you at least confine your remarks to those who appreciate them?'

With these parting words, she stalked away up the stairs to their rooms, and Andrea, watching her retreating back, pulled a wry face.

'Oh, dear! What did I say?'

'You know very well what you said,' replied Roy with a grin. 'But never mind that. What about tonight? Are you going to have dinner with me?'

'What about the others?'

Roy shook his head. 'I'm not interested in the others. Oh,

37

come on, Andrea. We needn't eat at the hotel. We could go to the Gasthof, too, if you like.'

'The Gasthof?' Andrea said the words slowly, thoughtfully, then she nodded, a wicked glint entering her green eyes. 'The Gasthof,' she said again. 'Yes. Why not? But not with Janet and the Baron, of course.'

'Are you joking?' Roy raised his dark eyebrows. 'Okay. What time? Better make it eight-fifteen or eight-thirty. I'd hate for us all to meet in the hall again.'

'Yes, so should I,' agreed Andrea, smiling. 'We'll make it half past eight.'

'Fine.'

They were about to separate when several young people came through from the bar where Janet and her escort had been earlier. Among them was Ruth Stevens. When she saw Andrea and her stepbrother, her eyes hardened angrily.

'So there you are, Roy,' she declared, in an overly loud tone. 'I've been looking for you all afternoon. You said you'd be back at one o'clock. Now it's after four. Where have you been?' Her eyes flicked to Andrea and their message was hostile. 'As if I didn't know!' Roy sighed, and excusing himself from Andrea went to speak to her. But before he left he mouthed: Eight-thirty, and closed one eye deliberately. Feeling slightly *de trop*, Andrea smiled at the rest of the gang and then continued on her way upstairs.

In their suite, Janet was sewing the strap of a slip which had broken earlier, but she looked up resentfully when Andrea came in. However, she didn't say anything, and it was left to Andrea to make the first overture. Shedding the thick parka, and shaking out her hair, she said casually:

'What are you going to wear this evening?'

Janet shrugged. 'I haven't decided. I might wear the sprigged cotton. I don't know.'

The sprigged cotton was one of the hostess gowns Janet had brought with her, and Andrea, who had been expecting her to say she was going to wear the apricot silk, was surprised. That particular dress had not been worn yet, and surely this was the ideal opportunity.

Realizing that it was her behaviour which had aroused Janet's indignation, Andrea expelled a resigned breath. 'Oh, Jan, do you want me to apologize, is that it?'

'I don't want anything from you.'

'Don't be silly. Look, I thought we agreed to change

identities to have some fun – not to take it all so deadly seriously.'

Janet's head jerked up. 'Oh, yes, that's all it is to you, isn't it? That's all everything is to you! But not to me! Can't you see, this is my only opportunity to – to meet with people like Axel, to go out with him on equal terms! And you're spoiling it!'

Andrea stared at her cousin through troubled eyes. Janet really was taking this far more seriously than she would have dreamed possible.

'Surely,' she began, choosing her words carefully, 'surely you can see what he's like, Jan. I mean, switching his attention back to you like this. Doesn't it prove anything to you?'

'I've told you, I don't care what it proves. I just want to enjoy it.'

Andrea turned away, her brows drawn together in a frown. 'I'm afraid – I'm afraid you're hoping – that something will come of this,' she ventured at last.

Janet's lips thinned. 'And what if I am?'

Andrea swung round. 'Janet, it's hopeless!'

'Why?'

'You know why. Obviously he needs money – a wife with money . . .'

Janet's expression softened slightly. 'But what if he should fall in love? I mean, *really* fall in love? Mightn't he then think some things were more important—'

'*No!*' Andrea was adamant. 'Jan, he's what? Thirty-three, thirty-four, thereabouts. A man doesn't live that long without – well, having affairs. Not if he's not married anyway. Even if he is attracted to you, even if he does fall in love with you, he'll have everything under control, believe me!' She paused. 'Besides, he's too old!'

'Fifteen years is nothing,' retorted Janet, tossing her head.

'With a man like the Baron von Mahlstrom it's a great deal,' replied Andrea. She tucked her thumbs into the belt of her pants. 'Jan, can you honestly see yourself as a Baroness?'

Janet's face was a little smug now. 'Oh, yes,' she said, nodding. 'I think I should like that very much.'

While Andrea took her bath she pondered Janet's attitude. Her behaviour was worrying to say the least, and she knew that if her father had any suspicion of what was going on, he would demand their return instantly. But what had begun as a kind of reckless dare had suddenly become a definite hazard and she didn't quite see how she could alter the situation without hurting Janet.

Besides, she told herself encouragingly, it was early days yet. The Baron might quite easily tire of Janet's company in a very short time, and then the problem would no longer exist. And why should she spoil Janet's chance to have fun? If the Baron was fortune-hunting he deserved no pity, and if he was not ; ... Well, Janet might have her opportunity after all.

When Janet emerged from her bedroom later she was wearing the apricot silk after all, and her eyes dropped before Andrea's appraising stare.

'Does it look all right?' she asked reluctantly, and Andrea summoned a smile.

'You look beautiful, Jan,' she told her enthusiastically. 'That dress really does something for you.'

Janet's lips twitched upwards. 'You look nice, too, Andrea,' she conceded, casting rather envious eyes on Andrea's plain black gown. She knew she could never wear anything so simple, but the narrow skirt that flared slightly at the knee accentuated Andrea's lissom curves. Narrow diamanté straps seemed scarcely strong enough to support the bodice, and her back was bare to her waist.

'Thank you.' Andrea accepted the compliment without conceit. 'I'm having dinner with Roy. But of course, you know that.'

Janet nodded, and picked up her coat. 'I'd better be going. It's almost eight.'

'Let him wait a few minutes. It won't hurt him,' suggested Andrea, but Janet ignored her. However, as her cousin was swinging the heavy tweed about her shoulders, Andrea added: 'Don't you have anything else to wear? I mean, an evening coat or something?'

Janet's face hardened. 'You know I don't.'

Andrea sighed. 'Well, wait a minute.' She went back into her bedroom and emerged a few minutes later with a dark blue velvet cape. 'Here, wear this! I hardly ever do. It's too – well, I'm sure it will suit you better than me.'

Janet's delight was evident. She draped the cape about her shoulders and hurried back into her room to examine her reflection in the long mirrors of the wardrobes. Then she came out again, beaming.

'Oh, it's super, Andrea. Just exactly what I needed.'

Andrea smiled, feeling vaguely maternal. 'There you are then. Off you go, Cinderella.'

After Janet had gone, Andrea wandered restlessly round the suite, half wishing she had suggested meeting Roy in the bar for a drink before they left. She had peered somewhat reluctantly through the window curtains a few minutes after Janet had departed, and had seen her emerge from the hotel accompanied by her tall, distinguished escort. They had entered one of the hired horse-drawn sleighs which were so popular with the tourists, and driven away amid a jingling of sleighbells. Watching them, Andrea had experienced a curious sense of unease which hadn't altogether to do with Janet's naïve aspirations.

Later, she donned a short fur jacket and went down to meet Roy. He looked unfamiliar in a dinner jacket and sheepskin coat after the casual clothes she was used to seeing him wearing, but his good looks could not be denied, and he attracted his own share of female admirers.

'Do we walk, or take a sleigh?' he asked, as they emerged into the cold night air, and Andrea endeavoured to thrust her own personal anxieties aside.

'We walk,' she asserted firmly, unconsciously shunning anything which reminded her of Janet and Axel von Mahlstrom.

The Gasthof was a conventional type of eating house, unlike the wine cellar which Andrea and Janet had visited with the rest of Susie's crowd a couple of nights ago. It was quiet and discreet, the tables set in upholstered booths, each with its own lamp and single hothouse rose. It was expensive, too, and Andrea paused to wonder exactly what Roy's occupation might be. She couldn't see Janet, or the Baron, but that was not surprising. The booths concealed their occupants from view.

The menu was extensive, *Schnitzel* of all kinds, as well as smoked pork and sausage, chicken and beef. There were puréed vegetables, sweet and sour cabbage, and stuffed peppers which added an Eastern flavour to the food. The desserts were mouth-watering – *strudel*, small sweet dumplings, dessert pancakes, stuffed with fruit and nuts, soufflés, and a selection of the rich gateaux Andrea had already sampled in the coffee houses.

Roy choose spit-roasted chicken as his main course, and Andrea decided to have the same. But when she saw the small whole chicken, glistening golden-brown on its bed of rice, she doubted her ability to do full injustice to it. Nevertheless, she made the effort, drinking quantities of the dry white wine which Roy had also ordered and which was served in litre-sized carafes. Afterwards, she tried the *palatschinken*, thin dessert pancakes rolled around a preserve of fruit and nuts and sprinkled with sugar.

The coffee was strong and black, the way Andrea liked it, and Roy produced a cigar and asked her if she minded that he smoked.

'No. Go ahead,' she exclaimed lazily, lying back in her seat and feeling infinitely more relaxed. 'Don't expect me to move for at least half an hour.'

Roy grinned. 'You enjoyed it?'

'Enormously. Have you been here before?'

'Once,' he conceded, lighting his cigar.

'With Ruth, one presumes.'

'That's right.'

'Why is her surname the same as yours?'

'Ruth's mother married my father when Ruth was only about three years old. It was simpler to make all our names the same, I guess.'

'I see,' Andrea nodded. 'And what do you do, Roy? I mean, do you have a job?'

'Not at the moment. I was working in an hotel in Bournemouth throughout the summer, but at the present time I'm unemployed.'

Andrea regarded him rather sceptically. 'So how do you come to be holidaying at the Kutzbuhl?'

He grinned. 'My father is a merchant banker. He wants me to join the company. This holiday is a kind of blackmail, to persuade me to do what he wants.'

Andrea digested this. If Roy's father was a merchant banker, he came from exactly the sort of background her own father would approve of. How delighted Patrick Connolly would be if he could see her now, she reflected with some irony. But she doubted he would approve of her behaviour towards the Baron even so.

A quartet had been playing throughout the meal, and now Andrea saw that couples were drifting on to the pocket-handkerchief sized dance floor. The music was slow and easy, rhythmic without being noisy, and when he had finished his cigar Roy suggested they danced, too.

That was when Andrea saw Janet and Axel von Mahlstrom. They were seated in a booth nearer the dance floor, and it would have been impolite not to acknowledge them, even through Janet avoided her cousin's eyes.

'*Guten abend, Fraülein,*' responded the Baron, in response to Andrea's casually spoken greeting, sliding out of the booth and getting to his feet.

He was taller than Roy, and the whiteness of his frilled shirt front threw the darkness of his tan into relief. The cool grey eyes were enigmatic as he looked down at her, but Andrea was aware of him as never before. She forced a smile to her stiff lips. She had not intended to interrupt them. But she had not taken the Austrian's inbred courtesy into account.

'You and your – friend will join us for a drink, *Fraülein?*' he suggested politely.

Andrea glanced at Roy's impatient face and then at Janet's pursed lips. 'I – why, no, I don't think so, thank you.' She slipped her arm through Roy's deliberately. 'We were just going to dance, weren't we, darling?'

Roy's expression changed miraculously. 'Yes, *darling*, we were,' he responded, holding her arm closely against his side, and Axel von Mahlstrom inclined his head.

'*Ich verstehe, Fraülein.* Some other time perhaps.'

Andrea permitted herself another small smile, moved her head to include Janet in the acknowledgment, and they moved away.

'Well – darling,' murmured Roy, as he drew her into his arms on the dance floor, 'so I do have my uses sometimes.'

'I don't know what you mean.'

'Yes, you do. You weren't really that desperate to dance with me. You just didn't want to join the Baron for a drink.'

'Did you?'

Roy's lips moved against her hair. 'Hell, no. But then I recognize competition when I see it.'

Andrea sighed. 'You couldn't be more wrong. Baron von Mahlstrom has no interest in me. Janet has much more to offer.'

Roy raised his eyebrows, looking down at her. 'Do I

43

detect a certain cynicism?'

Andrea shook her head. 'No. I'm perfectly serious.'

Roy shrugged, not without some bewilderment, but there-after they danced in silence.

It was later, after several more dances, that Andrea suggested they ought to be going. Roy was becoming mildly intoxicated with the amount of wine he had drunk, and in consequence harder to handle. Leaving him sitting at their table, she made her way to the foyer to collect her jacket and encountered the Baron apparently waiting for Janet to emerge from the cloakroom. She would have passed him by without speaking, but to her surprise he put out a hand and gripped her arm, halting her just in front of him. Andrea looked up at him half angrily, opening her mouth to protest, when he said:

'I believe you are having trouble with your escort, *Fraülein.* Permit me to take you home with your cousin.'

Andrea's breath escaped on a gasp. 'I think you're mistaken, Herr Baron. I'm not having any – trouble, as you put it.'

'Herr Stevens has had too much to drink, has he not?' Axel von Mahlstrom persisted quietly. 'I have watched the way he has been behaving on the dance floor, and your attempts to hold him off.'

Andrea's breathing had quickened, but it was as much with the knowledge that he had been watching her as with anger at his arrogant attempt to take control of the situation. But she chose to blame anger, and her eyes sparkled dangerously as she said: 'I should have expected you to be too engrossed in furthering your own interests, Herr Baron, to pay any attention to mine!'

His fingers round her arm tightened perceptibly, and it was all she could do not to cry out at the pain. 'You will apologize for that, *Fraülein,*' he stated coldly. 'I am not one of your weak-kneed Englishmen to take such insolence lightly!'

Andrea felt the hot colour flooding her cheeks, but her hand below his grasp was going numb. 'You can't make me,' she retorted.

'Can I not, *Fraulein?* We will see.'

Andrea hated the veiled threat in his words, and burst out: 'Don't try to tell me what to do! I can look after myself.'

A coldly mocking smile twisted his mouth and his hand suddenly fell away from her arm. 'As you wish, *Fräulein*. It is obvious you enjoy being mauled on the dance floor.'

Andrea didn't, and she despised the way her eyes filled with tears as feeling came back into her arm with agonizing thoroughness. She turned away, just as Janet emerged from the cloakroom, carrying the cape Andrea had loaned her. Her sharp eyes took in Andrea's unusually distressed appearance, and they narrowed as she asked: 'What's the matter?'

'Nothing.'

Andrea brushed past her, refusing to be drawn, and Janet was forced to leave her. In the cloakroom, Andrea dabbed furiously at her eyes with a dampened tissue, unable completely to erase the slightly puffy appearance of her lids. She didn't even know why she felt so upset. The pain in her arm had subsided, and while she was not convinced that she would not have a bruise there in the morning, it was not something to weep over. But the memory of Axel von Mahlstrom's contempt was an intrusive abrasion of her emotions, and collecting her fur jacket she left the restaurant without telling Roy she was doing so.

CHAPTER FOUR

OVER breakfast the next morning, Janet brought up the subject of Andrea's uncharacteristic behaviour the night before.

'Whatever was wrong?' she asked, buttering a roll before spreading it liberally with conserve. 'Was it Roy? Axel was standing in the foyer, you know, and I asked him if he had seen what happened, but he said not.'

Andrea poured herself a second cup of coffee. So far she had eaten nothing, and watching Janet ploughing her way through several thick rolls and butter had not improved her appetite.

'I'd got something in my eye, that was all,' she replied, without emphasis. Then, changing the subject: 'Did you enjoy your evening?'

Janet licked a crumb from her lips and nodded. 'Oh, yes. It was wonderful. Axel is such an interesting man. Do you know, he's travelled all over the world? Australia, South America, Japan ... He knows such a lot about other countries and their customs. Do you know once he worked as a roustabout on a sheep station in Queensland? And he went on an expedition up the Orinoco, right into the heart of Indian country. He's actually met head-hunters—'

'Do you mind?' exclaimed Andrea irritably. 'I don't wish to know Axel von Mahlstrom's life story. Just so long as you're enjoying yourself.'

'Aren't you?'

Andrea finished her second cup of coffee and poured a third. 'I never expected to have a ball, Jan. And I did enjoy skiing yesterday. But don't expect me to go into raptures over things like you do.'

Janet frowned. 'I thought you and Roy seemed to be getting along famously last night.'

'Yes. Well, you thought wrong.'

'You mean — you've had a row?'

Andrea's lips twitched, albeit rather reluctantly. 'I wouldn't say that exactly,' she remarked, and then, catching sight of the group of young people just entering the restaurant, she added: 'You'll see what I mean in exactly ten seconds.'

As she had anticipated, Roy came striding straight over to their table, resting his palms on the cloth and glaring at Andrea angrily. 'Well, you've got a nerve, I must say,' he muttered furiously. 'Walking out on me like that! What the hell do you mean by it? I was sitting there for hours, waiting for you to come back.'

Andrea cast a meaningful glance in Janet's direction, and he straightened slightly and muttered: 'Morning, Janet.'

'Good morning.'

Janet responded automatically, fascinated by this interchange, and Roy turned back to Andrea. 'Well?'

'You were drunk,' she said quietly. 'And I didn't feel like being – mauled.' She used the word deliberately, and a shiver ran up her spine at the remembrance of that awful scene with the Baron.

'I was not drunk!' he denied indignantly. 'Okay, so I'd had a bit too much *vino*, but that didn't make me drunk!'

Andrea's thick lashes lifted, and her green eyes gazed into his. 'So what word would you use, then?'

'I – intoxicated, perhaps.'

'All right, you were intoxicated. Why split hairs! Either way, I preferred to go home alone.'

'You should have told me.'

'What? Do you honestly think you'd have taken that, after the way you're behaving now? And this is the morning after!'

'Well – left a message then.'

'Yes, I could have done that,' she conceded. 'I just didn't think about it.'

'Thanks very much.' Roy clenched his fists and thrust them into his pockets.

Andrea sighed. After all, it wasn't altogether Roy's fault. 'I'm sorry, Roy,' she murmured. 'It was a rotten thing to do.'

'She had something in her eye,' put in Janet suddenly, as if this news might swing the balance. 'I saw her. She looked upset.'

'Did she? Did you?' Roy looked down at Andrea concernedly. 'I didn't know that.'

Andrea shook her head. 'It was nothing much. Look, your friends are waiting for you. Oughtn't you to join them?'

'What are you doing this morning?' he persisted.

Andrea glanced at Janet. 'I expect we'll be going out on to the slopes, won't we?'

Janet coloured prettily. 'Well, actually, Andrea, Axel's promised to give me some lessons today.' She giggled. 'Skiing lessons, I mean. Do you mind?'

'Would it make any difference if I did?' Andrea asked dryly. 'No. No, of course I don't mind.' But her stomach muscles tightened at the prospect of meeting Axel von Mahlstrom again.

'Then how about coming up the Feldberg with us, Andrea?' suggested Roy, with more enthusiasm, as Susie and several of the others drifted over from their table across the room to see what was going on.

'Yes, do come,' echoed Susie, with an impish grin. 'Roy's been like a bear with a sore head since he got up this morning. We've been in the pool, you see,' she explained.

Andrea hesitated, looking at Roy. 'Are you sure you want my company after last night?'

Roy sighed, glancing at Janet and Susie and the others and obviously wishing them far away. 'Yes,' he affirmed shortly. 'Will you come?'

'All right,' Andrea nodded. 'So long as Ruth doesn't bite my head off.'

'She won't,' Susie assured her. 'She's not coming. But I am, and Paul, and one or two of the more daring amongst us.'

It was another crisp cold day, with a wintry sun to lay a gilding on the trees and a sheen on the icy slopes. One of the group, Andrea had no time to worry about her own problems and determinedly entered into the spirit of things, infusing them all with her sometimes reckless enthusiasm.

In the cafeteria at the head of the ski lift, she forced herself to swallow one of the sausage-filled rolls she had eaten the day before. Surprisingly, it seemed to fill a little of the hollowness inside her, but that wasn't altogether a physical thing. Nevertheless, she felt less lightheaded after it, and that was a relief. The faint dizziness she had experienced on the downward plunge had convinced her that she had been foolhardy to attempt such an activity without first getting something substantial inside her.

They returned to the hotel in the late afternoon, making plans for the evening in the bar, and as they entered the reception area Andrea looked round expectantly for Janet.

But there was no sign of her and, frowning, she left the others, and went upstairs to their suite.

At first she thought Janet was not there either, but as she crossed the sitting-room to her bedroom, her cousin's voice called: 'Andrea! Andrea, is that you?'

Turning back, Andrea went to the door of Janet's bedroom and looked inside. Janet was lying on her bed, still wearing the *vorlagers* and thick sweater she had worn under her parka that morning. One of her trouser legs was rolled back, however, and her ankle swathed in bandages.

Andrea's eyes widened. 'Oh, Jan, what have you done?'

Janet sniffed miserably. 'I've twisted my ankle, badly. Axel said I was lucky not to have broken it.'

Andrea moved to the bed. 'You did this skiing, I suppose.'

'Yes. I was doing so well, too. Axel said so. But my skis just went out of control . . .' She propped herself up on her elbows, looking resentfully at the bandages. 'Of all the rotten luck! Just when I was beginning to enjoy myself.'

Andrea shed her own jacket, pulling the woolly hat off her head so that her hair fell silkily about her shoulders. 'Consider yourself fortunate that it wasn't a break,' she commented. 'You'd have had a plaster on for the rest of the holiday.'

Janet pressed her lips together for a moment, and then lay back with resignation. 'I suppose you're right. How long do you think this will take to get better?'

'Two or three days, I should think,' replied Andrea, walking towards the bedroom door.

'Axel said I should rest it as much as possible.'

'He's right. It's the only cure.'

'He said he would carry me downstairs for dinner this evening. Will you help me to get ready, Andrea?'

Andrea forced a smile, even though the knowledge that Axel von Mahlstrom would be coming into their suite was disruptive. 'Of course. Give me time for a bath and a few minutes' relaxation, and I'll be with you.'

Andrea had dressed in the purple velvet pants she had worn the first evening they were in Grossfeld, matching them with a nylon velvet tunic in rather an attractive shade of violet. She had been tempted to wear something quite outrageous, like the lime green see-through blouse which one of the gang back home had bought her on her last birthday, but for once she restrained her impulses. For Janet's sake, she told herself, but she couldn't deny that there was something about Axel von Mahlstrom which made a nonsense of her defiance.

He arrived soon after seven-thirty and Andrea had, perforce, to answer the door. Tonight he was less formally dressed in close-fitting leather pants, a cream silk shirt, and a leather jerkin with a thonged fringe. The silvery fair hair lay thickly against his head, one heavy strand persisting in lying over his forehead so that occasionally he thrust it back with an impatient hand.

'*Guten abend, Fraülein*,' he greeted her politely, and looking into his cool enigmatic features Andrea wished she knew exactly what he was thinking.

'Please – come in,' she invited formally, and he stepped into the sitting-room of the suite and closed the door behind him. 'Janet's almost ready,' she continued, aware of an awkwardness that was new to her. 'I'll tell her you're here.'

'*Danke.*'

Andrea paused. 'Are you eating in the hotel this evening, Herr Baron?'

He looked at her through those cold grey eyes. 'As a matter of fact, *ja*.'

Andrea digested this. 'With – Janet?'

'Ah – *nein*.' He shook his head. 'Herr Lieber has invited me to dine with him.' His eyes narrowed. 'Surely you do not depend upon your cousin for companionship?'

She couldn't decide whether he was being deliberately rude or not, so not deigning to answer this she walked quickly to Janet's bedroom door, knocked, and went inside.

'The Baron's here,' she announced flatly.

Janet was seated before the vanity unit putting the finishing touches to her make-up. Her eyes lit up. 'He is? Oh, gosh! Do I look all right, Andrea?'

Andrea surveyed the soft material of Janet's caftan with approval. It successfully hid the ugly bandage on her ankle. 'You look very attractive. Shall I tell him you're ready?'

Janet nodded excitedly, and Andrea opened the door again and went into the sitting-room. 'If you'll just go through, Herr Baron,' she suggested, and walked across to the windows.

There were a few significant moments after their greeting

when all Andrea could hear was the rustle of Janet's clothing, and then Axel von Mahlstrom reappeared, carrying his burden. Without being asked, Andrea hurried to open the outer door, and he afforded her a faint bow of his head as they passed through.

After they had gone, Andrea stood breathing deeply. She had to follow them down, but she was loath to do so. Not for the first time she wished she had not been compelled to come to Grossfeld.

Andrea and Janet ate dinner alone in the restaurant much to Janet's disappointment.

'I thought Axel was going to dine with us,' she exclaimed sulkily. 'I didn't know he knew Herr Lieber that well.'

'I imagine he knows just about everybody in Grossfeld,' remarked Andrea quietly. 'After all, he does live here, doesn't he?'

'Oh, yes.' Janet brightened for a moment. 'He told me he has a chalet not far from the ski school.'

'There you are, then.' Andrea looked idly round the room, wondering what had happened to the woman the Baron was escorting the first time they had met up with him. Perhaps he had found more lucrative pastures.

As her lips tightened she looked down at her plate. She was thinking far too much about Axel von Mahlstrom, whether or not her thoughts were malicious or otherwise. He was Janet's concern. Let her worry about him and his intentions.

After the meal was over, another of the guests carried Janet into the *après-ski* bar and later in the evening they were joined by Roy and Susie and the others. There was much amusement derived from Janet's ankle, but she took it all in good part and Andrea relaxed a little.

She was dancing with Roy when two men appeared in the archway that led through from the hall. One was Nicolas Lieber, the hotel's proprietor; the other, of course, was Axel von Mahlstrom. Roy saw the new arrivals, too, and grinned.

'Your cousin will be delighted,' he commented, nodding towards the newcomers. 'She likes being the centre of attraction, doesn't she? Is that what comes of having everything she wants all her life?'

'Everything she wants—' Andrea broke off, realizing what he meant. 'I – well, perhaps,' she finished lamely.

'She certainly likes attention,' Roy went on, unaware that Andrea was scarcely listening to him. All her attention was focused on Axel von Mahlstrom as he left his host and walked with indolent grace across the room to where Janet was sitting. She saw him bend and say something to Janet, something that made the colour suddenly burn in her cheeks and her eyes to sparkle brilliantly. 'She's not like you at all,' Roy was saying as she focused on him again. 'Isn't that always the way?'

Andrea frowned, feeling she had missed out on something. 'Isn't *what* always the way?'

'Girls. They're either good-looking, or disgustingly wealthy. Never both.'

Andrea had to hide a smile at this. 'Do you think so?'

Roy nodded. 'My father is desperately afraid I'll be caught by some fortune-hunting female with an eye to the main chance.'

'Is he?' Andrea moved her tongue over her upper lip. 'And what do you think?'

'I used to agree with him.' Roy shrugged. 'But since meeting you . . .'

'Oh, come off it!' Andrea almost laughed. 'I'm not that green, Roy. You're not serious about me and you know it. Let's just keep it light, hmm?'

She was glad when the music changed to a beat number and the couples on the floor separated to do their own thing. Giving herself up to the rhythm of the drums, Andrea allowed the sound to dominate her, and she knew when the music ended that she had never danced with more abandonment.

'You were terrific!' exclaimed Roy, catching her as she spun away from him and bringing her down to earth. 'Where did you learn to dance like that?'

'I don't suppose I learned it,' answered Andrea, fanning herself with a lazy hand. 'Isn't it some primeval urge to return to the forces of nature?'

'Well, don't forget to take me with you next time you take off,' commented Roy dryly, and they laughed. They were still laughing when they reached the group that had Janet as its focal point.

Axel von Mahlstrom was still standing, and he inclined his head towards Andrea in what she thought was a singularly contemptuous gesture. Of course. He would have seen her dancing. No doubt he considered her a typical example of reckless, free-living youth. Well, let him! She was still sufficiently high from the dancing not to give a damn!

'Isn't anybody going to buy me a drink?' she demanded, smiling provocatively up at Louis Graham, one of Roy's friends, and he responded with alacrity.

'What would you like?' he asked, and she allowed her tongue to protrude ever so slightly.

'Why, Louis! Don't you know?'

'It's vodka,' put in Roy shortly, his tone eloquent of his disapproval of her unexpected promiscuity. 'I'll get it.'

'Don't bother,' retorted Louis, already on his way to the bar, and Roy's expression darkened ominously.

Susie, sensing the quickening tension, said: 'We're going up the Oberlaufen tomorrow, Herr Baron. I expect you've been up there lots of times.'

Axel von Mahlstrom responded that he had indeed visited the highest point on the cable railway which swung some ten thousand feet up the Oberlaufen glacier.

'I'm sure I'll be terrified,' Susie added, with a nervous giggle. 'I even hate tall buildings. But I'm determined to go.'

Louis returned with a tall glass of liquid edged about with various pieces of fruit. He handed it to Andrea and she thanked him, extricating herself from Roy's possessive hold. Susie continued to hold the Baron in conversation, occasionally allowing someone else to get a word in, and Andrea sipped experimentally at her drink, gasping a little at its potency.

'Are you trying to get me drunk?' she asked Louis, in an undertone, but she was aware that both Roy and the Baron had heard her.

'Omit the word "drunk", and you may be right,' countered Louis wickedly, and they exchanged another smile.

'What do you think you're playing at?' demanded an irate Roy in her ear, and Andrea's eyes widened as she turned to look at him.

'Cool down, Roy,' she advised mockingly. 'Remember what Daddy told you.'

Roy took a step closer, grasping her wrist in exactly the same place as the Baron had gripped her the night before and she winced in agony. Then, as unexpectedly, Axel von

Mahlstrom was beside her, and his words caused Roy to release her at once.

'You will dance with me, *Fraülein*,' he said, an edge of ice to his politeness. 'You will excuse us, will you not, Herr Stevens?'

There was so much more to his words than a mere invitation to dance. They were a command, and a challenge, and Roy let go of her without argument.

Andrea wanted to refuse. She wanted to see Axel von Mahlstrom's face when she turned him down, but somehow his hand was in the small of her back propelling her on to the floor, while with his other hand he took her drink and handed it to a passing waiter.

The music had slowed again and while many of the younger people were drifting around wrapped in each other's arms the Baron held her at arm's length and moved very formally to the rhythm.

Andrea glanced back over her shoulder at the others and saw that Roy and Louis were presently engaged in an angry interchange. Janet meanwhile was talking earnestly to Ruth Stevens, and Andrea decided she didn't need to be a mind-reader to guess what they were saying.

Returning her attention to her partner, she exclaimed: 'Why did you do that?'

Axel's brows drew together. 'Ask you to dance?'

'Of course.'

'Don't you know?'

'If I did, I shouldn't be asking, should I? I don't want to dance with you. And I certainly didn't invite it.'

Axel's eyes narrowed. 'But you were inviting a certain number of other things, were you not, *Fraülein*?'

'Oh, stop calling me *Fraülein* in that ridiculously formal way! My name is Andrea, as I'm sure you know. As to the other, I don't know what you're talking about.'

'Yes, you do, *Fraülein*. You were deliberately playing Stevens off against Graham. I am not a fool, *Fraülein*. I could see exactly what you were doing. I chose to – how do you say it? – cool the situation, *ja*?'

Andrea's anger simmered. 'And what gives you the right to interfere in my affairs?'

Axel looked down at her with faint contempt. 'I dislike unpleasantness, *Fraülein*. You, I regret to say, create it.'

'Why, you—'

Andrea tried to pull away from him then, but his hold on her was strong and inescapable. In the momentary struggle, however, the wide sleeve of her tunic fell back to reveal the ugly bruising marring the soft skin of her left forearm. Axel saw this at once, and his eyes sought hers, darkening with an emotion she could not identify. But beneath his gaze her struggles ceased, and a peculiar tightness invaded her throat.

'Did I do that?' he demanded harshly, and she nodded.

'You can be pretty unpleasant yourself when you try,' she said unsteadily, and his fingers relaxed their hold on her, his hands falling to his sides.

'I am very sorry,' he apologized stiffly, and contrarily she no longer wanted to get away from him.

They had stopped in the middle of the floor but fortunately the discreet lighting and the other couples circulating about them hid them from the group around Janet. Andrea glanced about her, and then said:

'So – shall we begin again?'

Axel brushed back his hair with a careless hand. 'If that is what you wish, *Fraülein*,' he agreed politely, and Andrea felt a rising sense of impatience.

She moved closer to him so that he could put his arms about her. He put one arm about her waist, but when he would have taken her hand with the other she shook her head and placed both his arms around her waist so that they could dance in the way everyone else was dancing. He wanted to protest, she sensed it, and he held his body stiffly apart from hers, resisting her all the way. Andrea's palms rested against the soft leather of his jerkin. The cream silk shirt was open at the neck, but only one button, she noticed, with some amusement. His skin was very tanned, a startling contrast to his light hair, and his hair looked smooth and healthy, free of any hair dressing. She wondered how it would feel between her fingers, how he would look with his hair rumpled from sleep, with a growth of beard on his chin, his lean muscular body free of all constraint. A disturbing warmth enveloped her, and on impulse she allowed her palms to slide up his jerkin to his shoulders. She would have liked to link her arms behind his neck as she had done with Roy, but that required more courage than she possessed right at this moment.

He looked down at her then, a disturbingly unguarded

look that seemed to penetrate right to the inmost core of her being. Oh, God, she thought lightheadedly, and stumbled. His instinctive support brought her up against him, and his clothes were no barrier to the hardness of his body. Andrea gripped his jerkin to save herself, and closed her eyes against the wave of emotion that swept over her.

But almost before she had time to gather herself, he had put her away from him, and was saying: 'I am sorry, *Fraülein*, I am not much of a dancer, as you can see.'

Andrea's eyes sought his, but their cool grey depths told her nothing. 'It – it was my fault,' she protested.

'You are very kind, but I know my limitations,' he affirmed coolly. 'Shall we return to the others?'

CHAPTER FIVE

THE rest of the evening was an anti-climax.

Andrea had lost the urge to have fun with either Roy or Louis, and watching Janet with Axel von Mahlstrom brought a sickening little ache to her temples. She excused herself soon after eleven despite Roy's pleading for her to stay, and went up to bed. But not to sleep. She was still awake when Axel brought Janet upstairs, and she breathed a sigh of relief when it became apparent that Janet could manage alone. She heard Axel depart and rolled on to her stomach, burying her face in the pillow. What was that saying about the best laid plans of mice and men ...

The next morning Janet was up and about first. But this was hardly surprising. It had been well into the early hours before Andrea eventually got to sleep and when Janet came in, fully dressed, at nine o'clock, her cousin was dead to the world.

'Andrea!' Janet limped to the bed and shook her awake. 'Andrea, aren't you going to get up today?'

Andrea groaned and rolled on to her back, shading her eyes against the glare of sun on snow that was revealed when Janet drew back the curtains. 'What time is it?'

'It's after nine, and I'm starving!' Janet stared at her impatiently. 'Heavens, you weren't late to bed last night. I should have expected you to be up with the dark this morning!'

Andrea struggled into a sitting position, shivering and wrapping the quilt about her naked form. 'I didn't sleep very well,' she murmured reluctantly, brushing her hair back out of her eyes. 'How are you this morning? How's your ankle?'

'It feels heaps better,' said Janet with satisfaction. 'Another two days and I should be as good as new.'

'That's good.' Andrea blinked at her watch. 'Gosh, it's after nine. I'd better get dressed.'

'Herr Lieber said he would carry me downstairs this morning,' went on Janet conversationally. 'Axel introduced us last night, and he's a charming man. Older than Axel, of course, but nice.'

Andrea slid off the bed and pulled on her robe. She felt rather sick and headachy, but she put that down to her disturbed night.

'What time is Herr Lieber coming then?' she asked.

'He told me just to ring when I was ready. I've been waiting for you to wake up.'

Andrea sighed. 'Well, look – you go ahead. Ring him. Go and have breakfast. I just want coffee, as usual, so there's no need to wait for me.'

Janet hesitated. 'You're sure you don't mind?'

'Of course not.'

Andrea walked towards the bathroom, but as she reached for the door handle, Janet said: 'We didn't disturb you last night, did we? Axel and me? He brought me up, you see.'

Andrea shook her head, not looking at her cousin. 'No, you didn't disturb me.'

'I'm so glad. I mean, after what happened and everything. I suppose Axel made you feel pretty small, didn't he?'

Andrea swung round then, staring at Janet bemusedly. 'What are you talking about?'

Janet flushed. 'That silly affair with Roy and Louis. You were really making a fool of yourself, Andrea, weren't you? I mean, thank heavens Axel was there to break it up.'

'Is that what *he* said?'

'Well, yes.' Janet sighed. 'Look, I know you're the one who's supposed to know her way around, but really – acting like that! It was rather childish, wasn't it? Poor Susie thought Roy and Louis were about to come to blows, and they're the best of friends really.' She hesitated. 'That's why Axel asked you to dance, of course. For Susie's sake. And mine.'

'Oh, really!'

Andrea was tempted to pull back her sleeve and show Janet exactly what her beloved Baron had done in an unguarded moment, but restrained the impulse. Besides, Janet was right. He had asked her to dance to get her away from Roy and Louis, and he had succeeded in cooling the situation. So far as she was concerned he had doused every errant impulse inside her, except one . . .

'Is that all you wanted to say, Janet?' she asked now, and Janet looked slightly discomfited.

'Yes.'

'Good. Then I'll go and get my bath, if you don't mind,' said Andrea coldly, and jerked open the bathroom door.

After breakfast, which Janet had taken with Susie Nichols' parents and which Andrea had missed out en- tirely, it was suggested that Janet and Andrea join the trip to Oberlaufen. As they were going by car and then cable car, it would not entail a lot of walking for Janet, and there were plenty of able-bodied young men to carry her if necessary. Janet was keen, but Andrea was not.

'You go, Jan,' she said, when the idea was put to them. 'I – I've got rather a headache, actually. I'd rather stay in the hotel today, if you don't mind.'

Roy came to stand beside her. 'I shan't make a nuisance of myself, if that's what you're afraid of, Andrea,' he mur- mured quietly. 'Please come! I'd like you to.'

Andrea shook her head, touched by his sincerity. 'No, Roy, not today. Maybe – some other time.'

'Then I won't go either. I'll stay and keep you company,' he asserted.

'*No!*' Andrea softened the refusal with a smile. 'Honestly, Roy, I'd rather you didn't. I'm – not much company today. I'll be better alone.'

Roy heaved a sigh. 'Are you sure you're not just saying that?'

'Of course I'm not.' Andrea was conscious of Ruth watch- ing them. 'Go with your stepsister. Give her the pleasure of your company for once.'

Roy glanced across at Ruth. 'I don't know what's up with her. She's always moaning about something or other. I'm beginning to wish I'd never agreed to be responsible for her.'

'Spend a little time with her,' suggested Andrea mildly. 'I'm sure she'll come round.'

Roy hunched his shoulders moodily. 'I don't want to spend a little time with her! I'm not a kid, you know, Andrea. I need a woman's company, not a child's.'

Andrea half smiled. 'How old is Ruth?'

'Nineteen.'

'A year older than me, in fact,' she commented.

Roy sighed. 'Yes. But you know what I mean. You're not like Ruth. I don't believe you were ever like Ruth.' He flushed. 'You know what I mean. Don't make me spell it out.'

Andrea shrugged. 'I'm sorry. But the idea of spending the day with a crowd of people doesn't appeal to me. I – well, I'd prefer to be alone.'

Roy shifted from one foot to the other. 'That's your final word?'

'Yes.'

'Will I see you tonight, then? I understand there's to be some sort of fancy dress carnival at the Kursaal.' The Kursaal was a kind of nightclub in the town. 'Would you like to go?'

Andrea hesitated, then she gave in. 'All right. Providing my headache gets no worse. What time are you going?'

Roy brightened. 'We're all meeting in the hall after dinner. About nine-thirty?'

Andrea nodded. 'Fine.' Susie and Paul and Louis Graham had come to join them and she included them all in her smile. 'Have a nice day!'

Janet showed few qualms about leaving her cousin alone all day, but Andrea reflected that had their positions been reversed, she would have felt obliged to stay with Janet. Not that she wanted Janet's company, she told herself wryly, but it was another example of the differences that money could make. It had given her a guilt complex. Janet was not troubled by such a thing, nor by a conscience, it would appear.

Once the majority of the guests had departed about their various occupations, the hotel seemed very quiet. Andrea went up to the suite and collected a paperback novel she had brought with her, carrying it downstairs again to the lounge. She settled herself in a comfortable chair in one corner and began to read.

She was reading the first page for the umpteenth time, trying to keep her mind on what she was doing when it would persist in going off at a tangent, when footsteps sounded across the hall, and the swing doors into the lounge were pushed open. She looked up in surprise and encountered the cool dispassionate eyes of the Baron Axel von Mahlstrom. Immediately, the dull throbbing in her head which she had had since getting up that morning was magnified to painful proportions, and one hand gripped the arm of her chair nervously.

Axel allowed the doors to swing closed behind him and stood regarding her steadily. He was dressed in the thick parka and trousers he wore for skiing, and he drew sheepskin gloves from his long, lean-fingered hands.

'*Guten Morgen, Fraülein*,' he greeted her, with his usual politeness. 'You are alone today, I see.'

Andrea had herself under control now. 'Was there something you wanted, Herr Baron?' she inquired, with amazing coolness.

Axel brought his gloves hard against his thigh in a whipping gesture, and then took several more steps into the room. 'I understand your cousin and her friends have departed for the Oberlaufen glacier, *Fraülein*. Did you not wish to accompany them?'

Andrea shrugged. 'Obviously not.'

His eyes narrowed. He had short thick lashes, dark at the roots, but very fair at the tip, and they successfully concealed his expression. 'Are you not well, *Fraülein*?'

Andrea, who had deliberately returned her attention to her book in an effort to dismiss him from her thoughts, looked up with feigned impatience. 'Don't I look well?'

'Not altogether, no,' he told her honestly.

Andrea's eyes widened, and now her impatience was not feigned. 'Thank you,' she said sarcastically.

'You look pale,' he persisted. 'I do not think you slept well.'

'Oh, don't you?' Andrea's breathing had quickened, in spite of her determination to remain calm. 'And why would you suppose that, I wonder? Particularly as you took such care of me last evening!'

His expression hardened. 'Is it necessary always that you must be rude to me, *Fraülein*?' he exclaimed. 'My concern was perfectly genuine. I do not take pleasure in anyone's indisposition.'

'Not even your enemy's. No, of course. *You* wouldn't,' retorted Andrea, looking down at her book again in the hope that he would go away.

'Janet tells me you do a lot of skiing, *Fraülein*,' he went on, apparently unperturbed by her apparent absorption in her book. 'That you are quite an expert, in fact.'

Andrea lifted her eyes again. 'Janet exaggerates,' she said flatly. 'I can ski; end of sentence.'

Axel rocked back on his booted heels, surveying her appraisingly. 'I think you underestimate yourself, *Fraülein*, but we will not argue the point. Your – friend Stevens tells me you have skied the Feldberg. That is no place for amateurs, no?'

Andrea sighed. 'What does it matter—'

'It matters because I would like to take you skiing, *Fräulein*,' he said harshly. 'That is, of course, if you can drag yourself away from your so-fascinating book!'

Andrea stared at him in astonishment. 'Why should *you* want to take *me* skiing!' she demanded.

His eyes darkened angrily. 'Perhaps because I feel sorry for you, *Fräulein*. Deserted by your friends—'

'They have not deserted me! I chose not to go.'

'As you wish.' He made a negative gesture. 'Will you come?'

'No.' She took a certain amount of pleasure from refusing. 'I have a headache. That's why I didn't go with the others.'

Axel regarded her consideringly. *'Haben Sie?* That is why you look so pale, *ja?'*

'Perhaps.' Andrea did not look up from her book this time.

'Then I suggest the cold air outside might do more for you than this calculated warmth within,' he remarked.

This thought had occurred to Andrea, but she did not intend to give him that satisfaction. 'I'm quite happy here, thank you,' she replied shortly, and with a stifled expletive, the Baron turned and walked out of the lounge.

As soon as he had gone she felt a disagreeable sense of depression descend upon her and putting her book aside she got irritably to her feet and walked to the window. What was the matter with her? she asked herself angrily. Surely she hadn't wanted to go with him! Not after the way he had discussed her behaviour with Janet the night before! She should have nothing to do with him. She didn't like him and she didn't trust him. Just because his undoubted sex appeal could seed the most disturbing feelings inside her it did not mean that he was any less of a conceited swine. Did he honestly think he could come here and ask her to go skiing with him after the way he had treated her? It was ludicrous!

Nevertheless, his visit had disturbed her, and snatching up her book again, she ran up the stairs to their suite. The maid was just finishing their rooms, and she smiled and said: *'Guten Morgen,'* as Andrea smiled at her before going to change her clothes.

In her *parka* and *vorlagers*, dark glasses swinging from her hand, Andrea left the hotel, breathing deeply of the cold crisp air. Her headache did indeed feel better outdoors, and the activity of walking sent the blood coursing warmly through her veins. Perhaps she should have gone to Oberlaufen after all, she thought. But the prospect of being in a crowd and of having to be sociable to a lot of people did not appeal to her today.

She hired some skis, and took the lift up to the top of the Feldberg. While she drank coffee in the cafeteria, she overheard two Germans talking about an impending storm, and looking at the overcast sky she could believe it. So far they had been lucky with the weather, but once the snow set in it could be days before it stopped. Days of being confined to the hotel, confined to the company of Janet and the others – Andrea didn't find that prospect appealing either. She wondered if she cabled her father in those circumstances whether it would do any good.

Despite the disruptive influence of her thoughts, she quite enjoyed the day. Skiing was a solitary occupation, a singular test of skill that could not wholly be shared with anyone, and her mood did not encourage would-be admirers to interrupt her mental isolation.

It was getting dark when she took her final trip up the mountain, and below, in the valley, lights were beginning to glitter from a dozen different windows. Tiny flakes of snow were beginning to fall, too, and it was this as much as anything which had encouraged her to get as much out of the day as she could. Away to her left, the belt of trees which she and Roy had used in their obstacle races invited excitement, and pushing her sticks into the snow she swooped towards them.

It was dark in amongst the trees, but the tracks she and Roy had made were still visible. She slalomed to and fro, enjoying the rocking motion of her skis, feeling the power of body control. And then, without warning, one of the skis caught the protruding root of a tree which had been indistinguishable in the shadows. The ski was trapped, but her bodily momentum carried her forward, twisting her leg agonizingly before the ski snapped like a twig and she pitched into a snowdrift.

She thought she must have lost consciousness for a few minutes, because when she opened her eyes it seemed darker than before and the lights below her in the valley were no longer pinpricks of light but a mass of artificial illumination. It was snowing more heavily, too, the flakes thickening as they increased, and a sudden paralysing awareness of the desperate position she was in descended on her in a wave of pure panic.

Fighting back hysteria, she struggled to sit up, and scrambled out of the drift with difficulty. She stifled a sob as a shaft of pain shot up her leg from the knee, and when she tried to get to her feet she found the leg would not support her.

Holding on to the trunk of the tree which had caused her downfall, she looked about her, hoping that help might be at hand. But her careless disregard for her own safety had not been imitated by any of the other skiers, and as the light was almost gone, the slopes were deserted. Perhaps if it had not been snowing quite so heavily, there might have been one or two enthusiasts still about, but from where she stood she appeared to be alone.

She looked down at the lights in the valley, glimmering through the falling curtain of snow. Somehow she had to get down there, or die in the attempt. To remain where she was would be a futile exercise. No one knew she had come skiing today, She wouldn't even be missed until Janet's return, and even then it was possible that Janet might not immediately wonder where she was. And in her disabled position, she was quite likely to remain in the lounge, waiting for Andrea to come and find her. She was cold already, and the temperature was still falling. She had to go down.

The belt of trees stretched down into the valley, too. They did not follow the strict route observed by the skiers, but swerved away in a diagonal course. Nevertheless, they seemed to Andrea to be her safest method of descent. If she could somehow limp from tree to tree, she might conceivably achieve her objective.

But the going was rough. Her knee pained her terribly, and it was impossible to do anything more than lurch downward, grasping the trees like lifelines and praying that she would not lose the feeling in her hands. She had shed her skis, and her feet ached.

It seemed a terribly long way down. The snow had thickened even more, and she could scarcely see where she was going. Had it not been for the ground continually sloping away ahead of her, she would have thought she was going round in circles.

And then, when desperation was beginning to take her in its grip, she saw the lights of a chalet directly below her, sheltered by a copse of larch and fir trees. In her excitement, she tried to move more quickly now, and her gloves, wet and slippery with the snow, lost their grip and she tumbled downwards, rolling over and over, knocking all the breath out of her. Only the fence which surrounded the garden of the chalet brought her up short, and she lay there for several minutes before attempting to move, partially winded by her fall.

At last she was able to stagger to her feet again, and groped along the fence, searching for the gate. She found it at last, but its catch, stiffened by the snow, was awkward to open. When it did give at last, the gate fell back on its hinges with a noisy bang, and immediately a dog set up a noisy barking inside. It was not a very friendly sound, but just at that moment she would have forfeited friendship for the sight of a warm fire and another human face.

There were steps up to the door, but she couldn't make them, so she stretched across and knocked at the bottom of the door. The dog's barking grew even more frenzied, and a terrible thought struck her. If the dog was alone in the house, what would she do? She would die! She hadn't the energy to go any further.

But just when hope seemed gone, she heard the sound of a man's deep voice, speaking in German, she thought, bidding the dog to silence, and then the door opened.

'I – I'm sorry to trouble you—' she was beginning, eager that whoever was opening the door should not take her for an intruder, when weakness enveloped her whole body, and she sank down miserably on to the bottom step. For the man who had opened the door, and who was standing there in a navy bathrobe and bare feet regarding her in amazement, was Axel von Mahlstrom.

'*Andrea!*' he exclaimed disbelievingly. '*Mein Gott*, what has happened?'

Andrea shook her head helplessly, stupidly near to tears suddenly. 'I – I've made a fool of myself. I – acted recklessly. I had an – accident.'

Axel seemed to realize she was trembling with cold and fatigue and uttering an oath in his own language, he said:

'Please. Come in.'

Andrea tried to get to her feet, but her muscles refused to obey her. They had stiffened with the cold and with a scowl that brought his brows together, he came down the steps in his bare feet and bending, lifted her bodily into his arms.

'You are hurt!' he muttered impatiently, climbing the steps again and carrying her into the hall of the chalet. He kicked the door closed with his foot. '*Verdammt*, I should have known.'

Andrea scarcely heeded his words. He was so marvellously warm, the lapels of his bathrobe parting to reveal the muscled expanse of his chest. She dared not put her arms round his neck to support herself even had she been able to lift them. She was wet, and dirty from the bark of the trees, and as she had lost her hat at some point early in her descent, her hair hung in the rat's tails her father had teased her about. What must he be thinking of her? she thought miserably. That she deserved everything she got? She did! She knew it. But that didn't excuse her behaviour.

Axel opened a door to the left of the hall, and the wave of heat that emanated from the room beyond brought a painful tingling to her hands and feet. There was the excited scampering of feet and looking down she saw the dog which had been barking loudly earlier and which was now uttering smaller barks and growls at this unexpected intrusion into its domain. It was a grey German shepherd, and although it appeared reasonably friendly at the moment, Andrea would not have cared to meet it in less congenial circumstances.

Axel commanded the creature to silence and carried Andrea to a chintz-covered couch before a blazing log fire. The heat and the light hurt her eyes and they began to water, but Andrea raised a gloved hand and brushed the moisture away, unwilling that he should think she was crying.

Axel straightened for a moment, wrapping the bathrobe more closely about him, and she realized it was the only garment he wore. Then he came down on his haunches again, and ignoring her protests began to unlace her boots.

'Tell me what happened,' he said, pulling one of the boots off and instantly beginning to massage her foot. He understood how the return of feeling could be an exquisite pain, and his strong fingers dispersed the sharpness of

66

that discomfort.

Andrea was intensely conscious of him squatting before her, of the clean scent of his body, and the damp virility of his hair. There was pleasure, too, in his hands upon her, arousing a curious lethargy inside her.

'I – I decided to go skiing,' she began, half defensively. 'But I had an accident – one of my skis snapped, and there was no one to help me.'

'How did you manage to snap one of your skis?' he asked, drawing off her other boot, and glancing up at her through narrowed eyes as the movement jarred her injured knee and she started with the sharpness of the pain that ran up to her hip. He examined the ankle carefully, folding back her trouser leg to her calf, and then he went on: 'You have injured this leg. The knee, I think.' Andrea nodded. 'I will be gentle.'

Andrea looked down at her hands, fighting back self-pity. She didn't deserve his consideration and she knew it. And when Janet found out about this . . .

She looked with determined interest round the room, trying not to think about Janet. It was a comfortable apartment, sparsely but practically furnished with an unpolished table and two chairs, a small bureau, and this couch and a matching armchair. The wooden floor was polished and liberally strewn with skin rugs, and there were well-filled bookshelves at either side of the hearth. There was no evidence of a woman's touch anywhere, and the furnishings that there were were purely functional. But for all that, Andrea liked it. It was so refreshingly different from the luxury she was used to.

'I asked how you managed to snap one of your skis,' he prompted her quietly, and she avoided his penetrating stare.

'I – I told you. I was – foolish. I skied too near the trees.'

He completed his massage of her feet and straightened. 'So, that feels better?' She nodded, and leaving her for a moment to the shepherd's disturbing appraisal, he crossed to the bureau and taking a decanter and a glass from a cupboard at the bottom, he poured an inch of some amber-coloured liquid. He brought the glass back to her, handing it to her and saying: 'Drink this. It is cognac. It will complete the cure.'

Andrea took the glass without a demur. The fiery liquid was deliciously warming, but she was annoyed to see that her hands still trembled as she raised the glass to her lips.

'Now.' Axel stood with his back to the fire, the blazing logs behind him silhouetting his powerful frame within the loose-fitting bathrobe. Andrea tried not to stare at his body, as he went on: 'I suggest you use my bathroom, as I was doing when you arrived. If you will take off your trousers, I will try and find some way of supporting your knee.'

Andrea's eyes lifted to his face blankly. 'Oh, but I can't stay here. I mean, Janet will be wondering where I am. She'll be worried . . .'

Axel's expression hardened slightly. 'Believe it or not, *Fraülein*, but I do have a telephone. Providing it is still working, *naturlich*. I can contact the hotel and reassure your cousin of your safety.'

Andrea felt rather ridiculous. 'I see.'

'Have no fear, *Fraülein*,' he added, his eyes vaguely contemptuous in their appraisal, 'we Austrians are quite civilized!'

Andrea felt indignation replacing gratitude. 'I never thought otherwise, Herr Baron,' she retorted, and he inclined his head.

'So. Can you walk?'

Andrea shifted to the edge of the couch. One way or another, she was determined to do so, no matter how painful the exercise might be. Supporting herself with the arm of the couch, she managed to get to her feet, standing on her uninjured leg, swaying slightly. Warmth was spreading throughout her body now, and she held out the empty glass.

'If you will show me the way . . .' she suggested politely.

It was agonizing putting any weight on her injured leg, but she hoped he would not notice the difficulty she was having. He went ahead, opening the door, and she followed to the accompaniment of the dog's growling.

'*Schweig*, Prinz!' The Baron spoke sharply, and the dog contented itself with a plaintive whine.

However, the dog's misbehaviour had drawn his master's attention back to Andrea again, and he stifled a curse when he saw how pale she had become after only a few steps. Shaking his head, he came back to her and swung her up into his arms again.

'You have a saying in your country, do you not? Something about pride being painful?' he chided. 'Must you demonstrate it so foolishly?'

Andrea turned her face away from his. 'I could have managed,' she defended herself tautly, but she crossed her fingers as she spoke.

The chalet was not very big, mainly a one-storied building, Andrea guessed, with perhaps an attic room under the sloping eaves. Away from the comforting roar of the fire, she could hear the wind whistling round the chalet's walls, and the slap of snow against the windows. The Baron carried her along the hall which ran from front to back of the building, and pushed open another door leading into a bedroom. Andrea's stomach muscles tightened as he set her down on the side of the narrow bed, but when he straightened his expression was cool and enigmatic.

'The bathroom is through there, *Fräulein*,' he said, indicating another door. 'There is plenty of hot water, and you may borrow my robe so that I may examine your knee, *ja*?'

Andrea wet her lips with her tongue. 'Is – is this – your bedroom, Herr Baron?'

His eyes narrowed. 'It is the *only* bedroom, *Fräulein*. Why do you ask?'

Andrea sighed, not quite knowing what she wanted to say herself. 'I – I hope I'm not – putting you to a great deal of inconvenience,' she murmured awkwardly. 'Perhaps if you just phoned the hotel—'

His eyes darkened. 'Certainly I will telephone the hotel. But until the storm is over, you will have to make do with my company, *Fräulein*.'

'Oh, for goodness' sake!' she exclaimed, her confidence slowly returning. 'Can't you use my name? *Fräulein* this and *Fräulein* that! It's silly! You called me Andrea when you opened the door and found me on your doorstep.'

He thrust his hands into the pockets of his robe. 'Very well.'

Andrea looked up at him. 'And am I permitted to call you Axel? Or would that be carrying things too far?'

His eyes held hers for a long disturbing moment, and a wave of heat engulfed her. Then he shrugged. 'I am surprised you feel the need to ask my permission, *Frau*—' He

69

broke off. 'Do you need any assistance to get into the bathroom?'

Andrea stood up on her good leg. 'I can make it,' she assured him, and with another brooding look he left her.

It was wonderful to strip off her clothes and stand beneath the shower which was still steamy from his occupation. The clothes he had shed were still strewn carelessly on the bathroom floor, and she could smell a tantalizing odour of masculine talc and after-shaving lotion. She had put on her underwear, and was towelling her hair dry, when there was a knock at the door.

Her heartbeats quickened for a moment, but his voice was prosaic as he announced: 'Here is the robe!' from behind the panels.

She hopped to open the door a fraction and took the garment from his outstretched hand. It was still warm from the heat of his body, and she wrapped herself in it with a certain sensuous satisfaction. Her reflection in the mirror did not please her. Damp hair framed pale features that still bore the marks of strain from her ordeal on the mountain, and although the Baron's bathrobe came well below her knees, when she pulled the robe aside she could see the ugly swelling that was causing her so much discomfort.

Opening the bathroom door a few minutes later, she limped to the bed and sank down wearily on to its side. Exhaustion was beginning to catch up with her, and she thought she would have liked nothing better than to creep beneath the quilt on the Baron's narrow bed and sleep the clock round. The fact that it was almost dinner time, and hunger was beginning to make her feel really hollow now, mattered less than the physical weariness which was engulfing her. She wondered if the Baron had been able to get through to the hotel, and whether he had spoken to Janet or just Nicolas Lieber. Either way, it wouldn't much matter. Janet would not believe that Andrea had not planned this. But how could she have known that this chalet would be Axel von Mahlstrom's? Janet had said he lived near the ski slopes, but she had been very vague.

Andrea sighed and stretched her length on the narrow bed, closing her eyes. If she could just have a few minutes' rest, she thought, then she might feel more equipped to face what was surely to come . . .

CHAPTER SIX

ANDREA opened her eyes to a darkened room, and for several seconds could not remember where she was. Then realization came to her and she moved her limbs tentatively, discovering that the quilt she had previously been lying upon was now on top of her. Her fingers encountered the rough towelling of the robe the Baron had lent her, and it occurred to her that he must be responsible for covering her with the quilt. It was a disquieting thought, the idea of Axel von Mahlstrom lifting her sleeping body and putting her into his bed.

But where was he? She sat upright, endeavouring to distinguish shapes in the room. The brilliance of the snow outside was muted by the heaviness of the curtains at the windows, but it was possible to see that she was alone in this somewhat austere bedroom.

A sudden gust of wind brought a hail of snowflakes against the windows just then, and she wrapped the robe more closely about her and tried to make out the hands on her watch. It was a little after two o'clock and her brows drew together in dismay. Two o'clock! That meant she had slept for almost eight hours.

Another pang struck her, a physical one this time, and she pressed a hand to her empty stomach. She couldn't remember eating anything the day before, but now she was ravenously hungry. Perhaps that was what had woken her.

She ventured to swing her legs out of bed and winced as her knee, which had stiffened without treatment, sent a spasm of pain up her thigh. It was no better, and she sighed frustratedly. Well, there were other demands her body required relief from, and somehow she had to move.

She hopped to the bathroom, finding the light switch without too much difficulty. But on her return, curiosity took her to the bedroom door. Opening it, she peered out, listening for any sound of the German shepherd. Something told her that Prinz would not be half so obedient without his master's presence to control him.

Along the hall, a light glimmered beneath a door. The living-room door – and Andrea frowned more deeply. Was the Baron still up? As she was sleeping in his bed, had he decided to conduct an all-night vigil? She sighed. How could she allow that, when it had been her carelessness and nothing else which had brought about her accident? And besides, her own behaviour towards the Baron had left a lot to be desired.

Tightening the cord of the bathrobe, Andrea half limped, half hopped along the hall to the living-room door. Regaining her breath, she turned the handle tentatively, and looked round the door. The light came from a tall lamp standing near the bureau and the dying logs on the fire. At first she thought the room was empty, but then she distinguished the sound of someone breathing over and above her own uneasy palpitations, and saw two feet protruding over the end of the couch. They were stocking-clad feet, but unmistakably masculine in size and appearance.

Andrea opened the door a little wider and limped heavily into the room, unable to resist the temptation to look on the Baron in sleep. Dressed in tight suede pants and a matching suede jerkin that was open almost to his waist, one hand resting on his thigh, the other arm supporting his head, he looked relaxed and not visibly uncomfortable, although the three-seater couch poorly accommodated his length. His hair, fresh from the shower he had been taking at the time of her arrival, looked clean and healthy, and she had the strongest impulse to run her fingers into it. What would he do, she mused, if she woke him? A faint smile curved her lips. What other impulses might she arouse in him than the anger and contempt which she was growing used to inspiring?

With a sigh, she backed away from the couch, and went out into the hall again. It was much colder here, and she shivered. Where was the kitchen? she wondered, longing for something to eat. It should not be too difficult to find. As the bathroom was situated beyond the bedroom, the kitchen should be situated beyond the living-room. And it was. But it had an occupant. And when Andrea opened the door, Prinz leapt barking and snarling from his basket.

Andrea was not normally afraid of dogs, but Prinz was so big and powerful that she let out a cry of alarm. However, the shepherd's bark was obviously worse than his bite, because although it bounded about her, uttering menacing sounds, it made no attempt to attack her. Nevertheless, Andrea was unnerved and was still swaying unsteadily in the doorway when a masculine voice demanded:

'Just what do you think you are doing?'

Andrea limped round to face the Baron. His eyes heavy-lidded and less penetrating than usual, his hair a little tousled from sleep, he was devastatingly attractive, running a questing hand over the light covering of gold-tipped hair on his chest.

'I – I was hungry,' she explained defensively. 'I'm sorry I woke you.'

'You did not wake me, *Fraülein*. I was not sleeping.'

'You were! I saw you!' Andrea was indignant.

'No, I was not.' Axel's eyes probed hers. 'I was aware of you peering at me over the back of the couch.'

Andrea experienced annoyance and embarrassment all at once. What had her expression betrayed in those few revealing moments?

'Well, you might have spoken!' she declared shortly, and he conceded this with an inclination of his head.

'I did not wish to alarm you, *Fraülein*.' His eyes dropped disturbingly down the length of her body. 'You are feeling better?'

'I – yes, I suppose so. Less tired anyway.' Andrea was abrupt, but she couldn't help it. 'Do you suppose I could have a drink of water?'

Axel's lips twitched slightly. 'You think that will satisfy you, *Fraülein*?'

'You said you would stop calling me *Fraülein*!' she exclaimed. 'And no, of course it won't satisfy me. But – well, I don't want to put you to any more inconvenience.'

'Did I say you had inconvenienced me?'

'No, but I must have done, mustn't I? I mean, you're sleeping – or trying to – on the couch, and I'm using your bed.'

'Do not concern yourself, *Frau* – Miss Connolly. It is not the first time I have slept on my couch.' He stepped past her into the kitchen, bidding Prinz to return to his bed. 'Now, what can I offer you? Some sausage – cheese – eggs? An omelette, *viel-leicht*?'

'You mean, other women have stayed here?' Andrea persisted, unwilling to leave that subject so precipitately.

Axel had switched on the lights and was now swinging open the refrigerator door. But he raised his eyes to hers to say: 'Surely that is no concern of yours, Miss Connolly!' and her cheeks reddened like a schoolgirl's.

He returned his attention to the contents of the refrigerator after this, and his tone was mild as he asked: 'Well? Which is it to be?'

Andrea contained her resentment, and shrugged. 'Do you have any bread?' she inquired sullenly.

'Of course.' He extracted a long roll from a tin.

'Then I'll have a cheese sandwich,' she told him, and supporting herself against the door jamb, added: 'You needn't do it. I can manage.' And, belatedly: 'Thank you.'

Axel ignored her, lifting a slab of yellow cheese from the fridge and opening the lid of a dish to reveal creamy curls of butter. He took a breadboard from the top of a cupboard, and sawed several thick slices with a broad-bladed knife. Then he looked at her again.

'How is the knee?'

Andrea shrugged. 'It'll be all right.'

'I'll examine it after you've eaten.'

'There's no need—'

'There's every need!' he retorted sharply. 'I should have examined it earlier, but I thought you needed the rest more.'

Andrea made no answer to this, watching him as he spread butter thickly over the bread and then laid two slices of cheese between. 'It is not very professional,' he commented, cutting the sandwich in half. 'But I think you will find it enjoyable.'

'Thanks.'

Andrea would have limped into the room, but he shook his head. 'It is cold in here. We will go into the other room. I will put some logs on the fire.'

Andrea had no choice but to obey him. Trying not to show him exactly how painful her knee still was, she went ahead of him down the hall, hearing him speaking softly to the animal before putting out the light and closing the door.

The sandwich was good, and Andrea tried not to feel too conscious of him seated across from her in the armchair. He had poured her a glass of red wine to drink with the food, and by the time she had finished she was feeling infinitely more sure of herself. It seemed hardly possible that it was about two-thirty in the morning. She was as wide awake as after a night's sleep. Even so, she started when he got up from his seat and came to kneel on one knee in front of her.

'Now – the knee, *ja*?' he suggested evenly, and she had to suffer his hands drawing the robe aside to expose the injured knee. His fingers moved expertly over the swelling, probing and massaging the skin, watching her face for signs of acute discomfort.

Andrea leaned against the chintz-covered back of the couch, closing her eyes against the intentness of his. There was something unknowingly sensual in his touch, and she wanted to savour it to the full and not be conscious of his censure in doing so. When his hands fell away she opened her eyes with reluctance and found him getting to his feet.

'I do not think there are any bones broken,' he stated, smoothing his palms down over the seat of his pants. 'I would think you have wrenched the knee badly, possibly torn the muscles, I cannot be sure. Several days of rest such as I recommended to your cousin should produce a cure.'

Janet! Andrea's eyes widened. She had forgotten about Janet.

'Did you phone the hotel?' she asked, immediately, and Axel nodded slowly.

'I said I would.'

'You spoke to – Janet?'

'No. I spoke to Nicholas Lieber. He said he would convey my explanations to your cousin.'

'Thank heavens for that.' Andrea put a hand to her throat. 'I – I've not been very grateful, have I?'

He shrugged his broad shoulders. 'I did not expect your gratitude, *Frau – Miss* Connolly.'

Andrea looked up at him exasperatedly. 'Why do you find it so difficult to use my name? You use Janet's.'

He shrugged again. 'It annoys you, I know. I will endeavour to remember.'

Andrea sighed, and looked down at her hands. 'You like Janet, don't you?'

'Your cousin is a charming young lady,' he responded politely.

'Do you have any relatives?' she asked curiously. 'Or is this your only home?'

He seemed loath to reply, but eventually he said: 'I own a house – a *Schloss* – some distance from Grossfeld.'

'You do?' Andrea was intrigued. 'How exciting! A

Schloss! That's a castle, isn't it?'

His lips twisted. 'Your conception of my house and mine are vastly different, Miss Connolly. It is little more than a ruin, I regret. My parents died when I was very young, and I was brought up by an uncle in Bavaria. My family home fell into disrepair after the German occupation, and I was not able to redeem it.'

Andrea digested this. It was not an unusual story. In fact, she mused, it was probably true of many of the impoverished nobility of Europe. The war had exacted its toll, both in human lives and capital, and afterwards there had been no *schillings* to spare to repair the crumbling edifices of a dying breed. Was it any wonder therefore that a man in his position should prey on the wealthier members of her society?

'So you became a ski-instructor?' she murmured.

'Eventually,' he agreed. 'I have had many occupations. The one benefit of my background was an excellent education.'

'Janet told me you had been all round the world.'

'Janet is a good listener, Miss Connolly.'

'So am I.' She looked up at him, her eyes challenging. 'What are your intentions towards my cousin, Herr Baron? Do you care about her? Do you see Janet as the next Baroness von Mahlstrom?'

'I do not consider that it is any business of yours, Miss Connolly,' he retorted coldly, 'but I wonder why you ask?'

Andrea could feel the colour running up under her skin again, but mentally she stood her ground. 'Naturally, as her cousin, I feel a certain amount of responsibility for her,' she said, holding up her head.

'But surely, in your cousin's position, she is quite capable of looking after her own interests?' suggested Axel calmly. 'And as you yourself know, I know your cousin's father also. If—' he paused significantly, 'if I decide to have any intentions towards your cousin, Miss Connolly, naturally I will discuss them with her father first.'

Andrea regarded him irritably. Always he succeeded in making her feel inferior, and she didn't like it. She was tempted to blurt out that he was making a mistake in imagining that Janet could do anything for him, financially at least, but that would spoil the game she was playing. Besides, she had given Janet these few weeks. She could not take them away from her again.

'I will get an elastic bandage,' he said, leaving her to cross the room, and she hunched her shoulders dejectedly. It was just beginning to dawn on her what this incapacity would mean, and the prospects were not pleasing.

The bandage was wet and icily cold as he wound it round her knee, taking care not to bind it too tightly. He secured the end with a small safety pin, and then straightened, offering her his hand to stand also.

But Andrea chose to ignore it, and he stood looking down at her rather impatiently. 'You should go back to bed now, *Fräulein*,' he advised briefly, and her eyes flashed her irritation.

'Why? I'm not tired. You go to bed. It's your bed, after all.'

He sighed. 'I do not wish to argue with you, *Fräulein*—'

'Don't you?' Andrea's breast rose and fell with the tumult of her emotions. 'Why not? You haven't done so badly up until now! I don't have to do everything you say.'

That was childish, and she knew it. Axel absorbed her outburst in silence, but she wished he would make some wounding retort and relieve her conscience. But all he said was: '*Sehr gut, Fräulein*. Then perhaps you would be good enough to sit in the armchair so that I may use the couch. Unlike you, I am not on holiday, and I have no doubt there will be plenty for me to do in the morning.'

Andrea pressed her lips mutinously together, but she gave in, muttering: 'Oh, all right!' and struggled to get to her feet. Her knee gave out on her, and she clutched at him to save herself, but if she had expected any response from him she was disappointed. He allowed her to hang on to his belt to regain her balance, and then put her firmly away from him. She flopped down into the armchair, and Axel flexed his shoulder muscles before stretching his length on the couch, draping his legs over the end as before.

Andrea watched him helplessly, and then she said: 'Why don't you use the bed, Axel? I could sleep on there much more easily than you.'

He regarded her through narrowed lids. 'The bed is yours, *Fräulein*.'

Andrea gave an exaggerated sigh. 'My name is Andrea! Why won't you say it?'

He stifled a yawn. '*Gute Nacht*, Andrea,' he offered

dryly, closing his eyes, and she turned her face away from him.

The logs he had put on the fire burned slowly away, and Andrea shifted uncomfortably in the armchair. Soon after closing his eyes, Axel appeared to have fallen asleep, and she envied him his ability to relax in her presence. Outside the wind still howled, and its eerie exploration of the eaves was an unnerving sound.

The logs were dying when she had to make a visit to the bathroom, and when she came back she stared at the pile of logs in the hod beside the fire doubtfully. There was no point in allowing the fire to go out, she decided, but she had reckoned without the weight of the pine wood. One of the logs was particularly heavy, and she had to drop it to save herself from overbalancing. It fell with a deafening clatter, scattering several others, and horrified, she backed away. She almost jumped out of her skin when Axel's fingers closed round her wrist.

'What are you doing now?' he demanded, and she glanced round at him apologetically.

'I – I was just putting some more wood on the fire,' she explained miserably. 'But I dropped it.'

Axel lay looking up at her, his fingers still enclosing her wrist, a curious expression in his eyes. For someone who had supposedly been asleep, he seemed remarkably alert and aware of what she had been doing. He tugged gently at her wrist, bringing her down on to the side of the couch beside him. 'Why did you not go to bed?' he asked, and with dismay she realized she had not gone because she had not wanted to leave him! The knowledge was so startling that for a moment she stared at him in unguarded wonder, and his expression hardened abruptly. 'Do not look at me like that, Andrea,' he exhorted her softly. 'Not unless you are prepared to take the consequences.'

'What consequences?' she breathed. 'Oh, Axel – show me!'

With an exclamation which could have been protest, he lifted his body, jerking her towards him as he did so. His arms slid round her, and his lean mouth fastened itself to hers. She yielded against him completely, her breasts firm against the hardness of his chest, and he rolled over, imprisoning her body with the weight of his. Her lips parted under that demanding pressure, her mouth opening wide to

78

the possession of his. He held her face as he kissed her, winding a hand in her hair as he sought the hollows of her throat.

Andrea had not been kissed in this way before, not with such savage adult passion, and while her traitorous body arched beneath him, inviting him to do with her what he wanted, a small part of her consciousness urged her not to permit a man like him such intimacies. Hadn't she already experienced his bitterness and contempt, his scorn for her puny efforts at thwarting him? After all, he thought she was only the poor relation, Janet's cousin, someone to whom a taste of excitement was worth more than common sense or honour perhaps. He would expect her to revel in the experience, that the Baron Axel von Mahlstrom should have actually made love to her! Something to boast about when she resumed her normal everyday existence.

But she was Patrick Connolly's daughter. Her father was a millionaire building contractor. And she could have her pick of every impoverished nobleman in Europe!

Even so, his mouth was doing strange things to her metabolism, proving to her that he was no novice when it came to getting what he wanted from a woman. His hands stroked the length of her body from shoulder to thigh, loosening the cord of the robe she was wearing, the knot of which was digging into his flat stomach, seeking her small pointed breasts with his lips. She moaned in ecstasy, one of her hands gripping a handful of his hair and holding him closer, while the other made its own exploration until he stopped her, burying his face in her neck, muttering to her in his own language.

'Do you know what you are doing to me?' he demanded huskily, and shivers of uncontrollable excitement ran up her spine.

'I know what you're doing to me,' she answered softly. 'Oh, Axel, kiss me some more.'

Lethargy was creeping over her like a physical weakness. Her earlier resistance was giving way to desires she had never experienced before. Her palms were against his chest, loving the feel of his hard body, and she curled her nails like a cat, digging them into his skin.

He lifted his head then, looking down at her, his eyes slightly glazed by his emotions. '*Mein Gott*, do you want me to make love to you? I want you, you can feel that, I am sure, and I think you want me.'

'Yes, yes, I want you.' Aroused as she was, Andrea hardly knew what she was saying. Linking her hands behind his neck, she tried to pull him down to her, but now he resisted.

'So,' he said coolly. 'I was right. I can arouse you.'

His controlled words had an instant sobering effect on Andrea. And as that weakening lethargy began to leave her, she struggled to push him away.

'Please – let me get up.'

'Why pretend?' he asked mockingly, making no attempt to let her go. His eyes darkened as they rested on the creamy curve of neck and shoulder laid bare by his questing hands. 'Your protests come a little late, *Liebchen*. See – let me show you. Feel the dampness of your flesh.' He pressed one of her hands against her throat, and then brought it back to his body where she could feel the quickened throbbing of his heart. 'You see, I am trembling, too. We have that effect on one another. That is good.'

'Good for whom?' Andrea shifted helplessly. 'Does it please you to make love to several women at a time?'

He half smiled. 'Even I do not do that, *Liebchen*. What you mean is that you were jealous of the attentions I paid to your cousin Janet.'

'Me? Jealous?' Andrea's weakness disappeared. 'You're crazy! I'm not jealous of you and – and Janet.'

'I regret your inability to face the truth, little one, but I have to tell you that you were.'

'You're out of your mind!' Andrea twisted her body beneath him. 'Are you going to let me go?'

'All in good time, as they say in your country, *Fräulein*. You had your chance to go to bed, but you chose not to take it. And why? Because secretly you hoped that something like this would happen. Don't look so ashamed, *Liebchen*, I wanted it, too.'

'You don't know what you're saying!'

'On the contrary, I know exactly what I am saying. You and I have been aware of one another since your unhappy dismissal of your cousin on the day of your arrival. You know that as well as I do. Mentally, I have done all manner of things to you already – touched you, kissed you, caressed you.' He smiled. 'Do you deny that you have thought of me in this way?'

'Deny it? Of course I deny it. The only times I've thought about you were with – with loathing.'

He laughed then, but it was not an altogether pleasant sound. 'Oh, you are amusing, *Liebchen*. I like that. I should not like to get bored with your company.'

'Are you going to let me go?'

'Instead of – what?'

Andrea's face flamed. 'How should I know?'

'A few minutes ago you wanted me to possess your body—'

'*No!*'

'But yes. A tantalizing proposition.'

'I won't let you touch me!'

'You think not? But I disagree. If I wish you to submit, you will do so. Not because I have forced you, but simply because I can arouse you to a pitch where you will beg me to make love to you.'

Andrea twisted futilely. This could not be happening. Not to her. Oh, she had had moments in her past, what modern girl hadn't, but there had never been any occasion when she had not had the situation completely under control. She was not a prude. She genuinely believed that if she really loved someone she would be prepared to give herself freely and without restraint, always with the thought of marriage in the background. But she had never been promiscuous, and the way her body had responded to Axel von Mahlstrom's caresses had frightened her a little.

'Please,' she begged. 'What do you want of me?'

'I want to tell you a little about myself, *Liebchen*—'

'I'm not interested.'

'You will be. You see, I am tired of being a skiing-instructor. I am tired of living in Grossfeld. I am tired of the women who pay for my services, and expect more than skiing lessons.'

'That has nothing to do with me . . .'

'On the contrary, *Fraülein* it has everything to do with you. These women – very often they are middle-aged women, women past their youth who think they can buy it back again. Their money is welcome, as you will no doubt appreciate, their attentions are not.'

'Why are you telling me this?'

He stroked a lazy finger from her chin down to a spot between her breasts, and bending his head covered that spot with his lips. Andrea quivered, she couldn't help herself, but his next words were like a body blow.

'Who else would I tell, but the woman I am going to marry, *Liebchen*?' he murmured against her skin, and the warmth of his breath drifted upward to her nostrils.

A shudder swept over her, bringing goose bumps out all over her flesh as she stared at him in horror. 'You're mad! Mad! I wouldn't marry you!'

'Oh, yes, I think perhaps you will.' His tone was confident and insistent. 'Then I will no longer be a ski-instructor, and you will be a Baroness!'

'I – I wouldn't marry you,' she repeated faintly. 'You – you're a leech, a parasite! Living off women who haven't the sense to see how you despise them! Besides . . .' Her voice faltered. 'Besides, what point would there be in marrying me? I mean, I have no money.'

'Do you not?' His lips twisted. 'But your father does, *nein*?'

'I – I think you mean – my uncle. And – and he won't support you.'

'Your uncle? Joseph Connolly. Oh, no, I do not think Joseph Connolly's daughter could help me. But Patrick Connolly's daughter. That is a different matter. And you are Patrick Connolly's daughter, are you not, *Fräulein*? I was not duped for one moment. My apologies for letting you think I was.'

CHAPTER SEVEN

ANDREA felt limp, her strength drained from her. 'You – you know?' she gulped.

Axel sighed. 'I regret so. There is only one Miss Andrea Connolly, offspring of the president of the Connolly Construction Company. C.C.C. One of the most successful companies in the United Kingdom, is it not?'

Andrea moved her head weakly from side to side. 'But – even so . . .'

'I will put you out of your misery, *Liebchen*. I told you, I met your father once at the home of Fritz Steiner. Your father is very proud of you, little one. He carries many photographs of you in his wallet.'

'Oh! Oh – you beast!'

Axel shook his head. 'I am not to blame for your inadequate attempts to deceive me.'

'What a rotten trick! Just what did you hope to gain by it?'

'Much the same as you, I suspect, *Fraülein*. An opportunity to study you without your being aware of my doing so.'

'To study me?'

'*Natürlich!* As a von Mahlstrom, I had to be sure that you would prove a suitable candidate for my wife.'

'You can't be serious! I – I wouldn't marry you if I was a – a penniless peasant begging on the street corner!'

'If you were a penniless peasant begging on the street corner, you would not be given the opportunity.'

'Why, you conceited swine—'

'Have a care. Words uttered in the heat of the moment can often be regretted.'

'Do you think I'll regret anything I say to you? Nothing I say can possibly describe the baseness of your behaviour. And as for thinking I would marry you . . .'

Axel ran the back of his hand along the line of her cheek, but she knocked it angrily away. 'Don't! Don't touch me!'

'Why not?'

'I – I hate you!'

'No, you do not, *Liebchen*. That I am sure of. You may

83

wish you did so, but wishing will not make it so. See how your body betrays you to my touch—' He parted her lips effortlessly with his own. 'I could take you . . . so easily.'

His mouth hardened and the kiss became deeper, more passionate than he could have wished, and the words between them might never have been. His expertise was such that in a short time she was weak and clinging to him, pushing his jerkin aside and pressing her face against his skin.

'You see,' he said triumphantly, his voice thickened with emotion. 'You do not hate me, Andrea. But you may wish you did before we are through.'

'What do you mean?'

'You will see.'

'You don't imagine that any promise you can extract from me here will mean anything once I am free again,' she panted.

'I have reasons to assume it may.'

'All right, all right. I admit, you do – disturb me. And I can't stop you from seducing me if that's your intention. But I won't marry you.'

'I think you will.'

He was so insistent, and she was so confused. Beads of sweat moistened her brow, and her whole body seemed bathed in the heat of his. Objectively, if she could be objective about such a thing, she knew that there was some truth in what he said. Perhaps she had subconsciously wanted him to make love to her, certainly she had been aware of him right from the minute of their first encounter.

But there was still Janet to contend with, and this absurd, crazy idea he had about marrying her. Her father would never permit it, surely he must know that, and she would never marry any man who she knew was simply marrying her for her money. It was repulsive and degrading; and the fact that no word of love had passed his lips was proof that he was merely using his body to satisfy her needs as he had done with other women before.

Her thoughts were so distasteful to her that she allowed a faint sigh to escape her, feeling the burning heat of tears behind her eyes. The sound drew his attention, and he ran a lazy finger down the length of her nose.

'Do not look so depressed, *Liebchen.* I can make you happy.'

'But why? Why me?' she exclaimed desperately.

'Call it pique, if you like. I am a von Mahlstrom. The von Mahlstrom family was once strong and influential. They were not fortune-hunters, and no man cares to be dismissed as such.'

'I didn't dismiss you as a fortune-hunter—'

'No?' He shrugged. 'So why did you pretend to be your cousin?'

Andrea's cheeks flamed. 'It – it was a game. For fun!'

'But it has not turned out to be so funny, has it, little one?'

'You have no room to talk,' she defended hotly. 'As soon as you discovered which of us was worth cultivating . . .' She ran a hand over her hair, bringing herself up short. 'My father will – will kill you if you – touch me.'

'But I am touching you, *Liebchen*. I think you mean – if I make love to you.'

'Seduce me, yes.'

'This is no seduction scene, *Liebchen*. And I have proof of that. A recording of what has taken place, just in case I have to use it.'

'A recording? A tape recording?' Andrea was non-plussed.

'*Ja*, a tape recording.' He stretched a hand down under the couch and produced a pocket recorder. Andrea did not need to look at it to know the tape was turning. 'I wanted to be sure your father would believe me.'

'Believe you? You'd go to those lengths?' Andrea was horrified.

She hardly noticed him replacing the machine. If her father ever heard that tape he would be bound to think the worst. How could he do otherwise? She could remember only too clearly what she had said in those heated moments when Axel had aroused her.

Realizing her only hope of salvation lay in making light of his intentions, she said: 'All right. So you have a tape recording of the things I – we said to one another. What of it?'

Now his eyes darkened. 'You may pretend to be indifferent, Andrea, but you would not wish your father to be humiliated in this way.'

'Why should he be humiliated?'

'You know as well as I do how people love a scandal.'

'It would be a scandal for you, too.'

'Ah, yes. But as you are so quick to point out, I am only a ski-instructor. What possible damage can it do me? On the contrary, I might gain a certain – notoriety.'

'You – you're mean – despicable!' she exclaimed.

'Practical,' he essayed calmly. 'So – shall we come to terms?'

'What – terms?'

'My terms for not making you my mistress before you are my wife.'

Andrea grasped at straws. 'You can't really mean all this. You're – you're bluffing.'

'I assure you I am not. For once, Miss Connolly, you are not in control. Now, shall we go on?'

'You won't – I mean, you wouldn't—'

'Not yet, little one. Not, that is, until we are married, *nein*?'

She turned on to her back and stared appealingly at him. 'What do you mean?' she got out jerkily. 'Are you determined to force me to marry you?'

'That was my intention. Is it not what you expected? From a fortune-hunter?' His eyes narrowed. 'Or do you want me to take now what is unmistakably mine?'

'You – wouldn't!'

'You want to try me?'

Andrea touched her forehead distractedly. 'I don't know, I don't know. You're confusing me. I don't know why you're doing this.'

'Then think carefully, *Liebchen*, before you turn me down. I could make your life very unpleasant, *nein*?'

'Even if I agree, you can't be sure I would keep my word.'

'The tape recording will do for now, *Liebchen*. And before you leave here, you will telephone your father and tell him where you are and who you are with. You will confess that we have – anticipated our marriage vows—'

'But we haven't!'

'He will not know that, and when this is combined with the tape . . .' He shrugged again. 'From what I hear of your father, he will not flinch from getting you married to avoid a scandal.'

'You can't be sure!'

'I know that your father does not approve of the morals of the crowd you run around with in London. That was why he sent you to Grossfeld – to remove you from their influence.'

'And you think he will approve of you? A self-confessed adventurer!' she exclaimed.

He smiled without rancour. 'Only to you, *Liebchen,* only to you. To your father I shall be the Baron von Mahlstrom, the associate of his good friend, Fritz Steiner. I will convince him of my suitability as his son-in-law, and after the wedding, who knows? He may make me a director of his company.'

'You're completely unscrupulous, aren't you?' she asked bitterly.

'Completely,' he agreed, and with a groan he rolled off the couch to stretch his length on the hearthrug. 'And now, I think we should get some sleep, don't you? Much as I would prefer to make love to you, I am prepared to wait.'

'For bigger game,' muttered Andrea, struggling off the couch at last. 'Oh – oh, my knee hurts!'

'Did I hurt you?' he inquired, his eyes intent as they looked up at her, and she found that even now she could not sustain his stare. In spite of everything, she still found him the most disturbing man she had ever met.

'Married?' Her father's voice over the crackling wire sounded reassuringly astounded. 'You can't be serious, Andrea. My God, you've scarcely been there a week!'

'I know that, Daddy, but—'

'Who is he? This so-called baron? What do you know of him?'

Andrea was supremely conscious of Axel standing right behind her in the narrow hall of the chalet, and her hand on the receiver was shaking.

'You know him, Daddy. Or at least you've met him. At Fritz's house – Fritz Steiner.'

'I've met him.' Her father sounded sceptical. 'What did you say his name was?'

'Von Mahlstrom, Daddy. Axel von Mahlstrom.'

'Von Mahlstrom.' Her father repeated the name thoughtfully. 'It doesn't ring any bells. Oh – wait a minute. I think I do remember. Tall chap, very light hair. An arrogant devil, if I remember correctly.'

Andrea glanced over her shoulder at Axel, but she knew he must have heard. 'That's – right,' she conceded dryly.

'Yes, arrogant. I'd agree with you there.'

'And he's persuaded you to marry him?'

Andrea swallowed hard, but a nudge in the small of her back drove her on. 'I – yes. Yes, I'm – going to marry him.'

'And you know this – after only a week?'

Axel stepped forward and took the phone from her hand, and she had, perforce, to let him. It would not do for her father to hear them quarrelling already. 'Hello,' he said with cool assurance. 'This is von Mahlstrom speaking. You are Patrick Connolly? Andrea's father, *ja*?'

Andrea moved away and across to the doorway leading into the living-room. Her knee was easier after a couple of hours in bed, and she leaned against the door jamb staring blindly towards the windows. It was morning, but the storm had not abated, and the grey light filtering into the room was scarcely an illumination. The fire, and the lamp which had burned all night, shed their brightness over the worn cushions of the couch, burnishing the wooden legs of the table by the window. In other circumstances, she might have appreciated the attractive picture they created, but right now she was obsessed with her father's reactions to her behaviour. The tape recorder sitting on the bureau mocked her by its presence, but the tape which had occupied it had gone. She had discovered that earlier.

Glancing round, she tried to comprehend what was being said. She couldn't hear her father's voice, but Axel's deep tones were unmistakable.

'It was unforgivable,' he was conceding solemnly, although his eyes catching hers offered a mocking salute. 'But you know how these things happen. Marooned here together – caring for each other as we do. It was inevitable. That's no excuse, I know, but it's the truth.'

The truth! Andrea doubted he would know the truth if he saw it. His eyes tormented hers, and she turned her back on him. So it was done. And her father was probably absolutely furious. But what could he say? She had led him quite a dance since leaving school last year, and he might conceivably be relieved to get the responsibility for her off his back. But not being able to see his reaction, she couldn't know what he was thinking, and suddenly she yearned to do so. If only she could talk to him, she might be able to convince him she had not really done anything wrong. But to imagine him listening to that tape, hearing her impassioned words to Axel, did not bear thinking about.

Her brain turned full circle, but then her ears came alert as Axel spoke again. '*Was?* Ah, *ja.* I do not know exactly. Three – maybe four weeks. No sooner – *nein.* I promise.'

Andrea glared interrogatively at him, and he put one hand over the mouthpiece and said: 'Your father is afraid we might get married while he is away.'

'Away? Away?' Andrea's hopes of seeing her father soon plummeted. 'Where is he going?'

'To – America, of course. I thought you would know all about it.'

Andrea stared bewilderedly down at the wooden floor. Had her father told her of this proposed trip to America? She couldn't remember him doing so. But then she didn't always listen to everything he said.

'We won't be getting married at all!' she hissed angrily, and Axel removed his hand from the receiver to speak again.

'Andrea says she's changed her mind, Mr. Connolly. She has decided she doesn't want to marry me after all.'

Andrea was horrified, and her lips parted in dismay, as he continued: 'Naturally, I can't force her— What was that? 'Oh – oh, yes.' His smile towards her was tinged with malice. 'Andrea, your father wants to speak to you again.'

Andrea crossed the hall with speed, her knee forgotten. She almost snatched the phone from his hand. 'Daddy? Yes, yes, it's me. Daddy, listen to me ... Oh, no, *no*! You don't understand!'

'I understand only too well, Andrea.' Her father's voice was clipped and angry. 'Well, you listen to me, young lady, I will not have any daughter of mine earning a reputation for sleeping around. You're completely unreliable, do you know that? Either here or in Grossfeld!'

'Daddy, I haven't slept around!'

'I have only your word for it. And you did spend the night with this – this Baron von Mahlstrom, didn't you?'

'Well, yes, but—'

'But nothing. I don't want to hear another word, Andrea! God, at least the fellow is decent, and prepared to marry you!'

'Daddy, nowadays girls don't always marry the men they sleep with!' she protested frustratedly.

'Don't they? And you'd know all about that, I suppose!'

'Oh, Daddy, I want to come home . . .'

'No, Andrea.'

With a suppressed sob, Andrea dropped the receiver, rushing past Axel into the living-room and flinging herself on to the couch. She gave way to the tears that had threatened for so long. She didn't listen to the rest of what Axel said. She had her hands over her ears.

Axel's hand on her shoulder disturbed her, and she shook him off tearfully. 'Go away!'

'Come on, *Liebchen*. Pull yourself together, *ja*?' Axel was irritatingly cheerful. 'It could be much worse.'

'No, it couldn't.'

'It could. You might have been coerced into marrying a man you found repulsive to you.'

'You are repulsive to me,' she muttered, drying her eyes, and his lips tightened.

'Do you want me to prove otherwise?' he suggested, and she shrank away from him, shaking her head.

'You can't mean to go through with this!'

'Why not? At this moment your father is telephoning that national newspaper of yours, *The Times*, and arranging the usual announcement, and in a few moments I shall telephone the newspaper office in Vienna and do the same.'

'You're crazy! You can't force me to go through with it!'

'We'll see.' He turned away. 'And now – some breakfast, I think before I take you back to your hotel.'

Andrea blew her nose on her handkerchief. The Kutzbahl seemed another world somehow. A sudden thought struck her.

'What did you tell Nicholas Lieber to tell Janet last night?'

'I explained that you were injured and would be spending the night here, with me.'

'Is that all?'

'What else?'

Andrea shook her head. She didn't know what else she had expected, except perhaps some mention of the plans he had put into operation.

'What would you have done if I hadn't come here last night?' she asked suddenly. 'How could you possibly have known that such an opportunity would present itself?'

'I didn't know. But if you remember, I did ask you to come skiing with me yesterday.'

Of course! Andrea's brain was functioning again. And he was a man who knew these mountains. No doubt he had known the storm was due. It would not have been a difficult exercise to get her to visit his chalet once the snow started.

'You – you swine!'

'I wish you would stop calling me names, *Liebchen.* I don't like it.'

'Do you think I care what you like?'

'I think you will learn to do so,' he replied mildly, and she moved her head in a helpless negative gesture.

Andrea could eat no breakfast, but she drank a cup of coffee while Axel exercised the dog. He returned, the hood of his parka covered in snow, strong and virile and intensely masculine in his black ski clothes. Giving herself up to a fantasy contemplation of his being her husband, she had to concede there would be certain compensations. Except, she told herself severely, he had no morals, and could probably be relied upon to leave her at some future date for another woman with a higher valuation of his attributes. Then she brought herself up short. That would never happen, because she would never marry him. Whatever he said! Whatever he did!

Before Axel could take her back to the hotel, he had to dig a pathway through to the road. He had a Land-Rover, he told her, which he used to travel back and forward to Innsbruck, and if the snow-ploughs had cleared the road to Grossfeld, he would take her in that.

Andrea felt useless, sitting in the living-room, watching him wielding the long-handled shovel, but she told herself that it was not her fault if her presence meant he had more work to do.

Eventually he was able to bring the vehicle out of the corrugated-roofed garage that stood some distance from the chalet, and Andrea put on her parka and limped to the door. All around, as far as the eye could see, snow was falling in a steady curtain, and already the paths Axel had dug were covered with a light feathering of flakes. Vaguely visible in the distance, the somehow ugly masts of the ski lift stood lifeless and forlorn, and there were no shouts of laughter from the nursery slopes.

Axel eyed her thoughtfully as she stood there, shivering a little. 'Wait,' he said, stowing his shovel in the back of the land-Rover. 'I'll carry you.'

'Thank you, but that won't be necessary.' Andrea descended the steps very carefully. 'I don't want to owe you anything!'

Axel's expression was impatient now. 'I think you owe me quite a lot already,' he stated grimly. 'I know of no other man who would not have taken what you so blatantly offered!'

'Why, you—'

'No. That is enough. I will listen to no more.' His eyes glittered like chips of grey ice. 'Remember this, Andrea: you are my fiancée now. So far I have been very lenient with you, but no more, *verstehst Dn*? I am not one of your tame countrymen. I can be a dangerous enemy, *Mädchen*. Do not forget it.'

Andrea compressed her lips angrily. Until her father's arrival she was in an impossible position and she knew it. And even then . . .

'And what about Janet?' she demanded. 'What am I supposed to tell her?'

'Tell her nothing,' he replied surprisingly. 'I will talk to Janet in my own time. For the moment, you can behave as though nothing at all has happened.'

Andrea's lips trembled, much to her chagrin. 'Why? If Daddy's phoning *The Times*, they'll know soon enough.'

'I said – leave it to me,' he repeated bleakly. 'Now, get into the vehicle, if you do not require my assistance. I have no more time to stand arguing with you.'

Andrea brushed past him and grasped the door of the Land-Rover, swinging herself inside with difficulty. Her face mirrored the anger and frustration she was feeling, mingled with a not inconsiderable sense of unease. She wasn't afraid of him exactly. But she was afraid of the power he had over her, mental as well as physical.

The snow-ploughs were out in force, endeavouring to clear the Innsbruck road, and their drivers called a greeting. Obviously they all knew who Axel was, and one of them stopped his vehicle to come to the Land-Rover. Andrea understood a smattering of German, but the quickly exchanged patios lost her completely, and when they were on their way again she looked at him questioningly.

'There has been an avalanche at Meitbrugge,' he told her reluctantly, in answer to her raised eyebrows, mentioning the name of a resort some thirty miles from Grossfeld. 'I understand that three people have been killed.'

'Oh, how terrible!' Andrea was genuinely concerned. 'When was this? Last night?'

'Do you really care?' Axel's cool grey eyes probed hers. 'You who take so many risks yourself?'

'I don't know what you mean.'

'I mean that had you been discovered to be missing last evening, a search party would have been organized, and men would have risked their lives to save yours.'

Andrea looked down at her hands in her lap, resenting the censure in his voice. 'I – I was unlucky, that's all.'

'You were reckless! Uncaring that by risking your own safety, you selfishly involved others.'

'If you have such a low opinion of me, I'm amazed you want to marry me, then!' she declared angrily, and he laughed mockingly.

'Your other – attributes more than make up for a certain lack of forethought, *Liebchen*. Besides, I am confident that given time I can mould you to the kind of woman I would like you to be.'

Andrea would not dignify this statement with a retort, and turned her attention instead to the outskirts of Grossfeld. The small town was practically deserted, everyone seeking the warmth of their hotels or firesides. One or two stalwarts trudged determinedly through the snow, seeking the delights of the pastry houses and coffee shops, but most of the stores were empty.

Axel turned the Land-Rover into the yard of the Kutzbahl, and Andrea looked up reluctantly at the windows of the suite she and Janet were occupying. Now that she was here she had the most ridiculous desire not to get out of the vehicle, but she put this down to the explanations she would have to make to her cousin and the others. She was not looking forward to them at all. All the same . . .

Axel had stopped the Land-Rover, and now half turned to regard her out of the corners of his eyes. 'Well?' he challenged. 'Do you wish that I should carry you into the hotel?'

Andrea's lips parted, and impulsively she laid a hand on

the smooth material of his sleeve. 'Axel,' she began appealingly, but he gave a curt shake of his head, and removing her hand slid out of the Land-Rover.

He came round to her side and opened the door, but before he could help her out, voices hailed them from the doorway of the hotel.

'Hi there!'

'Hey, Andrea, what's wrong?'

'Do you need any help?'

'Andrea! What on earth have you been doing?'

Andrea pressed her lips together and managed to give Susie, Roy, and the others a faint, tight smile. Axel's hand was gripping her elbow, as he helped her down the steps, and he ignored the chorus of voices. Once he looked up into her eyes, allowing her a glimpse of the intensity of feeling which could reduce her limbs to water, and then his expression hardened slightly as he turned to face the group of young people thronging the hotel lobby.

Now Andrea could see Janet, just behind Susie, her ankle obviously much improved, although she was still limping. There were a few good-natured jeers when Andrea limped across the forecourt, and then Axel was helping her up the steps into the hotel, and she was taking off her hood and shaking the flakes of snow from her dark hair.

'What the devil have you been doing to yourself?' demanded Roy at once, taking up a position to one side of her, as Axel relinquished his hold. 'You missed the Carnival last night.'

'Did you fall down a mountain?' chided someone else, and Susie offered her a rather relieved smile.

'We were so worried about you, Andrea,' she exclaimed. 'I mean, we got your message via Herr Lieber, but no one mentioned what had happened – that you were injured.'

'Did you take a fall?' asked Ruth Stevens, and Andrea sensed that she was hoping this was so.

'Give her a few moments,' suggested Axel, standing just inside the door of the hotel, his expression dark and ——ful, and Janet spoke for the first time.

'I'd like to thank you, on Andrea's behalf, for taking ——— of her, Axel,' she said, glancing rather spitefully towards her cousin. 'I mean, obviously Andrea's forgotten about that in the excitement of being with her friends again.'

Andrea's lips tightened as she limped round to face both

94

her cousin and the Baron, and her tone was taut as she said: 'I already – thanked him, Janet. Didn't I, Axel?'

She was aware of Janet's surprise at her use of the Baron's Christian name, but Axel was inclining his head politely, and Andrea felt frustration reasserting itself. Already he had adopted that slightly detached air of hauteur which he could assume with such ease, and she could hardly believe that last night she had lain in his arms and felt the hard urgency of his desire.

But now Axel was making his apologies before departure. 'There is work to be done,' he explained to Janet, who was expressing her disappointment that he couldn't stay longer. But as he was about to take his leave, Nicolas Lieber strode into the lobby.

'Ah, Miss Connolly!' he exclaimed, stopping before her and taking her hand. 'What a good thing it was that you reached the home of my friend von Mahlstrom! Tell me, did you hurt yourself at all?'

Andrea managed a smile. 'I wrenched my knee, but it's nothing—'

'But nonsense!' Nicolas Lieber was concerned. 'We must arrange for you to see the doctor as soon as possible.'

'I don't think that's necessary,' Andrea was beginning, when the Baron broke in.

'I think that's an excellent idea, Nico,' he assured his friend warmly. 'I don't think there is any irreparable damage, but one can never be absolutely sure without an X-ray.'

Andrea opened her mouth to protest, but Nicolas Lieber had moved to join his friend. 'You are leaving, Axel?' he inquired, and as they moved towards the door, Andrea turned away.

'Have you had breakfast?' Roy was asking, and Andrea dragged her thoughts back to him.

'Yes,' she nodded. 'If you don't mind, Roy, I'd like to go straight up to my room. I need a shower, and a change of clothes.'

'I'll come with you,' said Janet at once, and Andrea shrugged her agreement. If Janet expected explanations she was going to be disappointed yet again.

CHAPTER EIGHT

WHEN Andrea came out of the bathroom, Janet was lounging impatiently on her bed. Her lips tightened as Andrea shed the bath towel for a silk robe before sitting down at the vanity unit and beginning to brush her hair.

'I thought you had a headache,' she burst out resentfully.

Andrea half turned to stare at her. 'What?'

'Yesterday. You said you had a headache.'

'Oh.' Andrea swung round again. 'I did.'

'Yet you went skiing – on your own?'

'Yes.'

Janet snorted. 'I may be naïve, Andrea, but I'm not stupid! You did that deliberately, didn't you? Turning up at the Baron's chalet!'

Andrea gasped and put down the brush. 'I didn't even know it was his chalet!' she protested indignantly. 'I didn't even know he had a chalet!'

'You did, you did! I told you.'

'Well, all right, I forgot. Whatever.' Andrea heaved a sigh. 'Believe me, Jan, I didn't know where he lived. Good lord, do you think I sought him out, is that it?'

'That's exactly it,' muttered Janet, digging her nails into the coverlet on Andrea's bed.

'You're crazy!' Andrea almost went on to say how much she disliked and despised the Baron, but the memory of that tape recording made her cautious. 'Janet, I promise you, I did not hurt myself deliberately.'

'Oh, I'm not saying you did.' Janet shrugged her shoulders. 'And I suppose your knee is painful.' Andrea had taken off the bandage before taking her shower, and the swelling looked bruised and angry. 'No, all I'm saying is that it was very peculiar, wasn't it? Your ending up there.'

'It wasn't peculiar at all. It was purely coincidence,' replied Andrea shortly.

'So? What happened?'

'What happened?' Andrea played for time, snatching up a jar of moisturizing cream and smoothing it into her cheeks, hoping Janet would not notice her heightened colour.

'Yes. What happened? What did you do? What did you talk about? Did he tell you you could use his Christian name?'

'I think that just – happened,' murmured Andrea, drawing a slightly unsteady breath. 'Nothing much happened really.' She bit her lip. 'I – he bound up my knee, and then I fell asleep. He slept on the couch in the living-room. I used his bed.'

Janet frowned. 'What's the chalet like? He has promised to take me there, but I haven't been yet.'

'It's ordinary.' Andrea could at least be honest about that. 'A living-room, kitchen, a bedroom. The usual offices, as the estate agents say. Honestly, Jan, it's just somewhere to live.'

'I wonder if he's always lived there,' mused Janet thoughtfully, her curiosity momentarily diverted. Andrea considered mentioning Axel's childhood in Bavaria, and the crumbling *Schloss* which had been his family's home, and then decided against it. The less involvement she appeared to have with Axel von Mahlstrom, the better. Changing the subject, she asked:

'Did you have an interesting time yesterday? At Oberlaufen?'

Janet wrinkled her nose. 'It was all right, I suppose. The view was magnificent, but being with a crowd like that isn't like being with Axel. I mean, he knows all about these places. He can tell you their history, describe incidents that have happened, bring a place alive for you. When we visited the Hofburg, in Innsbruck, you know, I really felt a sense of atmosphere. Did you know the Emperor Maximilian had three wives – well, two really, because one was only by proxy and never consummated, and that the Tyrol was his favourite place?'

Andrea shook her head. 'No, I didn't know that,' she conceded quietly, wondering rather hysterically what Janet would say if she suddenly announced that she was going to marry Axel von Mahlstrom.

'Well, anyway, Axel's a far more interesting companion,' continued her cousin, pleating the bedspread. Then she looked up, and her eyes were intent. 'Did – did he say anything to you – about me, I mean?'

Andrea's colour deepened. 'I – I don't think so. No.' She paused. 'What did you expect he might have said?'

Janet moved her shoulders in a dismissing gesture. 'I don't know. Knowing you're my cousin, he might have tried to pump you about our fathers. You know – about Uncle Patrick – and how we came to come to Grossfeld.'

Andrea tapped the handle of her brush against the cut glass tray on the vanity unit. It was a nervous action and she stopped it almost immediately when she saw Janet watching her.

'I've told you,' she said, guilt sharpening her tones. 'We didn't do a lot of talking.'

Janet looked sceptical. Narrowing her eyes, she studied her cousin's evident unease. 'You know,' she said at last, 'if I were a suspicious person, I'd say you were hiding something.'

Andrea gasped, but she couldn't help it. 'Hiding something?' she echoed helplessly. 'Oh, don't be silly. What is there to hide?'

'I don't know.' Janet licked her lips. 'Did you tell Axel that I wasn't really Uncle Pat's daughter? That you were?'

'No!' It was the truth. She had told him nothing.

Janet looked relieved. 'Oh, well, that's something, I suppose.' She got to her feet. Then she paused again. 'Andrea, can you honestly tell me that your visit to Axel's chalet wasn't deliberate?'

'Yes. Yes, I can.' Andrea was vehement.

Janet nodded. 'Oh, well ...' She limped to the bedroom door. 'I think I'll go downstairs and join the others. We're going to play Scrabble. Come and join us when you're dressed.'

'I might do that.'

Andrea forced a smile, but after Janet had gone she flung herself on the bed. The last thing she needed right now was the cheerful interchange of trivialities common to the group. She needed time to be alone, to think, to wonder what on earth she was going to do. Was it really only twenty-four hours since she had set out from the hotel on that fateful journey to the ski-slopes? It seemed aeons ago. So much had happened in those twenty-four hours that the whole period had assumed the proportions of a nightmare.

She shivered. It might well turn out to be just that. That that man should have done such a thing! She would not have believed it possible. Oh, she had heard stories, read newspaper articles about diplomats and statesmen, other notable people, getting involved with blackmailers, having compromising pictures taken of themselves in equally compromising situations; she had even heard of tape recordings made of damning conversations. But that such a thing could have happened to her. It just didn't seem possible. But it was.

She sighed and turned on to her back, staring up at the ceiling. She saw it all now. His assumed relaxation, the ease with which he had feigned sleep. He was a consummate actor. She should have been warned by the earlier occasion when she had thought he was sleeping. Obviously when she made her trip to the bathroom he had taken the heaven-sent opportunity to put his little plan into action, and the remembrance of what was on that tape recording filled her with disgust. How could he do such a thing? she asked herself. How could such a man, a supposed member of one of Europe's noblest families, stoop so low? It was despicable!

But the fact remained that he had done it, and aside from her father she could think of half a dozen London newspaper editors who would pay dearly for the chance to print what was on that tape. Patrick Connolly had not reached the position he enjoyed without making enemies, and a chance to get at him through his daughter would be a chance not to be missed. And then there was Aunt Lavinia . . .

Of course, she would say it served Andrea right. She would denounce her niece in no uncertain terms, given the opportunity, and Andrea's father would be bound to see it as just one more black mark against her.

So what were the alternatives? Marriage with the Baron, or God knows what! Dishonour? She half smiled. An old-fashioned word in this day and age, and yet it still meant something. And although she had always maintained that she didn't care what people thought of her, she found she did. At least, to the extent of not wanting anyone else to hear that impassioned conversation with Axel von Mahlstrom.

Remembrance of that conversation momentarily blanked out her anxieties, and she rolled on to her stomach, pressing her fingers to her lips. If he were not such a swine she might remember his lovemaking with a certain sense of wonder. Undoubtedly, he had aroused her as she had never been aroused before, and although she was still basically naïve about the consummation of lovemaking, with him it had held no fears for her. In fact, she had wanted him to force himself upon her, and that knowledge brought its own self-derision. What had he done to disturb her so? What had his kisses achieved that another man's hadn't? She had no real answer. Except that the touch of his hands upon her had driven all sane and sensible thoughts from her head. And the realization that he might be able to do this at any time he chose was sufficient to arouse a strong sense of resentment inside her. Oh, God, she thought desperately, if she told all this to her father, would he even try to understand? She didn't know. And if he was leaving for North America she might have a long time to wait to find out.

When Andrea did arouse herself sufficiently to go downstairs it was lunchtime, and she went straight to the restaurant where Janet was waiting for her at their table. As though rejecting her previous image, Andrea had discarded her usual jeans for a calf-length skirt of Welsh tweed and a soft cream cashmere sweater, coiling her hair into a knot on top of her head. The hairstyle and more elegant clothes added years to her appearance, and Janet raised startled eyebrows.

'Well, well,' she commented, as Andrea seated herself at the table, acknowledging the greetings from across the room. 'What's happened to you?'

Andrea shrugged, running a hand over her knee to check that the bandage she had re-wound was not showing. 'I felt like wearing a skirt for a change,' she replied. 'The bandage on my knee made pants too uncomfortable.'

'Really.' Janet looked unconvinced. Then, unnecessarily: 'It's still snowing.'

'So I see.' Andrea smiled up at the waiter and asked for soup to start the meal. 'Did you play Scrabble?'

Janet nodded. 'Yes. Oh, and Herr Lieber came looking for you. He's made arrangements for a doctor to call and examine your knee this afternoon.'

'That's not necessary—'

'He seemed to think it was.'

'Is your ankle all right now?'

'More or less. I'll certainly take more care in future. I suppose I'm lucky really. I mean, the weather changing and everything. It's meant that I've not missed so much, hasn't it?'

'You and me both,' commented Andrea dryly, and applied herself to the pungently smelling consommé of beef put before her.

During the afternoon, Andrea found herself having to explain what happened the day before to Susie and the others. The compulsory confinement in the hotel made any diversion welcome, and the only good thing, Andrea felt, was that Axel von Mahlstrom was not there to hear her stumbling replies to their questions.

'You should have come with us to Oberlaufen,' said Roy unequivocally. 'I told you before, it's madness to ski alone. You could have died of exposure – anything!'

'I realize that,' said Andrea patiently. 'I know I behaved foolishly, but we all do that at some time or another, don't we?'

'Some more than others,' put in Ruth Stevens maliciously. 'How fortunate you happened to struggle to the Baron's chalet! Some people have all the luck.'

Andrea let this go, deciding there was no point in creating any more ill feeling between herself and Roy's stepsister, and Susie hastily asked what the Baron's home was like. Andrea told them what she had told Janet, conscious of a certain reluctance to discuss his affairs with them which she put down to the ambiguous position she found herself in. Sooner or later they were going to learn exactly what plans the Baron had for her, and those who did not find the situation ludicrous would no doubt do their best to make her life as uncomfortable as possible.

The weather remained bad for the rest of the day, and reports started to come in of roads being blocked by avalanches and villages cut off from essential supplies. In other circumstances, Andrea might have found the situation just as novel as did the others, but her own problems outweighed all else. Nevertheless, she couldn't help feeling a twinge of apprehension regarding Axel's safety as darkness fell, and Janet's spoken anxiety on the same subject didn't help.

The doctor Nicolas Lieber had contacted pronounced her knee to be in a satisfactory condition. He approved the supporting bandage, and assured her that she would be skiing again within a week. It was reassuring to know, but Andrea had little enthusiasm for the sport any longer.

She was dressing for dinner when Janet came into her bedroom wearing a striped cotton gown with a smocked bodice. It was one of the hostess gowns she had brought with her, and as the stripes were horizontal they did nothing for her plump figure. She grimaced when Andrea showed instinctive surprise at her choice of dress, and said defensively:

'I can't wear those two gowns you bought me all the time.'

'Wear a pair of pants, then – and that cream blouse with the red scarf,' suggested Andrea at once.

'No.' Janet was adamant. 'This looks all right, doesn't it? Mummy paid six pounds for it last summer.'

Andrea studied her thoughtfully. 'Janet, there's nothing wrong with the dress. It's you. You shouldn't wear circular stripes.'

'Well, I don't intend to go down to dinner looking as casual as that, when you're likely to turn up in some extravagant evening gown.'

As Andrea hadn't yet decided what she was going to wear she looked slightly taken aback. 'What do you mean?'

'Well, at lunchtime you got all dressed up, didn't you? How am I supposed to know what you're going to wear this evening?'

'Oh, I see.' Andrea sighed. Then she shook her head. 'Look, if it'll make you take off that dress and wear your pants and blouse, I'll wear trousers, too.'

Janet looked suspicious. 'I thought you said you couldn't wear trousers, because of the bandage on your knee.'

Andrea shrugged. 'Jeans are tight, as you've pointed out before. I've got some flares that don't cling around the knee at all.'

Janet hesitated. 'And you really think I'd look better?'

'I'm sure of it.'

'All right, then.'

Janet went away and Andrea opened the sliding doors of the fitted wardrobe unit. She had intended to wear a soft jersey gown this evening, but she couldn't let Janet go downstairs looking out of season and dumpy in the hideous striped cotton.

Orange flared pants and a vivid green shirt looked bright and practical, and she re-wound her hair into its knot. She was ready by the time Janet came back looking infinitely more attractive in dark brown pants and the cream blouse Andrea had suggested.

After dinner, there were festivities in the Tyrolean Bar.

Everyone was supplied with masks and streamer-trimmed hats, and a troupe of folk singers and dancers soon had the room vibrating to the stamping of their feet. Because of her injured knee, Andrea had an excuse not to join in, which was a relief, feeling as she did. Roy insisted on sitting out with her, despite her pleas to the contrary, and his stepsister's, but at least it prevented her from spending too long looking at her watch. She was wondering how soon she could reasonably excuse herself and go up to her room, and although some small traitorous part of her longed to be reassured that Axel was safe and well, by far the strongest emotion she possessed was one desirous of escape.

By ten o'clock she felt justified in pleading tiredness and excusing herself left the party. She had turned the bend in the stairs when she heard voices below her in the lobby, and the unmistakable tones of Axel von Mahlstrom. She stumbled up the rest of the stairs and reached her room with a feeling of intense relief, congratulating herself in just getting away in time. But at least she knew he was unharmed, and surprisingly she fell into a deep slumber the minute her head touched the pillow.

Because of her early night, Andrea was awake early the next morning. Sliding out of bed to see what manner of day it might be, she found her knee felt much easier, and that she could put her weight on it without too much discomfort.

Outside, a grey overcast day confronted her, but at least it had stopped snowing. The wind blew flurries of snow from the roof of the hotel opposite, and its coldness seemed to penetrate the walls of her room. Grossfeld was gradually coming to life again, but as recollection of the previous night's events returned to her, Andrea felt more like crawling back into bed. She had little doubt that Axel would consider her behaviour an admission of defeat, an admission that she was afraid of him, and it would be all the harder to meet him today.

Thrusting such disquieting thoughts aside, Andrea put on her swimsuit. A dip in the pool would do her good. It would stimulate her circulation, and perhaps disperse the headache which was hovering just beyond the realms of painful consciousness. Leaving her room, she crossed the lounge to Janet's door. Janet was still sleeping, the quilt drawn high above her ears, and Andrea decided not to wake her. Right now, she preferred to be alone.

The pool was deserted, and soon Andrea had shed her towelling robe and was stroking powerfully across its green depths. The exercise was in itself soothing, and she began to feel a little more optimistic. Axel von Mahlstrom could not really *force* her to do anything, not if she was determined enough. When her father arrived she would tell him everything, including that unsavoury business of the tape recording, and if he chose not to believe her, then he would have to cope with the consequences.

Of course, that was easier said than done. Patrick Connolly was not the most patient or understanding of men, and he was known to be ruthless in business. He had been pretty ruthless with Andrea, too, on occasion, and it would not be easy to convince him that she was the innocent party.

She sighed, turning on to her back and floating for a while. It was here, in this pool, that she had put the whole disastrous affair into operation, and that knowledge brought her upright with a start, half afraid that Axel was there again, watching her, assessing her . . .

But apart from one of the hotel porters she was alone, and suddenly she was depressed again. Damn Axel von Mahlstrom, she thought angrily. Damn him, *damn him*!

Back in the suite, Janet was awake, her bedroom door standing ajar. When Andrea came into the lounge she called: 'Andrea! Andrea, is that you?'

Andrea limped to her cousin's bedroom door. 'Yes, of course. Who were you expecting?'

Janet was pulling a sweater over her head, and her face emerged, flushed with exertion. 'Where have you – oh, the pool!' She pulled a face as the water trickled down Andrea's legs and on to the carpet. 'Doesn't swimming make your knee ache?'

'Not particularly. I needed the exercise.' Andrea walked across to her own room. 'Did you have a late night?'

Janet emerged from her bedroom and followed the other girl, obviously prepared for a chat. 'Quite late,' she answered. Then: 'By the way, Andrea, Axel brought a friend with him last night. A Count! Graf Heinrich von Reiter.'

Andrea, towelling herself dry in the bathroom, felt her nerve ends tighten at the mention of Axel's name. 'The – the Baron came last night, then?' she suggested, pretending ignorance. After all, she was supposed to have been in bed before he arrived.

'Oh, yes,' went on Janet eagerly, evidently enjoying being the conveyor of this news. 'He came just after you'd gone to bed. I told him you were tired, and he understood.'

'I'm so glad.' Andrea tried to keep the sarcasm out of her voice, but Janet didn't appear to notice.

'Anyway,' she went on, 'he brought this friend, Count Heinrich von Reiter. Graf means Count, you know.'

'Yes, I did know that,' put in Andrea dryly.

'Well,' Janet was not deterred, 'as I said, they came about a quarter past ten. Apparently the Count is spending a few days in Grossfeld so that he and Axel can see something of one another. They were at school together, or something. He's a German, not an Austrian, but he's ever so nice. Not as attractive as Axel, I don't think, but – you know – friendly.'

Andrea emerged from the bathroom and began to dress. 'Is he the same age as – as the Baron, then?' she asked, feeling obliged to show some interest.

Janet nodded. 'Yes. But they're not at all alike. I mean, Axel is tall, whereas Heinrich is only about five feet eight, and he has rather reddish coloured hair and a beard.' She giggled. 'I've never actually known a man with a beard before.'

Andrea finished dressing and began to brush her hair. Trying to sound casual, she said: 'Did – er – did the Baron make arrangements to – to come to the hotel today?'

Janet's brows drew together. 'No. Why? Did you want to see him?'

Andrea forced a note of indifference into her voice. 'Why should I want to see him?'

Janet relaxed. 'You might have wanted to thank him again – for taking you in like that. I mean, you were lucky he was who he was, weren't you? The chalet could have been occupied by anyone. Some horrible lecherous old man, for instance. Were you in any fit state to fight anyone off?'

'No.' The word came out on a sigh, but Janet's words had heartened her a little. Was that why he had found it so easy to humiliate her? Because she was weak and tired, robbed of the strength to resist him? It made a doubtful kind of sense. But . . . She outlined her lips with a colourless rouge. 'Shall we go down?'

During the morning, Andrea attempted to compose a letter to her father, but it was hopeless. It was impossible to put what she wanted to say down on paper, and every time anyone came into the writing room, she started violently. She was convinced it was only a matter of time before Axel appeared and demanded an explanation for her non-appearance the night before, and the prospect was nerve-racking.

But no one came to disturb her, and by lunchtime she was feeling distinctly uneasy. Janet had gone with Roy and Susie and the others to the lake at Seegold. Some of the more enthusiastic members of the group were hoping to do some skating, and although Andrea had not wanted to go with them, even without the incapacity of her knee, these hours spent in her own company had become wearing. Where was Axel? she fretted frustratedly. Why didn't he come and get it over with? What kind of cat and mouse game was he playing with her?

Andrea had lunch in the restaurant. She had contemplated asking for it to be served in the suite, and then decided against it. Just now she didn't want to have time to think.

But she did not enjoy the meal. Half-way through, Axel came into the restaurant accompanied by a stocky red-bearded man who Andrea realized was the Count Janet had been chattering about. But to her astonishment, and regrettably dismay, he merely acknowledged her presence with a brief inclination of his head, and instead of approaching her, led the way to a table against the far wall. The two men seated themselves comfortably, and then entered into consultation with the waiter regarding the menu.

Andrea pushed her soup plate aside and stared down at the whiteness of the cloth beneath. Her hands were tightly clenched in her lap and it was all she could do not to get up and walk out of the restaurant. A number of uncomplimentary epithets describing his behaviour tormented her brain, and the waiter had to speak twice to her before she became aware of his presence beside her.

Gathering herself with difficulty, Andrea omitted ordering a meat course and asked instead for some cheese and biscuits. She couldn't have faced anything solid, and the thought of the sugary confections eaten as desserts made her feel sick. If the waiter was surprised by her order he gave no sign, and she concentrated in his absence on the wine in her glass. Just what game was Axel playing? What was he trying to do to her? She felt like getting up and marching over to his table and demanding to know why he had no more than acknowledged the woman he was supposedly going to make his wife. What explanation would he give then in front of his aristocratic German friend? What explanation could he give? Was he ashamed of her or something? Was she not the sort of wife this German Count would consider acceptable to a member of the Austrian nobility? All manner of thoughts erupted and were discarded with angry emphasis. She had never been in such an ambiguous situation before, and she cast a malevolent glance in Axel's direction.

He was seemingly unaware of her emotional upheaval, lounging carelessly in his chair, smoking a cheroot, talking casually to his companion who was doing likewise. They might not have been aware of Andrea's presence, and her nails bit deeply into her palms. The beast, she thought furiously. The pig! He was doing this on purpose to humiliate her. Her breathing quickened. Well, she would not sit here any longer and be subjected to his indifference.

Thrusting back her chair, she got to her feet, half expecting Axel to rise too when he saw that she was leaving. But he did not. So far as she was aware, he did not even notice her departure, and she forced herself not to limp too obviously as she walked quickly to the door.

In her room, she paced the floor impatiently. She wished that Janet were there, that Roy was in the hotel; just someone to talk to, to expunge her frustration. But most of all, she wished she dared approach Axel von Mahlstrom and tell him exactly what she thought of him!

Eventually, her anger dispersed to leave in its place an even more disturbing feeling of helplessness. What was she going to do? How was she supposed to cope with these weeks until her father's arrival?

Andrea was sitting in the lounge of the suite trying to read when Janet arrived back. She looked flushed and attractive after her day in the open air. The weather had remained fine, and they had all had a good time, she said.

'You should have come with us, Andrea,' she added, as she shed her outdoor things. 'Staying here alone. You can't have had much of a time.'

'I haven't,' agreed Andrea mildly, trying not to think about lunchtime. 'Did you skate?'

'Not me, no. But some of the others did. They had to sweep the ice first, but it was still inches thick. I've never seen a frozen lake before. It was quite beautiful.' She paused. 'So what did you do?'

'Stayed here, as you can see,' replied Andrea shortly.

'You haven't – spoken to anyone?'

'No.' Andrea shook her head. 'Except a waiter at lunchtime.'

'Er – Axel's downstairs.'

'Is he?' Andrea managed to speak carelessly.

'Yes. With Heinrich. Are you coming down to have some tea?'

'No, thanks.'

Janet sighed, and began combing her curly hair. 'As you like. But Roy will be disappointed.'

'I thought you felt sorry for Ruth. I thought you didn't approve of me associating with him.'

Janet shrugged. 'Oh – well. She's not half as nice as I first thought she was. I mean, last night she was positively ogling the Count, just because he admired a necklace she was wearing. It was one of those metal medallions, you know the sort of thing. He said it reminded him of the Iron Cross. He said his father won that medal in the last war.'

'Fighting on the other side, one presumes,' commented Andrea dryly, half amused by Janet's obvious jealousy.

'Oh, yes, I suppose so. But that's all over and done with, isn't it? You can't keep fighting the war, can you?' She patted her hair complacently, as though its appearance satisfied her. 'I don't have any prejudices of that kind. People are people. Heinrich can't be held responsible for the politics of his parents.'

Andrea put her book aside. 'Heinrich?' She raised her eyebrows. 'Do I take it you call him by his Christian name, too?'

Janet flushed. 'Well, yes. Axel introduced him as Heinrich. Naturally, he uses my name, too.'

Andrea digested this. 'I see. And what is his occupation? Or don't you know?'

Janet smoothed her hands down over her hips. 'He's not destitute, if that's what you mean. He drives a Lamborghini sports and he's staying at the Berghotel. And everything he wears – and uses – oh, Andrea, he's simply loaded, I just know it.'

Andrea made a moue with her lips. 'Oh, well. At least you'll have something to talk about when you go home.'

'Hmm.' Janet sounded thoughtful. Then: 'So you're not coming down?'

'Not right now, no.'

'What shall I tell Roy?'

'Tell him – oh, tell him I've got a headache. I have, too. I – I may have another early night.'

'Oh, Andrea!' Janet stared at her impatiently. 'People will think you're deliberately going out of your way to avoid them.'

'Perhaps I am, at that.'

'Well, I think you should come down. You can't spend the whole evening sitting here.'

'Why not?'

'What will everyone think?'

'I don't particularly care,' retorted Andrea tightly.

But she did. And she knew it.

CHAPTER NINE

IN the event, Andrea did go downstairs for dinner.

After Janet had left her to join the others for afternoon tea, Andrea could no longer settle to reading her book. Not that the couple of chapters she had read so far had meant very much to her, but after Janet's intrusive conversation and subsequent departure, she felt more restless than ever.

Going into her bedroom, she stripped off her clothes and then went into the bathroom. A shower provided a brief respite from the uneasy torment of her thoughts, and she turned the cold tap full on so that the spray of water was like icy spikes against her heated flesh. She wanted it to hurt her, she wanted to feel a physical pain which would oust the mental torture she was going through. She thought she could understand why ascetics sometimes scourged themselves with hair shirts.

She was towelling herself dry when there was a knock at the outer door of the suite. Thinking it might be the maid come to check that everything was all right, she called: 'Come in!' but it was not the maid. Wrapped in a bath towel, peering round the bedroom door, she was awestruck when Axel von Mahlstrom entered the suite, closing the door silently behind him.

At once Andrea drew back behind the door, but not quickly enough. He-had seen her, and in bored tones he called: 'The sight of your partially clothed body is no novelty, Andrea. Come out here and stop behaving like a modest virgin. It doesn't become you.'

Gritting her teeth, Andrea opened the door and stood in the doorway, the huge bath-towel more than adequately concealing her still stinging limbs from his raking gaze. 'What do you want?'

Axel was still wearing the dark brown corded suit he had worn at lunchtime, and the sight of him stirred her to fresh resentment. How dared he come here and behave as if he owned her? She would see that her father learned every detail of his behaviour!

'Why are you skulking up here like some temperamental

opera star?' he inquired in cutting tones. 'You sneak away to bed at night to avoid seeing me, and then behave like an injured prima donna because I choose to ignore you at lunchtime—'

'Is that what you did?' Andrea managed an indifferent shrug. 'I didn't notice.'

'Oh, yes, you did.' There was scorn in his eyes now. 'And it doesn't improve your image in my eyes to know that you also tell lies with consummate ease.'

'I? Tell lies? How dare you accuse—'

'Be silent! I am telling you that you do. Be assured, I do not.'

'Will you get out of here?' Andrea had had just about enough. 'I don't have to stand here and listen to you behaving like some Victorian tyrant! What are you doing in this suite anyway? What would you do if Janet suddenly appeared behind you? Scuttle down the nearest hole like the rat you are?'

He covered the space between them with a speed she had not expected, but she had the good sense to put her bedroom door between them before he could touch her. The diversion was only a temporary thing. There was no lock on her bedroom door and he forced it open without much effort, so that it crashed back against the wall behind. She had no time to reach the bathroom, and instead she stood trembling in the middle of the bedroom floor, waiting for the retribution which she was sure was to come. But what form would that retribution take? She did not dare to guess.

His advance into her bedroom took on the proportions of some scene in a horror movie. Her fingers clung to the towel, draped sarong-wise about her, but she expected any moment for him to snatch it away and expose her mercilessly.

He halted in front of her, so close he was almost touching her. But he didn't, quite. He looked down at her with eyes blazing with anger, and she swayed unsteadily. His nearness unnerved her. His quickened breathing, brought about by the energy he had used in crossing the room and flinging open her door, matched hers, and her eyes were irresistibly drawn to a pulse throbbing near his jawline. Her eyes dropped, following the line of his tie which lay against the cream silk shirt, lower until the buckle of his belt came into view. She remembered only too well the feel of the skin that covered the muscles of his chest and stomach and warmth flooded her body. He was a disturbing man, and her anger against him was slowly evaporating as he made no move to chastise her. Indeed, she knew the most wanton impulse to move against him, to feel the instinctive hardening of his body, and submit to whatever he might demand of her.

As though she had no control over herself, she swayed towards him, but his hands, suddenly gripping her forearms with knowing cruelty, held her off.

'Oh, no,' he told her harshly. 'Not that. Not now. What's the matter? Don't I look like a rat any longer?'

'Oh – oh, you beast!' Tears of frustration came to her eyes as she wrenched herself away from him. 'Why don't you go away and leave me alone? Oh, God, I wish I'd never laid eyes on you!'

'Do you?' His eyes mocked her. 'Why? Because I don't conform to your ideas of what an impoverished nobleman should be?'

'You don't conform to anyone's ideas, noble or otherwise,' she retorted angrily.

'You forget, *Fraülein*, my race is descended from the Huns. You have heard of them, of course – of their nomadic life and great skills as hunters—'

'—the way they pillaged and raped Europe?' she interrupted him. 'Oh, yes, I've heard of them!'

He half smiled. 'I admit, some of their practices were not subjects for debate in mixed company, but you have to admit that they usually got what they wanted.'

'Until they were defeated!'

He shrugged. 'Greed defeated them, *Liebchen*, and I am not greedy. I shall be quite happy with my share.'

'You have the morals of a – of a—'

'—*Gassenjunge?*' he supplied mockingly.

'What's that?'

'It is your word for – er – guttersnipe? Is that correct?'

'I can think of less polite epithets.'

'Then why did you not use them?'

Andrea shrugged. 'I – well, I don't use language like that.'

He drew a sceptical breath. 'So – to more immediate matters. You will come down for dinner this evening, *ja?*'

'You can't make me.'

'Oh, do not let us go into all that again.' He sounded impatient now. 'You will come down for dinner, and you will stop behaving like a spoilt schoolgirl. The future Baroness von Mahlstrom should behave with dignity and good breeding.'

'I am not going to be the future Baroness von Mahlstrom!' she stormed at him furiously. 'You think you've got it all tied up, don't you? You think that tape recording and that call I made to my father wraps it up. But it doesn't. It doesn't! When he comes here, I shall tell him everything, do you hear? Everything! And then we'll see which one of us he believes.'

Axel allowed her her moment's triumph, and then his hands descended on her bare shoulders, holding her at arm's length, caressing the soft skin with purposeful insistence.

'Let me tell you something, Andrea,' he said steadily. 'I know quite a lot about you – and your father. Sufficient at least to be aware that while you assume a certain independence from him, you would not do anything to hurt him. Can you imagine how he would feel if you made a complete fool of him? If you denounced me as a blackmailer the day after your father announced our engagement? And believe me, there is no other way you could do it. Even so, I would deny it all. And then where would you be? Without any proof? Facing a charge of defamation of character, I should suppose.'

'You – you bas—'

One of his fingers silenced her. 'Please. I do not like to hear such words from a woman's lips. Particularly not in respect of myself.'

She dashed his hand away from her face, but he caught her fingers in his and sitting down on the bed behind him, he drew her resisting body between his legs. Holding her there with the muscles of his thighs, he raised her hand to his lips and opening the fingers pressed a kiss to her palm.

Andrea quivered. His mouth against her palm was a sensuous thing. It weakened her resistance against him, made her want to run her fingers through the thick, smooth hair bent over her hand. Then he raised his head and looked at her, the heavy-lidded eyes dark and passionate. Her lips parted involuntarily, her breathing quickened, and when he pulled her down on to his knee she went willingly, her arms sliding round his neck drawing his face to hers.

His lips played with hers, light inconsequential caresses that aroused her need for him but did nothing to satisfy it.

She tried to hold his face between her hands, to cover his mouth with hers, but he evaded her, seeking the curve of her neck, the creamy tanned skin of her shoulder and throat, one hand cupping the nape of her neck while his thumb explored the hollows of her ear.

'Axel,' she found herself pleading, 'Axel, please, stop tormenting me . . .'

'Very well.'

With a lithe movement, he rose to his feet, turning to deposit her unceremoniously on the bed, and before she had time to protest, he strode towards the door. Andrea stared after him, unable to believe that he was leaving her.

'Axel—' she began in protest, but he shook his head.

'I will see you at dinner,' he stated formally, and she heard the outer door slam behind him.

Only then did full realization of what he had done come to her, and with a bitter sob she rolled on to her stomach and burst into tears.

When Janet came upstairs to get changed for dinner, Andrea was already dressed in a long cream gown with a halter neck that left her shoulders and most of her back bare. It was a dress her father had bought for her in Bermuda last year, but she had only worn it a couple of times. Janet had never seen it before, and her eyes widened in surprise.

'Do I take it you're going down for dinner, then?' she exclaimed impatiently.

Andrea nodded a trifle wearily. 'I thought I might.'

Janet made an angry sound. 'I hope you realize I've just told everyone that you have a headache and won't be joining us! Honestly, Andrea, you are a nuisance!'

Andrea controlled the instinctive retort that sprang to her lips. 'I'm sorry if I've put you out, Jan. I'll explain that I'm feeling much better.'

'It's not just that,' mumbled Janet reluctantly, scuffing her toe against the carpet. 'I – well, I accepted an invitation to have dinner with – with Heinrich.'

'You did?' Andrea's reaction was one of relief. 'Well, that doesn't matter. You go ahead. Dine with Heinrich.' At least that way, if Axel expected her to dine with them, it would not look significant. Had he planned it that way? Manipulating people was nothing new to him.

Janet stared at her cousin doubtfully. 'Are you sure?

Won't you mind dining alone?'

'No. No, not at all.'

Janet hesitated. 'I suppose Roy would always sit at our table if you asked him,' she suggested, but Andrea wanted none of that.

'Just leave my affairs to me,' she said, trying not to sound too abrupt. 'Er – have you been talking to Heinrich just now?'

Janet nodded, folding her arms around her waist. 'Yes. Actually, he took me to see his car. I had expressed an interest in it, so he suggested I might like to take a short drive with him.'

'I see.' So that was why Axel had felt so confident in coming to the suite. He had known Janet was safely out with his friend. Andrea's lips tightened, but she tried to remain calm. 'But you didn't have a coat, Jan,' she exclaimed.

'No. Heinrich loaned me his.' Janet hugged herself. 'It was gorgeous, Andrea. One of those super skin coats, lined with lambswool.' She walked slowly into her bedroom. 'He really is awfully nice.'

Andrea went downstairs with Janet when she was ready. Her cousin had arranged to meet Heinrich in the bar, and Andrea accompanied her, steeling herself to face the triumph in Axel's face when he saw that she had obeyed him after all. However, although Heinrich von Reiter was in the bar, broad and immaculate in a dinner suit, there was no sign of Axel. But Roy was there, with Susie and Paul and the rest of the gang, and his face mirrored his delight in Andrea's unexpected appearance. He left the others to come towards her, but Janet tugged her cousin across the room to be introduced to the Count von Reiter.

Heinrich clicked his heels and bowed politely over Andrea's hand, clearly not recognizing her as the girl Axel had acknowledged so distantly in the restaurant at lunch-time. She was relieved.

'I am most happy to meet a cousin of Janet's,' he said, with evident honesty. 'You are enjoying your holiday?'

'Yes,' Andrea smiled. 'Are you staying long in Grossfeld, Herr Count?'

'A few more days only. I have to return to Munich. There are business matters to which I must attend, regrettably.'

Andrea glanced at Janet. 'I understand you are a friend of the Baron von Mahlstrom.'

'Axel? *Ja, Fraülein*, that is correct. Do you know him?'

'I've — met him.' Andrea hesitated over the last words. 'Actually, I — er — I thought he would be with you this evening.'

Heinrich shook his head. 'Ah, no. This evening Axel is entertaining some colleagues at the Gasthof. He will not be joining us. Janet and I are dining at my hotel, the Berghotel, do you know it? And naturally, I should be delighted if you would care to join us.'

Andrea's knees were feeling so weak, she felt that if she didn't sit down soon they would give out on her. It couldn't be true! Axel couldn't be entertaining colleagues at the Gasthof. It must be a ploy to deceive Janet. He wouldn't force her to come down for dinner and then abandon her, would he?

But something told her that that was exactly the sort of thing he would do, just to humiliate her, and rage and frustration drained all the colour out of her face.

Heinrich was regarding her with some concern now. 'You look distraught, *Fraülein*. Are you not well? You are pale.'

'No — no, I'm fine.' Andrea spoke quickly, not wanting to arouse Janet's curiosity, and became aware, with some relief, that Roy was standing just behind her. She stepped back jerkily, and slid her arm through his, welcoming his support. 'I — er — thank you for your invitation, but I'm having dinner with Roy, aren't I?'

Her eyes challenged Roy's and his widened in surprise. 'If you say so,' he conceded, half amused, and she breathed a sigh of relief.

'Can I get you a drink, then?' suggested Heinrich, encompassing them all with his generosity, but Roy declined, waving the glass already in his hand, and Andrea excused them both, moving away towards the bar.

'You know, I could get a complex about being used as a convenience,' Roy murmured in her ear, as they approached the others. 'And did you mean that about dinner, or will I be abandoned as I was at the Gasthof?'

One of Roy's friends moved to allow Andrea to take his seat at the bar, and she slid on to the tall stool thankfully. Then she looked up at Roy and gave him an apologetic smile. 'I'm sorry. But they're dining at the Berghotel—'

'I heard that.'

'—and I didn't want them to feel responsible for me, alone here.'

'So you didn't mean it?'

'I didn't say that.' Andrea glanced quickly round the room. 'Could I have a drink, please?'

'Oh, hell — yes!' Now it was Roy's turn to look apologetic. 'What'll it be?'

Andrea ordered a Martini cocktail, and saw to her relief that Janet and Heinrich were leaving. She waved in answer to Janet's farewell, and then concentrated her attention on the swinging coloured lights above the bar. Axel wasn't coming, and she might as well accept it. There was no point in getting angry or het up about it. That was just playing into his hands. If he chose to try and make a fool of her, it was up to her to show him that so far as she was concerned she was glad he wasn't here.

Roy handed her a glass containing the colourless liquid she had ordered, and she sipped the cocktail gratefully. She refused the cigarette he offered, and then started when Susie said: 'Here comes Herr Lieber. I wonder what he wants.'

Nicolas Lieber halted before Andrea and looked down at her smilingly. Her nerves tightened, and she could feel the muscles of her face stiffening. Now what? A message from Axel? An apology, perhaps. And if so, what would Roy and the others make of it?

'Good evening, Miss Connolly.' Nicolas bowed. 'I see you are feeling better. That is good. Your knee — the *Doktor* he tells me there is no serious injury. It is feeling easier, *ja*?'

'Thank you.' Andrea forced the words.

'*Bitte sehr.* I am happy to tell you all that the weather forecast is improving. I think there will be skiing tomorrow. *Auf wiedersehen!*'

After he had gone, Andrea put both hands to her glass. She was trembling and she despised herself for the weakness that possessed her. She was allowing this whole affair to get a hold on her, and not even Roy's uncomplicated presence could disperse the sense of unreality which gripped her.

'Are you all right, Andrea?' Susie asked, looking at her rather anxiously. 'You do look pale. Janet said you had a headache and wouldn't be coming down for dinner, and I was quite surprised when I saw you.'

Andrea put down her glass without spilling any of its

contents. 'I felt – better,' she answered jerkily. 'But it is rather hot in here, isn't it? If you'll just excuse me, I'll go and – powder my nose.'

Roy was waiting for her when she came back, but the others had apparently already gone into the restaurant. 'Come on,' he said, taking her arm. 'I'll share your table. You can't eat alone.'

'Thanks.'

Andrea allowed him to lead her into the restaurant, trying to ignore the speculative stares which accompanied Roy's seating himself at her table. She wondered what he would say if she confided in him. If she blurted out that she, and not Janet, was Patrick Connolly's daughter, and that the Baron Axel von Mahlstrom was attempting to blackmail her. Even to her ears it sounded ludicrous, and she doubted he would believe her. Besides, she could not take the risk. Until she had spoken to her father, her hands were tied.

Throughout the rest of the evening she managed to behave as though she was enjoying herself, and if she found herself occasionally glancing over her shoulder, no one else seemed to notice. Nevertheless, she was not sorry when Janet returned, flushed and excited after her date with Heinrich, and she could go to bed without arousing comment.

In their rooms, however, Janet was far from feeling sleepy. She insisted on describing the details of the meal she had had, and then went on to tell her cousin how she had danced with Heinrich and how he had told her he found her *bezaubernd*.

'It means enchanting,' she explained, swinging round on her heels. 'Oh, Andrea, I really think he likes me!'

Andrea was in no mood to be tactful. 'I thought you fancied yourself as a Baroness,' she commented dourly.

'I did – I *do*.' Janet was quite serious now. 'But Axel doesn't have any money, does he? And besides, Heinrich's different. Axel's so attractive. He could have any woman. Whereas Heinrich – he's more ordinary.'

'An ordinary Count who drives a Lamborghini!' Andrea grimaced. 'Oh, come on, Jan! Grow up!'

'Well.' Janet pursed her lips. 'You don't have to be nasty about it, just because neither of them appear to fall over themselves to date you!'

Andrea turned away, feeling sick with reaction. She had asked for that, and she was being bitchy. But everything had gone terribly wrong with this holiday, and there seemed no way to make it right.

CHAPTER TEN

IT was three days before Andrea saw Axel again. Three days in which she almost succeeded in convincing herself that he had decided he had taught her a lesson and that was the end of it.

Every morning she searched the previous day's edition of *The Times* which was available to the hotel guests, and every morning she felt a curious sense of anti-climax when she found no announcement from her father. She couldn't understand why he hadn't inserted it before leaving for the United States, and that was when the doubts and uncertainties manifested themselves. Strangely enough, they did not fill her with the relief she would have expected. All she felt was an emptiness, an absence of feeling, a kind of suspended animation that nevertheless made her impatient and restless. But for what? For Axel's return? She plagued herself with thoughts like these. Where was Axel? What was he doing? The ambiguity of her position made asking too many questions suspect.

Her knee improved rapidly, which was a blessing, and with the resilience of youth she was soon out skiing again. But she avoided the trickier slopes, and refused Roy's suggestion that they go up the Feldberg. She supposed her accident and subsequent events had taught her a lesson – she was no longer willing to take unnecessary risks.

Janet continued to see quite a lot of Heinrich. But since Andrea's criticism of her maturity, she did not discuss the things they said and did with her. Heinrich was always polite to Andrea, and she did not think Axel had discussed their involvement with him.

Axel arrived while Andrea was having dinner with her cousin. Janet was telling her that she was not seeing Heinrich that evening, that he had other plans, when Andrea looked up and saw Axel standing in the doorway of the restaurant. Immediately, some of the colour drained out of her face, and Janet, noticing her sudden tension, glanced round.

'Oh – it's Axel,' she murmured speculatively. 'Why are you looking so alarmed? He's probably not looking for us.'

Andrea crumbled the flaky pastry of the dessert she had been enjoying, now feeling slightly sick. Was she to be granted an acknowledgment this time, or was Janet right? Was he looking for someone else?

She was conscious that he had entered the restaurant, and her fingers sought the stem of her empty wine glass. She wished she had had the forethought to refill it earlier. Now she could not do it, her hands were too unsteady.

She sensed rather than heard his approach, but when he reached their table it was Janet who spoke first.

'Why, Axel,' she exclaimed warmly. 'I haven't seen you for days. Heinrich told me you were busy.'

Axel inclined his head politely. 'That is correct. I have been – busy, Janet. I trust you are still enjoying your holiday?'

'Immensely.' Janet was enthusiastic. 'I expect you know I've seen quite a lot of Heinrich. He's been very kind. I don't suppose I'd have had half so much fun without him.'

There was a pregnant silence after this, but Andrea didn't make any effort to break it. However, she did lift her head and look at him, and felt alarm feather along her veins at the expression in his eyes.

'*Guten Abend*, Andrea,' he greeted her softly. 'Are you well?'

Andrea squared her shoulders. 'Yes. Yes, I'm fine.'

'The knee – it is not troubling you?'

'No. It's better.' Andrea paused, and then catching Janet's reproving eye, she added, 'Thank you.'

'That is good. I was concerned.'

Andrea couldn't let that go. 'Were you?'

'But of course.' Axel's amusement infuriated her. 'Oh, I think you mean because I have not inquired for you during the past few days. Be assured you were – in my thoughts. As you are a visitor to my country, naturally I feel a certain – responsibility.'

Andrea looked down at her hands, now clasped tightly together in her lap. He was so sure of himself, she thought resentfully, so confident that she would do nothing to upset his plans.

'Your solicitude is entirely unnecessary, Herr Baron,' she retorted, much to Janet's dismay. 'And is it several days since I saw you? I really can't remember.'

If she had expected, even hoped for, some angry retort,

she was disappointed, but his humour disappeared. 'I have been to Vienna, *Fraülein*,' he told her with emphasis. 'To see a newspaper friend of mine there. I did not realize my absence would create such bitterness between us, particularly as you know as well as I do why I made the journey.'

Janet looked astonished at this unexpected turn of events. She didn't say anything, but her attitude boded ill for when she and Andrea were alone once more.

Andrea's cheeks were flaming. 'I'm not interested in your reasons for going to Vienna,' she said, pushing back her chair and getting to her feet. 'Now, if you'll excuse me . . .'

Ignoring Janet's startled confusion, Andrea hurried across the room, reaching the door only seconds before Axel. As she reached for the handle, his hand forestalled her, and she stood back to allow him to open the door for her. Outside in the hall, however, his politeness fled, and his fingers fastened unyieldingly round her upper arm.

'You did not think I permitted you to leave the restaurant by accident, did you, *Liebchen*?' he taunted harshly. 'What I have to say to you, I prefer to say in private.'

'I'll bet you do!' Andrea raised angry eyes to his. 'Let go of me! Or do you want me to call the manager?'

'Nicolas? You can if you like. But what will you tell him? That I am molesting you? Hardly. Besides, he will know in a couple of days that you are my-fiancée, and you would look rather ridiculous accusing your fiancé of annoying you.'

'But you do!' she stormed. 'Annoy me, I mean. When my father gets here . . .'

'Yes? What will you do?'

'I'll tell him the truth.' She paused. 'In any case, I don't believe *he* has any intention of announcing our engagement. I've checked in the columns every day, but there's been no announcement.'

'I expect you missed it,' retorted Axel comfortably.

'I didn't. I couldn't!'

'Then perhaps it has been delayed.'

'Yes,' she said scornfully. 'Indefinitely.'

'You wish me to contact your father's publicity department?'

'*No!*' Andrea dared not risk that. In a few more days perhaps, when she was sure. But now . . . 'Oh, let me go!'

'I want to talk to you,' he replied imperturbably, glancing

round the hall. 'Come with me.'

She had no choice but to go with him into the small writing room. At this hour of the evening it was practically deserted, its only occupants two boys playing chess in a corner.

'Now,' he said, when they were ensconced on a deep leather couch, 'I have an invitation for you.'

'An invitation? For me?' Andrea was taken aback. 'What – kind of an invitation?'

Axel hesitated. 'As a matter of fact, the invitation is from my aunt.'

'Your aunt?' Somehow Andrea had not expected him to have any living relatives.

'Yes, my aunt. Sophie von Mahlstrom. She lives in Mahlstrom, at the *Schloss*.'

'But—' Andrea licked her lips. 'You told me it was a ruin!'

'It is.'

'Then how can anyone live there? Particularly not an elderly lady!'

'It is not entirely derelict. One wing is habitable. That is where my aunt lives.' His smile mocked her. 'It will give you an opportunity to see what money could do to the place. *Your* money.'

'I won't go!'

'Won't you? You will risk my contacting my friends in London?'

Andrea hunched her shoulders. 'Oh, Axel, please! Stop this charade!'

'What charade?' He forced her face up to his. 'Is the idea of seeing my family home so distasteful to you? We would be virtually alone, for two, maybe three days. Does that idea not appeal to you?'

'*No!*'

But it did. Insinuatingly came the thought that she could quite easily overcome all her worries – by accepting that Axel intended to marry her, and giving in to it. For the first time she really considered the idea, and she found, to her intense disgust, that it was no longer something she abhorred. In spite of his behaviour, in spite of his callous disregard of her feelings, these past few days had been empty without him, and after all, as he had said, there was little she could do about it – at the moment.

Straightening up, she moved away from him on the couch, trying to bring coherency to her thoughts. 'I – why should your aunt want to see me?' she asked tremulously.

'You know why. Naturally, she wishes to know the woman who has captured her nephew's affections.'

Andrea turned on him then. 'I haven't – captured your affections.'

'No. But your money has, and it's all the same thing. Besides, I do find you utterly enchanting—'

'Must you always be such a – a swine?'

'What would you have me say? That I am madly in love with you? That I can't live without you? I can't. But not for the reasons people will think.'

'People will know you for what you are!' she exclaimed, her voice rising, and then she coloured as she attracted the attention of the two boys across the room. 'I mean, you can't expect anyone to believe that I – that I – want you!'

'Oh, but you do,' he murmured, his hand sliding down over her wrist, his fingers sliding between hers, a curiously sensuous gesture. 'And I can assure you, I make quite a satisfactory lover. I can give you the names and addresses of several women who would vouch for my – er – credentials.'

She pulled her hand away from him, and he laughed. 'So – can you be ready to leave the day after tomorrow? Unfortunately tomorrow Heinrich is leaving, and I must be here to say *Lebewohl*!'

'And what will Janet do in my absence?'

'I have told you before. Leave Janet to me.'

Andrea's breast rose and fell as frustration aroused a sense of panic inside her. 'Axel, I can't go with you!'

'Oh, but you must. It's all arranged. Tante Sophie is expecting us the day after tomorrow, and we cannot disappoint her.'

Andrea got to her feet and paced restlessly to the window. The glass was frosted with rime, and outside the temperature was still falling. Even so, there was no absence of activity along the busy main street of the small town as holidaymakers went about their evening's entertainment. Axel came to stand beside her, and his tone was almost gentle as he said: 'You will like my aunt. She is a charming person. And I have no doubt that she will approve of you.'

'I notice you don't say *like*,' muttered Andrea bitterly.

'But of course, she doesn't need to like me, does she?'

Axel sighed. 'I do not enjoy all this bickering, Andrea. Why can you not accept what is to be? You could do worse.'

'Could I?' She looked up at him, and on impulse he bent his head and brushed her lips with his.

Even that transitory caress disturbed her, and his eyes narrowed. 'Oh, yes,' he murmured huskily. 'A lot worse.' He paused. 'So – the day after tomorrow, mmm? At – let me see – shall we say – nine? I will pick you up here, at the hotel.'

'You have a car?' Andrea's eyes were wide.

'I have – transport,' he amended. 'The Land-Rover.'

'You can't mean – you don't intend to drive to – to Mahlstrom in the Land-Rover?'

'Why not? You would prefer to walk?'

'You – you're impossible!'

'Well, that's better than illegitimacy,' he commented dryly.

'Andrea!'

Roy was standing just inside the doorway to the writing room, and to Andrea he appeared like a lifeline to a drowning man. Belatedly, she remembered promising to go with him and the others to one of the taverns in the town to hear some genuine gipsy music, and evading Axel's instinctive move to detain her, she went towards him.

'Hello, Roy,' she said breathily. 'Have you been waiting for me?'

'I've been looking for you,' agreed Roy, glancing over her head towards the Baron. 'I – Janet said you went off with – with—'

'Axel?' Andrea glanced over her shoulder now, feeling more confident with reinforcements on hand. 'Yes, I did. But we've finished now.'

Axel came towards them. 'Where are you going?'

'To a tavern to hear some Romany music,' replied Roy, before Andrea could answer. 'I expect it's all pretty old hat to you. You'll have heard it all before.'

'Old hat?' Axel frowned. 'What is this?'

Roy grinned. 'Sorry. Colloquial English, I'm afraid. It means – old style, boring. I'm sure you've been to these kind of affairs.'

'Ah, yes, I see,' Axel's mouth turned down at the

corners. 'And Andrea is going with you?'

'Yes, I am.' Andrea resented being spoken about as though she wasn't present. 'If you'll excuse us . . .'

'Any time,' responded Axel politely, with a slight bow of his head. 'Ah, here is your cousin. I want a few words with her also.'

A twinge of something Andrea refused to recognize as jealousy swept over her at his words. What was he going to say to Janet? What explanation would he give for the invitation he had offered her cousin?

But Roy gave her no time to speculate. 'Get your coat, Andrea,' he exclaimed. 'The others are waiting.'

Andrea hesitated. 'But Janet . . .'

'I'll take care of Janet,' rejoined Axel smoothly. 'Have a — good time.'

Not unnaturally, Andrea did not have a good time. She fretted to get back to the hotel, to talk to Janet, and the boisterous smoky atmosphere did nothing for the sick headache which had invaded her temples. Pleading tiredness, she left before the others did, arriving back at the hotel before midnight, only to find that Janet was already in bed and apparently asleep.

The next morning she was up at seven, having spent a more than restless night, and invaded her cousin's bedroom before dressing. Janet was half awake, but her expression was not encouraging.

'Oh, honestly, Andrea!' she exclaimed, when her cousin drew back the curtains letting in more light. 'What do you want? I don't want to go swimming, whatever you say.'

'What — what did Axel von Mahlstrom tell you last night?' There was no way of wrapping it up, and Andrea stared down at the other girl with weary resignation.

Janet sniffed, and struggled up on to her elbows. 'What did Axel tell me? What do you think he told me?'

'That's what I'm asking you.' Andrea sank down on to the side of the bed. 'Oh, Jan, I'm sorry!'

'It can't be helped. It was bound to come out sooner or later. Anyway, the fact that Axel knew all along and still made dates with me proves that he's not one of your fortune-hunters, doesn't it?'

Andrea digested this in silence. 'I — what do you mean, Jan?'

'What's the matter? Aren't you wide awake yet? He told

me he'd known all along that you were Patrick Connolly's daughter.'

'Oh! Oh, I see—'

'Anyway, it doesn't matter. If he knows, Heinrich must know, too, and it solves any problem of me having to tell him. I'm seeing Heinrich this morning, you know. Before he leaves. He says he's going to try and get back again before the holiday is over. Do you think he will?'

Andrea was dazed. What *had* Axel told her? Nothing about their enforced relationship, she was sure. Janet would never let that go uncommented upon. But then how had he explained her coming trip to Mahlstrom? Or hadn't he?

Realizing Janet was waiting for her to make some reply, she shrugged her shoulders confusedly. 'I – I don't know. If he likes you . . .'

'Oh, he likes me. I'm sure of that.' Janet half smiled. 'I know what you said about him being a Count and all, but he really does seem – sort of – naïve. Not worldly wise or sophisticated or anything. He's lived with his mother all his life, his father's dead, you see, and perhaps that's why he's so – gentle.'

'Yes.' Andrea managed a suitable response. Then: 'Jan – about tomorrow—'

'Oh yes, tomorrow,' Janet interrupted her, yawning. 'Axel told me about that, too. He's driving you to Salzburg, isn't he? To see your father? What's Uncle Pat doing in Salzburg anyway? And why can't he come to Grossfeld if he wants to see you?'

Andrea was silent for a few moments and then she swallowed convulsively. 'Axel told you – Daddy was in – Salzburg?'

'Of course. Why shouldn't he?' Janet frowned. 'Honestly, Andrea, what's the matter with you? If you ask me you've got up far too early. You're acting as if you're still half asleep.'

'Am I?' Andrea got up from the bed, her brow furrowing. 'I suppose I am. Sorry.' She pushed her hands into the pockets of her dressing-gown. 'So you don't mind? About my going to Salzburg, I mean?'

Andrea was trying desperately to think. If Axel had told Janet he was taking her to Salzburg to see her father, it could mean one of two alternatives. Either he had been lying all along and it was to Salzburg they were going – or this was just a story he had concocted for Janet's benefit. She wished she knew which it was. Was it possible that he had only been teasing her? That her father really was in Salzburg? That that was their real destination? Her spirits rose – but only fractionally.

Janet shrugged now. 'Would it make any difference if I did? No, I don't mind. It's not as though I'll be alone. I've got friendly with Susie and the others. They're quite good company.' She studied Andrea's expression. 'Don't look so anxious, Andrea. Uncle Pat's not going to eat you, is he?' She paused. 'Why does he want to see you? Do you know?'

Andrea shook her head. That at least was easy to answer. 'I've no idea.'

'Well, I shouldn't worry about it. I mean, apart from wrenching your knee and having to spend the night in Axel's chalet, you've done nothing he can complain about, have you?'

'No. Oh, no.'

Andrea paced restlessly about the room and Janet snuggled back under the covers again. 'Well, if that's all you wanted me for, I'm going back to sleep again. Are you going down to the pool?'

'What? The pool? No – no, I don't think so.' Andrea felt totally disorientated. 'Sorry for disturbing you.'

She went out, closing Janet's bedroom door behind her. In the lounge she stood hesitantly, looking about her. What did it mean? Was she conceivably going to see her father tomorrow? Oh, if only she was!

Andrea didn't see Axel at all that day. Janet went off in the morning to lunch with Heinrich at the Berghotel. It was to be a sort of farewell lunch, and when she returned, she said that Axel had been there too. Immediately Andrea felt resentful. Why couldn't she have been invited to lunch with them instead of left to kick her heels at the Kutzbahl, not knowing when or if Axel was to appear. If she was to be his fiancée, why didn't he treat her as such instead of ignoring her for seventy-five per cent of the time?

The next morning Andrea was up and dressed by eight o'clock. She pushed a spare pair of trousers, a shirt and a couple of sweaters into an overnight bag, and then added the cream dress she had worn the night Axel had taunted her into going down to dinner and then not turned up.

Janet was dressing when there was a knock at the door of their suite. Andrea went to answer it and found one of the hotel porters outside.

'*Verzeihen Sie, gnädige Frau*, the Herr Baron is waiting in the foyer. You are ready, *ja*?'

Andrea's lips worked soundlessly, then she gathered herself. 'But I haven't had breakfast.'

The porter looked apologetic, and with a helpless shake of her head, Andrea went to Janet's door. She knocked and poked her head round. 'Jan, I'm going.'

'Already.' Janet was pulling on her skiing trousers. 'What about breakfast?'

'I don't think I'm to be given time to take any. Look, Jan, it's okay. I can get something on the way, perhaps.' She bit her lip. 'Be seeing you!'

'Yes.' Janet came and patted her hand. 'Good luck!'

'I may need it,' murmured Andrea dryly, and closed the door. Then she lifted her overnight bag and handed it to the porter. 'That's all,' she nodded in answer to his silent query, and picking up her shoulder bag and sheepskin coat, followed him out of the suite.

Axel stood in the foyer, tall and impressive in a black leather coat and dark suede trousers. Andrea couldn't suppress the quiver of excitement that ran through her at the thought that this man wanted to marry her, for whatever reason. She could imagine what her friends back home would say. They would wish him luck. But then they had a real contempt for anyone with more money than they needed.

'You are ready?' inquired Axel, directing the porter outside to where the Land-Rover was waiting.

Andrea shrugged. 'I haven't had breakfast. But I suppose that's a minor detail.'

Axel surveyed her in her red woollen slack suit with its fringing of black suede without expression, and then he inclined his head towards the restaurant. 'Go ahead, have your meal. I'll join you for coffee.'

But Andrea was remembering Roy's displeasure the night before when he had learned that she was leaving this morning with the Baron, and she shook her head. She had no wish to invite another confrontation with him.

'It's all right. I'm not desperate. Perhaps there'll be somewhere along the way ...' Her voice trailed away. 'Will it take long? This journey to wherever we're going?'

'Wherever we're going?' Axel raised his eyebrows as she passed him on her way to the door. 'You know where we're going, Andrea.'

'Do I?' she countered, glancing up at him. 'You told Janet you were taking me to Salzburg.'

'You would have had me tell her we were going to Mahlstrom?'

'It would have been more honest. You said you didn't tell lies.'

'Since when has honesty troubled you?' he returned, and she flounced outside.

It was a beautiful morning. The sun was glinting on the snow-covered slopes around them, and their brilliance was dazzling. Andrea hastily pushed dark glasses on to her nose, blinking rapidly. The narrow streets of Grossfeld were already busy, even at this hour, and several people recognized Axel as he drove between horse-drawn carts and sleek, trans-continental coaches. Shopkeepers were replenishing their windows, delivery boys were carrying trays of rolls and pastries into hotels, and the delicious aroma of freshly ground coffee drifted to Andrea's nostrils. It made her stomach offer a noisy protest, and she went bright red and apologized in a low tone.

Axel made no comment, but once they were clear of the town square and climbing the steep gradient out of the valley, he reached forward into the glove compartment and produced a flask. 'Help yourself,' he directed, and the deliberately slow motion of the vehicle did not interfere with the pouring.

'Thanks.'

Andrea was surprised and a little touched by his thoughtfulness, particularly when she offered him some and he refused saying he had had breakfast. Obviously he had guessed that she would not have had time, but as usual he offered no explanation.

'There's a sandwich, too,' he told her, as she sipped gratefully at the fragrantly milky liquid. 'It's rather chunky, I'm afraid, but at least the bread is fresh.'

Surprisingly, Andrea felt suddenly hungry. For days she had eaten sparingly, enjoying little of what she had consumed, but this semi-alfresco repast tasted like ambrosia, and her spirits were rising by the minute. Even the jolting of the vehicle, sprung for tougher use than passenger transport, did not disturb her unduly, although she did wish she had thought to bring a cushion to sit on.

When she had finished the sandwich, and the papers and flask had been stowed away, she wiped her mouth and then turned to look at her companion. 'Will it take us long to get to Mahlstrom?' she asked, with what she hoped was casual interest.

'In these conditions – four, maybe five hours.'

'So long!' Andrea was shocked. 'How far is it?'

'A little over eighty miles. It is a remote district, little frequented by tourists and the like.'

A twinge of alarm fluttered in her stomach. What did she really know of this man, to be making such a journey with him? What she did know was not encouraging, and looked at objectively, she was mad to go with him. But something was driving her on, and it wasn't just the thought of that tape recording.

She sighed, a little of that sense of wellbeing dispersing, and he glanced sideways at her.

'There is no need for anxiety, little one. I promise, you will enjoy the trip.'

Andrea stared mutinously at him. 'How do you know I will enjoy anything with you?'

'Because you wanted to come with me. Deny it, if you can.'

'Why, you arrogant—'

'Oh, please let us not start arguing again. Accept that you are here, we are together, and make the best of it.'

The journey was enchanting, even Andrea could not deny that. She had never driven through the mountains in winter before, with banks of snow reaching up to the far peaks, and sheer cliffs of white falling away into the valleys. Grey spires of hidden churches spoke of villages unseen, and clumps of spruce and fir trees now and then revealed some woodland creature, eyes gleaming in the shadows. The sun was brilliant, the sky an unbroken arc of blue. Andrea thought that no one could remain immune from the beauty of it all. Once, she saw the turrets of some remote castle, pepperpot spires visible above a shielding belt of trees; a fairytale glimpse right out of The Sleeping Beauty. What secrets might those grey walls hold, what hidden mysteries might be enacted far from the laws that governed lesser mortals? Andrea smiled at her own wilful imagination, and then coloured when Axel caught her doing so.

'So — you are happier now,' he commented, and she nodded reluctantly.

'How much further is it?'

He glanced at his watch before replying. 'Two hours maybe. We should be there by one o'clock.'

Andrea pressed her palms down on the seat, lifting her rear end tenderly. 'Two hours? So long!'

Axel looked over his shoulder, checked that they were not being followed, and then pulled the Land-Rover off the road into a narrow layby. They were at the head of a pass leading down into a valley, and he reached for his cheroots.

'If you would like to get out for a few minutes and — stretch your legs, you are at liberty to do so.'

Andrea hesitated, and then seeing that he was in no hurry to join her, she opened her door and did as he suggested. She was stiff. Her spine ached, and there was a certain numbness around its base. The cold air was sharp and made her nose tingle, and her breath made steamy clouds about her. But it was good to walk a little, to feel her circulation moving again, and she looked round doubtfully for some hidden crevice as other demands made themselves known.

Axel wound down his window and surveyed her lazily. 'Round the back — you'll find a copse of trees. Will you go first, or shall I?'

Andrea turned scarlet, and without deigning to answer him, set off in the direction he had suggested. Her boots sank into the soft snow as she left the road, and she had to roll up the legs of her trousers, but she was determined not to ask him for any advice. She was fastening the waistband of her pants when a rustling behind her made her swing round in alarm. For a moment she thought it was Axel, come to disturb her, but the grey form, half hidden in the shadows, was the incarnation of every nightmare she had ever had. With an involuntary scream escaping her lips, she plunged back to the road, and Axel caught her as she reached the Land-Rover. She clung to him desperately, pressing her face against his chest, and his brows drew together in a frown.

'What is it?' he demanded, shaking her a little. '*Mein Gott*, Andrea, what happened?'

Andrea drew an unsteady breath. 'There – there was a – a wolf!' she got out, half incoherently. 'Back – back there – in the trees—'

'A wolf!' Some of the concern had left his voice. 'Impossible.'

He shook his head, but when he would have put her aside to go into the trees, she caught his arm. 'It was, it was a wolf!' she averred desperately. 'Wh – where are you going?'

'I'm going to see this creature—'

'Oh, no! No! You mustn't!'

'Why not?'

'You know why not. Wolves – are killers!'

'You are concerned for my safety?' His eyes narrowed as he continued to look down at her, and she nodded her head helplessly. 'Get in the Land-Rover,' he told her, somewhat harshly now, she thought. 'I won't be long.'

He was adamant, and with reluctant steps Andrea made herself walk to the vehicle and get in. But she stared tautly over her shoulder watching for his return, and when he appeared, walking with his usual easy indolent stride, she felt the flooding warmth of relief inside her. He climbed into the Land-Rover, slammed the door behind him, and then gave her a half mocking smile.

'No wolf,' he announced, turning the ignition. 'You probably disturbed a chamois, rooting for food. You can't usually get so close to them. They're very shy creatures. You probably frightened it out of its mind.'

'What's a chamois?' asked Andrea suspiciously.

'A kind of deer, I think. They're usually a reddish brown in colour, but in winter their coat turns grey for camouflage, I suppose.' He sounded amused. 'I trust you accomplished what you went to accomplish.'

Andrea pressed her lips tightly together. 'Don't be so sarcastic. Anyone can make a mistake.'

'Including a chamois,' concluded Axel dryly.

CHAPTER ELEVEN

IT was almost half past one, and Andrea was beginning to feel distinctly faint from hunger, when Axel indicated a building below them in a narrow valley, where a river rushed with torrential haste across rough stones and rugged boulders.

'The Schloss Mahlstrom!' he announced, with a sigh. 'We are almost there, little one. Soon you will be fed and warmed.'

Andrea strained forward in her seat, trying to see beyond the trees that hid the *Schloss* from sight, and Axel uttered a mocking chuckle.

'I trust you will not be too disappointed, *Liebchen*. There is no central heating at Mahlstrom, and the things you take for granted like electric light and television are unknown here.'

Andrea refused to let him dishearten her. In spite of everything which had gone before, she was eager to see his home, the place where he had been born, to meet this aunt who appeared to be his only surviving relative.

The road wound down steeply, and it was as well that Axel had chains on the wheels of the Land-Rover. Even so, the valley was comparatively sheltered, and the river was not frozen like some petrified falls they had seen.

As they drew nearer, Andrea made out a turreted roof, sloping steeply above narrow, shuttered windows. Some of the shutters were broken, and hanging free she saw, as they got closer, the broken panes behind showing like gutted holes in the grey stone. Part of the roof had crumbled away, but smoke still curled from two of the chimneys, which proved the place was not as derelict as it looked.

Axel drove under an arched way, and Andrea saw now that they were in a courtyard. Once the outbuildings would have accommodated horses, but now they, like the rest of the building, were falling into disrepair.

As soon as Axel stopped the Land-Rover, Andrea got out. She was glad to ease her aching back, and the sounds of the river, which was obviously not far away, came strongly to her ears. No doubt in summer it provided excellent fishing for anyone who cared to try their luck, but right now it was too cold to contemplate.

She stood looking up at the fortified walls of the *Schloss*, at the deep-set windows that remained, and the heavy front door which was barred against them by a piece of wood which had been nailed across.

'Disappointed?' inquired Axel, in her ear, and she started violently.

'You told me what to expect,' she reminded him. 'How do we get in?'

'This way.'

He led the way along a covered passageway to a smaller door which opened into a kitchen area. The heat of the room swept over them as Axel urged her inside, and she saw that it came from an enormous log fire burning in the wide grate. An elderly man straightened from adding more logs to the fire, and his rheumy eyes brightened when he saw Axel.

'*Ach*, Herr Baron!' he exclaimed, coming towards them. '*Willkommen, willkommen! Ich freue mich, Sie zu sehen.*'

'*Hallo*, Carl. *Wie geht es Ihnen?*'

'*Danke, danke.*'

The old servant bowed his head over and over again, drawing them into the room, taking their coats, urging them to the fire. Andrea could understand most of what was said – the usual inquiries about the old man's health, how bad the weather had been, and finally, Axel asked about his aunt.

It appeared that the old lady was resting at the moment, but Carl assured them that she was quite well, and would no doubt join them later. In the meantime, there was a delicious aroma emanating from a pan set to one side of the fire, and Axel suggested that they should eat first and meet his aunt later.

Andrea was only too willing. The stew that Carl served into striped earthenware bowls smelt wonderful, and just then the physical needs of her body had banished any sense of nervousness.

As they ate, and Axel talked to Carl, Andrea looked round the huge kitchen. She imagined it was much the same now as it had been many, many years ago, the enormous range beside the fire providing the main cooking and heating facilities. There appeared to be no hot water, only a cold tap ran into the huge porcelain sink, and lighting, when it was needed, would be provided by paraffin lamps. It was a strange, incongruous setting, and she found her eyes shifting continually to Axel. Did he really see this place stripped and modernized? Was he really prepared to marry her to re-establish his heritage? It would certainly take an immense amount of money to simply install an adequate plumbing system, and if this kitchen, with its dust-strewn beams, was an example of what was to be expected in the rest of the building, it would take a small fortune to make it habitable.

Axel had observed her absorption with her surroundings, and now he said: 'What are you thinking? That it will take a great deal of money to put this place into good order?'

'As a matter of fact, yes,' she nodded.

Axel contemplated the stew in his bowl. 'Yes, I confess I discussed the matter with your father.'

Andrea gasped. 'You did what?'

'I discussed the cost of renovation with your father.'

'With – my father? But – but how?'

'By telephone.'

'To the United States?'

'No. To London.'

'But you said he was going to the United States!'

'Did I? Well, he must have changed his mind. No doubt our sudden engagement made him call his trip off.'

'And you've spoken to him again, without telling me!'

Axel shrugged. 'Naturally, we had things to say to one another. Things better said between the two of us.'

Andrea clenched her fists. 'Financial things, I suppose!'

'Among other things. I think your father quite likes the idea of his daughter becoming a Baroness and living in an ancient Austrian castle.'

'It – it will cost the earth to renovate this place.'

'Your father considers he can afford it.'

'You're completely unscrupulous, aren't you?'

'I think you've asked me that before.'

Carl made coffee to have after the stew, and then Axel got to his feet. They had been sitting at the scrubbed wooden table, and Andrea had been amazed at how easily he had adapted to his surroundings.

'Come along,' he said. 'I will show you something of the place.'

Andrea went with him willingly, accepting his injunction to put on her coat again first. She was curious in spite of herself, and she cast a rather doubtful smile at Carl as she followed Axel through a door which led into another corridor.

It was a stone-flagged corridor upon which a piece of shabby carpeting was laid, and its fragility did a little to protect the feet from the cold which struck upward from the flags. The walls were stone, too, and the ceilings seemed shrouded in shadow because of the few narrow windows that overlooked the side of the *Schloss*. They passed several closed doors and a narrow staircase which twisted out of sight before they reached a heavy wooden door which successfully blocked their way. Axel brought a handful of keys out of his pocket, inserted one in the lock, and the door swung creakily inward.

It was lighter here because of the broken shutters on the windows, and Andrea looked around what had once been the main hall with wide eyes. It was in a distressing state. Cobwebs hung from every available beam and rafter, shrouding the space above their heads with a grey curtain. The stone floor was strewn with debris blown in by the wind on stormy nights, a long table and chairs were mouldering to dust, and the staircase which followed the curve of the wall to an upper gallery promised an even greater deterioration. But for all that, the main stonework of the building was intact, and only the roof over their heads which allowed glimpses of the blue sky, and the broken windows, required immediate repair. Structurally the walls were sound and would probably stand for at least another hundred years.

'No one enters this part of the building these days,' remarked Axel unnecessarily. 'As you can see, it is a refuge for beetles and spiders. I can hardly remember the way it used to be myself.'

'It would take an army of cleaners to scrub down these walls and floors,' exclaimed Andrea, turning round slowly. 'And central heating would need to be installed. It's so cold!'

'Yes.'

Axel was surveying her with faint mockery, but she was hardly aware of his regard at that moment. 'I remember once visiting some stately home in England,' she went on thoughtfully. 'There were radiators, but they were concealed inside what appeared to be antique carved cupboards, with fluted rails instead of doors to allow the heat to escape. There should be something like that here, something that wouldn't spoil the atmosphere of the place.'

'Hmm?'

Axel sounded interested, but now Andrea became aware of his amusement, and realized that for a few minutes she had allowed herself to be carried away by her own enthusiasm.

'What a pity you didn't tell me my father was in London before bringing me here,' she said shortly. 'It would have saved you the trouble. When I get through telling him what you've said – and done—'

'You'll have plenty of time to talk to your father,' put in Axel mildly. 'I happen to know that he intends coming to Austria in the very near future.'

'What?' Andrea was confused. But of course. Her father still assumed she was serious about marrying Axel. He was bound to be curious to see them together. She would soon disabuse him.

Or would she? Her fingers curled into her palms. The memory of the tape recording brought a shudder of distaste. Could Axel seriously intend sending it to some newspaper if she attempted to thwart his plans? Could she allow her father to hear it and trust to his judgment? And if she didn't, did that mean she was thinking seriously about marrying this self-confessed adventurer? She looked resentfully at him. He was so cool, so assured. So confident of his hold over her. How could he behave so calmly when he knew as well as she did what was at stake? His coolness unnerved her, as it was intended to do, she supposed.

'I'm going to tell my father the truth!' she declared, but her words lacked conviction.

'Let us not go into all that again,' he said, taking her arm, ignoring her resistance. 'Come, we will go and find my aunt. I am sure she is dying to meet you.'

They went back through the heavy wooden door, and Axel relocked it. Then he opened another door and they were in another corridor, and at the end there was a flight of steps leading upwards. A first floor landing displayed several doors, and Axel walked confidently to the first of these and knocked lightly. Andrea heard a sound from within, and then Axel was urging her before him into his aunt's sitting-room.

Andrea's first impressions were of how much brighter this room was, and how warm. Light streamed in through several narrow panes set in the curved outer wall, and the walls were concealed behind faded tapestries. There was a warm carpet covering the floor, and although the furniture was old, it still maintained a certain dated elegance. The heating came from a square tiled stove set in one corner, and beside this stove a woman was sitting sewing.

Sophie von Mahlstrom bore little resemblance to Andrea's imaginings of her. For one thing, she was much younger than Andrea had expected, in her sixties, but no more, she thought, and her clothes and appearance were as elegant as her surroundings. She rose to her feet as they came into the room, and her smile was a facsimile of her nephew's.

'Ah, Axel! You are here. I thought I heard the Land-Rover a little while ago.'

Axel went to kiss his aunt's cheek. 'Carl told us you were resting,' he explained. 'We have had something to eat, and I have been showing Andrea a little of the *Schloss*.'

'Yes, Andrea.' Sophie left her nephew to approach the girl who was hanging back awkwardly behind him. 'So you are Andrea, my dear.' She spoke with only the slightest accent. 'I am delighted to meet you.'

'I – well – how do you do, Baroness.'

Andrea didn't quite know how to address the older woman, but Sophie shook her head. 'You may call me Tante Sophie, as Axel does, my dear. The title means little nowadays, as I am sure you are aware.'

'Thank you.' Andrea forced a smile, linking her hands together and seeking desperately for something else to say. 'What – er – what a nice room.'

'I assume you mean compared to the rest of the building,' remarked Sophie dryly. 'But yes, I suppose it is quite a pleasant room. It was Axel's mother's sitting-room originally, but unfortunately, during the war, we had some unwelcome visitors, and I am afraid I tend to remember that too well.'

'Sit down, Andrea.' Axel indicated one of the tapestry-covered armchairs, and when Sophie von Mahlstrom resumed her seat, Andrea did as he suggested. Then, to her surprise and unwilling regret, he walked towards the door.

'I have duties to attend to, you understand?' He addressed his aunt, and she nodded. Then he turned to Andrea. 'Until later, little one. *Auf wiedersehen.*'

When the door had closed behind him, Sophie smiled rather apologetically at her young visitor. 'Forgive my nephew, but it is so seldom he comes to Mahlstrom and naturally there are estate matters to attend to.'

'There's an estate?'

Andrea spoke involuntarily, but Sophie seemed to notice nothing amiss. 'A small one, I regret to say. Once the von Mahlstroms owned this whole valley, but now we have to content ourselves with the land immediately surrounding the *Schloss*, and so many metres of river bank. The fishing is very good here. Did Axel tell you?'

'I'm afraid not.'

Sophie shook her head. 'No, of course, he wouldn't. Fishing wouldn't interest you, would it? No doubt he has discussed that with your father.'

Andrea's eyes widened. That Sophie von Mahlstrom should sit there so calmly and suggest that Axel might have discussed fishing rights with her father! Was every member of this family so sure of themselves? What had fishing to do with what Axel intended? Did they conceivably imagine that it might influence her father? It was ludicrous!

'I don't think my father is especially interested in fishing, Baroness,' she ventured carefully, and Sophie clicked her tongue.

'No? You surprise me. Lots of people are, you know. It's always an advantage to be able to offer every facility. You can even swim in the river in summer, although I must confess the water is hardly ever above freezing point. But we're sheltered here, and it does get very hot sometimes. I've known Axel take a dip in the river to cool off.'

Andrea made no answer to this, looking with interest round the room. In truth, she was loath to enter into any discussion about the future with Axel's aunt, and she felt impatient with Axel for abandoning her like this. But then that appeared to be a habit with him. He seemed to enjoy disconcerting her.

'Is this your first visit to Austria, my child?' Clearly Sophie suffered no sense of unease at the situation. 'Axel tells me you are staying at the Kutzbahl in Grossfeld.'

'Yes. Yes, I am. But no, this isn't my first visit to Austria. I've been here several times. With – with my father.'

'But not to Grossfeld.'

'No.'

'Axel tells me you have not long left school.'

'Last summer.'

'And do you have a career in mind? Or is university your goal?'

Andrea's lips parted. What was that supposed to mean? Having listened to Sophie von Mahlstrom speak with such authority in her language, she could not believe she had mistaken the tenses. So why was she asking such questions? Did she suppose that Andrea might go on with a career after marriage? Or had she doubts that Patrick Connolly might agree to Axel's plans? She must know of her nephew's intentions or she would not speak of Andrea's father's interest in renovating the *Schloss*.

Fortunately there was a tap at the door at that moment, and at his mistress's summons, Carl appeared. 'You would like some tea, madam?' he asked in his own language, and Sophie nodded.

'Thank you. That would be most welcome,' she nodded, and the old servant withdrew. 'Carl is a treasure, you know. Who else would live here, miles from anywhere, without anyone of his own to talk to?'

Andrea licked her lips. 'He's – the only servant?'

'At present, yes. Poor Carl. He was married, you know, but his wife died during the war, and they had no children.'

'He's very – old.'

'But so loyal. He remembers Mahlstrom as it used to be, as it will be again – with your father's assistance.'

While she served tea from the tray Carl had provided, Sophie talked of her own ambitions for Mahlstrom. Her enthusiasm was infectious, Andrea found in spite of herself, and the older woman's voice betrayed an emotion it was hard to ignore. Andrea found herself sympathizing when Sophie explained how the German army had stripped everything of value from the *Schloss* when they left, and how hopeless it had been to try and go on as before when the war was over. She made her see that the destruction was not only a betrayal of the past, but of the future as well. By the time Axel returned, Andrea was discussing her own ideas of modernization, and she flushed when he came into the room and interrupted her. He was carrying a lamp which revealed his mocking smile, and she saw to her surprise that it was already getting dark.

'If you will excuse us Tante Sophie, I will show Andrea to her room,' he said, applying a lighted match to another lamp standing on a nearby bureau. 'We will all meet again at dinner. Carl tells me he has concocted something special for us.'

Sophie nodded. 'Very well, Axel. I shall look forward to continuing our conversation over the meal. It is so seldom I am with company these days.'

Outside the room, Axel indicated that Andrea should follow him up the second flight of stairs which led from this landing. Another landing appeared, much the same as the one below, and Axel led the way into a room, holding the lamp high so that she could see it was a bedroom. Her overnight bag was already deposited there, but the room struck chill after his aunt's sitting-room.

Axel set down the lamp on the bedside table, and then crossed the room to an old-fashioned washstand where a pitcher of hot water was steaming. 'I'm afraid a bath is out of the question,' he told her politely, 'but I have provided you with some hot water to wash with. There is no bathroom up here, and you will have to come downstairs as before if you require . . .'

Andrea turned away, staring at the square posts of the wide bed, the heavy *armoire* with its carved doors, the spotted mirror above the scratched dressing table. 'You're too kind,' she said flatly. 'And I doubt very much that anyone would willingly take off their clothes in these temperatures, even to take a bath!'

Axel's lips twisted. 'I assure you people do. People who have not been softened by too much easy living.'

'People like yourself, I suppose.'

He did not answer this, but walked towards the door. 'Can you find your way back to the kitchen? I regret we will be eating in there, but I'm sure you will appreciate it is much the warmest place.'

After he had gone, Andrea stared mutinously at the door. It was useless trying to score points with him. He just ignored anything he didn't want to hear. She turned back to look at the room, noticing with a shudder that there were cobwebs here, too. Of course, Carl was old, and couldn't be expected to keep the place as it should be kept, but surely Sophie von Mahlstrom should notice these things and make a special effort when visitors were expected.

She walked to the windows and saw that from this height it was possible to see the river in the distance. Dusk was shadowing the trees, but there was still sufficient light to see the width of the torrent, swollen no doubt by the recent snows. Its greedy onward surge gave her an eerie, cut-off feeling, and the shadows cast by the lamp seemed longer as she turned to look again at the bedroom. She paused a moment, wondering where Axel's room might be, wishing with a sense of guilt at the realization that he would not be too far away.

By the time she had had a thorough wash and brushed her silky hair, it was completely dark, and not wanting to stay overlong alone in these strange surroundings, she quickly put on the cream gown she had brought with her, and applied a green eyeshadow to her lids. She shivered in the chill of the room, and put on her coat again to go downstairs.

She hesitated on the lower landing, wondering whether she ought to knock at Sophie von Mahlstrom's door, but then decided against it and continued on her way downstairs.

Because this wing of the building was cut off from the rest, it was comparatively easy to find the kitchen again, and besides, a delicious odour of herbs and spices attracted her nostrils in the right direction. When she entered the room it was to find the long wooden table lit by a silver candelabrum, and set rather incongruously with silver cutlery. There was no sign of Carl or anyone else, and rather awkwardly she moved towards the fire, holding out her hands to the blaze. Outside the wind was whistling round the solid walls of the *Schloss*, but there was something immensely reassuring about this candlelit room.

Even so, she started when the door behind her opened and Axel came into the kitchen. She had shed her coat and her heart pounded rapidly at the intent look in his grey eyes. She was absurdly conscious of the expanse of flesh revealed by the backless gown, and although he had changed into a dark suit, she felt overdressed. And yet she could hardly have insulted his aunt by coming down to dinner in the same clothes she had worn to travel in, and her only alternative was jeans.

'You appear to have coped quite admirably with your toilet,' he remarked, closing the door and advancing towards her. 'You must feel warmer now.'

'It's very warm in here,' replied Andrea jerkily, and it was true – even without her overheated emotions.

'Yes,' Axel nodded, looking around. 'Something smells delicious. Are you hungry?'

'A little,' she admitted.

'Did you enjoy talking to my aunt this afternoon?'

Andrea stiffened. 'Very much.'

'I am glad. She is a gentle woman, a lonely woman in some ways, although she would be the last to admit it.'

'I'm not surprised – living here!'

'You would find it lonely?' he probed, standing in front of her.

'Of course. Anyone would.'

'Even with my presence?'

Andrea's cheeks turned slowly pink, and she looked away from his knowing eyes. 'You should spend more time here,' she went on hastily. 'Your aunt would appreciate it.'

'What would I appreciate?'

Andrea had not heard the door opening, and now she faced Sophie von Mahlstrom feeling decidedly disconcerted. 'I – er – I was just telling Axel that you would appreciate his spending more time at Mahlstrom, Baroness.'

Sophie's lips tightened at Andrea's unconscious use of her title, but she did not comment upon it. Instead she said: 'But, my dear, Axel comes when he can. He is a busy man—'

'My aunt is very loyal,' Axel interrupted her abruptly, and the look they exchanged was incomprehensible to Andrea. 'Ah, here comes Carl. I must confess, I am ready for dinner.'

The old manservant was carrying a bottle of wine. '*Der Chateau Rothschild!*' he announced triumphantly, and Sophie clapped her hands. '*Nichts als das Beste*, eh, Herr Baron?'

Considering the limited facilities and Carl's advanced years, the meal that followed was quite amazing. They began with tiny pancakes stuffed with cheese that melted in the mouth, and progressed through tender chicken, served in its own consommé, with tiny garden peas and buttered noodles, and finished with a tart which Sophie explained was originally made in the Black Forest area of Germany. Coffee was served with fresh fruit and cheese, but Andrea could eat nothing more.

'It was good?' suggested Sophie, smiling at their young guest, and Andrea nodded, rubbing a rueful hand over her stomach.

'I've eaten far too much,' she exclaimed, cradling her coffee cup between both hands. 'Please express my thanks to Carl for serving such a marvellous meal.'

Carl, who had eaten with them, seated at the end of the long table, not taking any part in their conversation, now nodded his head in a gratified way, and Andrea wondered whether he understood English after all.

Later, Axel produced a bottle of cognac, and they sat round the fire drinking the fiery spirit. Andrea was not used to such strong alcohol, and she found herself chattering on about her life in England, about the relationship she shared with her father, and the fact that she had never known her mother. She talked about her childhood, about Janet and her parents, revealing, unknowingly, what a lonely little girl she had been.

Then Axel got to his feet and announced that it was time they were going to bed. Andrea was amazed to discover it was after midnight, and she apologized to Sophie for talking so much.

'Not at all, my dear.' Sophie patted her hand gently. 'I've enjoyed getting to know you. I hope we'll see some more of one another.'

Andrea thought this was an odd thing for Axel's aunt to say, particularly in the circumstances, but she just said: 'Yes,' and Sophie said good night to her nephew and Carl and went on her way.

'Come,' said Axel, after his aunt had left them. 'I will escort you to your room.'

'It's not necessary,' Andrea began, but then remembering that lamplit apartment she was silent.

Axel did not bother to light a lamp to show her upstairs. He lifted the candelabrum from the table and carried that, the flames flickering crazily in the draughty passageways. They climbed the stairs, passing the landing where a light showed under Sophie's door, and continuing on to the second floor where Andrea's room was situated. Axel opened her door and set down the candelabrum while he fumbled for matches to light her lamp. A sudden draught of air extinguished all but two of the candles as he sought for his matches, and Andrea uttered a startled cry.

'Don't panic,' he told her calmly, succeeding in lighting her lamp without undue haste. 'There – is that better?'

Andrea was hovering in the doorway, her coat about her shoulders, trembling as much with apprehension as with the cold that crept about these high-ceilinged corridors. Even in the subdued light, her face was pale, and Axel paused before her, shaking his head half mockingly.

'Why are you trembling? Do old buildings have this effect on you? I noticed earlier that you started when I came into the kitchen.'

Andrea drew an unsteady breath. 'I – I'm used to modern buildings, buildings that aren't shrouded in cobwebs and the dust of the past.'

Axel glanced up at the ceiling of her room. 'Yes, the housekeeping does leave a lot to be desired.'

Andrea endeavoured to calm herself. 'Has – has anyone died here? In – in this room, I mean.'

Axel stifled an amused chuckle. 'Not that I know of, little one. Why? Do you think there may be ghosts?'

'Don't joke about it!' She stared at his white shirt front. 'I – where is your room?'

'My room?' He raised his eyebrows. 'Why?'

'You know why,' she exclaimed. 'I'm all alone up here, with – with only your aunt one floor below.'

'Ah, I see. Well, I must confess, I intended sleeping on the ground floor, in a room near the kitchen which I have occupied many times before.'

'Oh!' Andrea bent her head. 'I understand.'

She heard his swiftly indrawn breath, a strange, almost impatient sound, and then his hands closed over her shoulders and she was jerked towards him, his mouth seeking and finding the moist opening of hers. Andrea felt her senses swimming at his touch. Her fears, the amount of alcohol she had consumed, the heated scent of his body, her own traitorous needs, all combined to make her want their embrace to go on and on, and she wound her arms around his neck, and moulded her body to the hardening angles of his with increasing urgency. He parted his legs to keep his balance, and she pressed even closer, uncaring at that moment what interpretation he might put on her behaviour. His hands slid her coat from her shoulders, moving over her back, caressing the smooth flesh with an insistence that revealed his own heightened emotions. His hands slid over her hips, holding her more firmly against him, exciting her with the awareness of his desire. With a groan his hands sought the zip of her dress, and she did not protest.

'Axel! *Mein Gott, bist Du verrückt?*'

Sophie von Mahlstrom's outraged voice brought Axel to his senses, and his hands slid away from Andrea's body as he took an automatic step backwards. He was pale, more pale than Andrea had ever seen him, and his eyes burned with a brilliance which revealed his barely leashed control. She realized with a pang that for once he had not been in control of the situation any more than she had, that in spite of his calculated approach she had been able to make him forget the reasons they were together. It was an intoxicating realization, and turning to face the Baroness she knew that she regretted the older woman's intrusion.

The moment's silence which followed Sophie's outburst had a sobering effect on all of them, however, and when his aunt spoke again, she was much calmer.

'You will forgive me for interrupting you, I know, but I really think it is time you retired to your own room, Axel.'

Andrea's cheeks flamed, and she glanced up at Axel to see how he accepted this. But he was in control now, and she could not sustain his mocking scrutiny. 'You are right, of course, Tante Sophie,' he said smoothly. 'My regrets if we disturbed you.' He ran a smoothing hand over his hair. 'I bid you both – good night.'

Picking up the candelabrum, he bowed once more and left them, and Andrea felt that with his departure he had taken some essential part of her with him. But she took a deep breath and when Sophie turned to her she appeared outwardly composed.

'You are all right?' Sophie regarded her piercingly.

Andrea stifled an hysterical gulp. 'I – yes. Yes, I'm all right.'

'Good. It is late. You must be tired. If you – want anything in the night, please – call me.'

As Sophie's light disappeared down the stairs, Andrea closed the door and leaned back against it. She felt weak and trembling and not at all ready for sleep. She closed her eyes for a moment and allowed herself to relive those minutes in Axel's arms. Oh, she wanted to be there again. She wanted to feel the warmth, the hardness of his body close to hers. She wanted to stay with him, be near him, never let him go.

It was a shattering awareness, and she straightened as a wave of nausea swept over her. The alcohol, she thought dazedly. That must be what it was that was making her feel as though her heart had been torn out of her. How Axel would laugh if he could know how she was feeling at this moment, how much she longed to leave this cold and lonely bedchamber and seek the warmth of his bed. Insidiously the idea came to her that he would not turn her away if she did just that . . .

With a gasp of dismay, she walked to the washstand and splashed cold water over her face and neck, allowing it to trickle down over her breasts. She must be mad, thinking such things, wanting such things. But after she had taken off her clothes and slipped beneath the covers of the bed, her feet welcoming the hot bottle that Carl must have placed there for her, she had to accept that no amount of self-recrimination would destroy the feelings he had carelessly aroused inside her.

CHAPTER TWELVE

ANDREA slept late the next morning, which she considered was hardly surprising when she had lain awake for hours the night before. But she awoke feeling infinitely brighter and more confident – and ridiculously eager to see Axel again.

She dressed in the warm trousers and sweater she had worn to travel in the day before, and then, draping her coat about her shoulders she descended the stairs. There was no sound from Sophie von Mahlstrom's room, so she continued on down to the kitchen. Carl was there, building up the fire, and she smiled at him quite cheerfully and wished him *'Guten Morgen'*.

'Guten Morgen, Fräulein.' Carl straightened to offer her a polite bow. *'Wie geht es Ihnen?'*

Andrea sighed. 'I do not speak very good German,' she said carefully, in his language. 'Do you speak any English?'

'A little.' Carl surprised her by answering in her own language. 'You sleep well, *ja?'*

'Oh, yes. Very well.' Andrea gathered herself, and as she did so she noticed the remains of a hastily taken breakfast on the table. 'Er – is the Baron already up?'

'Oh, *ja,'* Carl nodded, looking slightly discomfited.

'Then – where is he?'

Carl hesitated. 'He is taking the Baroness to the railway station, *Fräulein.'*

Andrea could not have been more surprised. 'To – the railway station?' she echoed. 'I don't understand. What railway station?'

'Mahlstrom, *Fräulein*. The station for Mahlstrom. The Baroness is returning to her home in Salzburg.'

'Her – home?' Andrea swallowed convulsively. 'I – thought this was her home?'

'Oh, *nein, Fräulein*. No one lives at Mahlstrom – only myself.'

Andrea shook her head, trying to make some sense out of all this. 'You're telling me that – that Baroness Sophie lives in Salzburg?'

'Ja, ja, Salzburg.'

Andrea frowned deeply, feeling the beginnings of a headache probing just beyond consciousness. Why had Axel told her that his aunt lived at Mahlstrom, if she didn't? What was the point of bringing her here to meet her, if Salzburg would have done just as well? It didn't make sense.

'Tell me,' she addressed Carl again, 'how long has the Baron been gone? Is it far to the railway station?'

Carl shrugged. 'Two kilometres, maybe three. He went thirty minutes ago.'

Thirty minutes! Andrea consulted her watch. It was a little after eleven. Surely it would not take much more than thirty minutes to drive at the most six kilometres!

'He shouldn't be long, then,' she said, but Carl turned away and did not answer her.

Feeling completely confused, she seated herself at the table, and when Carl had finished the fire he washed his hands before offering her rolls and coffee.

'Just coffee, thank you. No rolls,' replied Andrea tautly, and when the coffee came she drank it black. Over and over in her mind she was asking herself the same questions, but she could come up with no logical answers. And after Sophie von Mahlstrom's behaviour of the night before, it seemed totally out of character for her to depart and leave Andrea alone with her nephew. Unless he intended taking her back to Grossfeld today. That sounded reasonable. But that still didn't explain why he had lied to her about his aunt living here.

She finished her coffee and looked again at her watch. It was after half past eleven now, and there was still no sign of Axel returning. Her nerves were tightening with every minute that passed, and there was an awful helplessness about being confined here, with no means of transport to make her escape.

She left the kitchen on the pretext of going up to her room and went instead to Sophie's sitting room. The tiled stove was cold this morning, and there was no sewing strewn around, nothing in fact to show that the room had been occupied. Adjoining the sitting-room was a bedroom, and here the tumbled bedcovers showed that Sophie had slept the night there. That was a relief. Andrea was beginning to feel vaguely imaginative.

She peered through the windows, her breath misting the panes. Tall firs blocked most of the view, but if she listened hard she could hear the river still churning endlessly on its way. Oh, where was Axel? she fretted miserably. What was he doing?

It was nearing twelve when she returned to the kitchen, and found Carl laying the table for three. Obviously he expected Axel to return, and her spirits rose a little. Even so, she could not prevent the questions which trembled on her lips.

'Wh – where is Axel? Why is he taking so long?'

Carl shrugged expressively, and Andrea tried to slow her quickened breathing. Something, some inner instinct, warned her that all was not as it should be, that Axel's absence was a deliberate thing, and she paced restlessly about the kitchen floor, feeling the prick of tears behind her eyes. For the first time she had been eager to see Axel, eager to be with him, to talk with him, she had even been prepared to find excuses for his previous behaviour. His lovemaking the night before had convinced her that he was not indifferent to her, and she had known for some time that she was not indifferent to him, no matter how she tried to deny it. But now he had disappeared, and although that sounded dramatic, she was terribly afraid it was true.

'You would like some food, *Fraülein*?'

Carl was addressing her politely, and Andrea had to drag her thoughts back to the present. 'Er – not now,' she refused. Then: 'Thank you, Carl, but I don't feel hungry.'

'You should eat, *Fraülein*.'

'Should I?' Andrea's demand was bitter. 'Well, maybe later. When your employer comes—'

The sound of chains on wheels and a labouring engine halted her in mid-sentence. With a relieved cry, she ran to the back door, wrenched it open and sped along the covered passageway to the courtyard. The Land-Rover was just pulling up before the barred doors leading to the main body of the building, and she ran forward excitedly, almost losing her balance on the slippery surface. Then she stopped in confusion. The man driving the vehicle was not Axel, but Tim Brady, her father's lawyer and personal assistant, and the man climbing down from the passenger seat was her father himself. Yet it was the same Land-Rover. She recognized the scratches along its sides – and the bottom seemed to drop out of her world. With a little sob, she ran towards her father, and when he gathered her up into his arms, she burst into floods of tears.

Some little time later, Andrea was seated beside her father on the settle in the kitchen, and Tim Brady was wandering tactfully round the room, pretending not to listen to their conversation.

'But where is Axel?' Andrea wanted to know, when her tears had ceased, leaving her drained of emotion.

'On his way to Salzburg, I should imagine,' replied her father, taking back the handkerchief she had borrowed, and replacing it in his jacket pocket.

Andrea shook her head helplessly. 'But why? And what are you doing here?'

'First things first,' said her father briskly. 'I'm hungry, and I'm sure Tim is hungry, too. We've been travelling since early this morning. I suggest we eat lunch. Carl is impatient to serve it, I'm sure. Then afterwards we can talk.'

'But how do you know Carl?' exclaimed Andrea frustratedly. 'Have you been here before?'

'Several times,' Patrick Connolly conceded dryly, then pushed her to her feet. 'Now, no more questions until after lunch.'

Carl served the stew they had had the night before, but Andrea almost gagged on the food. She felt sick and confused, and her mind was plagued with unanswered questions. Her father on the other hand ate with obvious enjoyment, complimenting Carl in his own language, and accepting a second helping. She thought Tim Brady had some sympathy for her. He, after all, was quite a young man; an attractive man, she supposed, if one liked stocky men of medium height with a dry sense of humour; but to Andrea, he had always been simply her father's assistant, and being allied with him was treated in much the same manner as she treated her father.

Her father was someone she had always secretly admired. It had been a great disappointment to the female acquaintances he made that he had never thought of getting married again, and at fifty-five he was still an attractive man. Dark, like his daughter, quite grey now about the temples, he enjoyed physical exercise, and consequently was still as lean as he had been thirty years before.

But for all that, Andrea and her father were too much

alike to often see eye to eye. She enjoyed thwarting him, and the more he laid laws down for her to follow, the more rebellious she had become. Even so, a strong bond of affection existed between them, and they had spent many happy times together.

By the time her father had finished his stew and several wedges of new bread, plus some cheese and coffee, Andrea's nerves were stretched to fever pitch, and she could hardly sit still at the table. Tim Brady, noticing her distress, got to his feet.

'I think I'll go and have a look around the rest of the building,' he said. 'I want to check on those ceilings in the east wing.'

Patrick Connolly relaxed. 'Yes, you do that, Tim. And don't forget to inspect the woodwork.'

'I won't.' Tim looked down compassionately at Andrea's taut face. 'Cheer up, Andy. Nothing's ever as black as it seems.'

Andrea forced a faint smile, but when the door had closed behind him, she turned on her father. 'Now! Will you tell me what's going on!'

'Yes, yes. If you remain calm. Otherwise I shall get very impatient with you, Andrea. I could do, anyway. You deserve it.'

'What do you mean?'

'You ask me that!'

She flushed. 'I suppose you mean – my engagement to – to Axel.'

'Among other things.' Her father took out a case of cigars and put one between his teeth. 'You really try my patience, don't you?'

'I'm not a child, Daddy.'

'Then why do you continually act like one?'

'I don't.'

'Do you deny pretending to be your cousin, and persuading Janet to pretend to be you?'

Andrea gasped. 'That was only a game! How – how do you know? Have you seen Janet?'

'No.'

Andrea frowned. 'Axel – told you?'

'That's right.'

'But – but when? Oh, when he spoke to you about coming here?' She paused. 'You said you'd been here before. How can that be?'

'If you allowed that intelligence you possess to surface occasionally, perhaps you'd begin to see what's obvious to even the most ignorant among us.'

'I don't understand.'

'Oh, Andrea! Andrea! Will you never learn? Axel said you needed a lesson. I'm glad I agreed with him.'

'A – lesson?' Andrea stared at him. Then an awful cold feeling invaded her stomach. 'What are you saying? What kind of a lesson? What has Axel to do with it?'

Her father sighed, and after applying a match to the end of his cigar he inhaled deeply. 'You tell me.'

'What – what do you want to know?'

'Suppose we'd met in – Grossfeld. How would you have explained your involvement with von Mahlstrom?'

Andrea licked her lips. 'I – we—' She halted uncertainly. 'He asked me to marry him.'

'Why?'

'What do you mean – why? Why do people usually get married?'

Her father shook his head. Then he felt in his pocket and brought out a small tape recorder. As he placed it on the table in front of them, Andrea stared at it in horror, feeling waves of nausea sweeping over her. What game was Axel playing now? Why had he given this to her father?

Patrick Connolly tapped the tape significantly. 'Do you recognize this?'

Andrea's lips worked soundlessly. Then she nodded. 'I – I think so.'

'Do you know what's on this tape?'

'I – yes.'

'Do you want to tell me about it?'

Andrea bent her head. 'Do I have to?'

'I'd like you to.'

She cupped her face in her hot hands. 'It – it was the night I spent at – at Axel's chalet. He – he recorded – what – what happened.'

'What did happen?'

'Nothing. Nothing – I told you.'

'I believe you.'

'You believe me?'

'Of course. It's the truth, isn't it?'

'Well, yes. But – the tape—'

Ignoring her automatic attempt to stop him, Patrick pressed the button which set the recorder in motion. Axel's voice was so clear, he might have been in the room with them. But what he had to say cooled Andrea's blood.

'Andrea,' he began, 'I told you once that I didn't care to be taken for a fortune-hunter. So, with your father's permission, I contrived to play a little trick on you. I have known your father for years, and when he sent you to Grossfeld, he asked me to keep a fatherly eye on you.'

'What?' Andrea raised her eyebrows at her father in dismay, but he put a finger to his lips, indicating that she should listen.

'Unfortunately,' Axel continued, 'you resented my introducing myself, and I decided to resort to subterfuge, too. My only intention was to give you a fright. There was no tape recording, no announcement in the Austrian papers, nor yet in *The Times*, as you were quick to observe. I kept your father advised of what was going on, but I had to play the cards as they were dealt to me. It was not difficult. You are a very beautiful girl. Oh, by the way, your father *is* going to spend money renovating the *Schloss*. He plans to turn it into a hotel, a private hotel, for people who require peace and relaxation away from the tourist haunts I am forced to inhabit. One thing more, my cousin, with whom you saw me the day you arrived at Grossfeld, was quite flattered when I told her you had mistaken her identity.'

The tape went on turning, but there was nothing more. Patrick turned it off, and only then did Andrea realize she was trembling, violently. So it had all been planned, a calculated exercise to teach her a lesson for the way she had treated him. She had thought he had been cruel to her in the past, but never as cruel as this!

And yet shouldn't she be glad? He had released her, after all. Freed her from the anxieties she had been suffering, given her back the right to come and go as she pleased. Just when she no longer wanted it . . .

Her father was examining her drawn features with concern now. 'What's the matter?' he demanded. 'It's all over! Much sooner than I expected, believe me!'

'What do you mean?'

'I mean, I wouldn't have let you off the hook so soon. You behaved abominably, Andrea, to a man I both like and respect. You tried to make a laughing stock of him, and instead he turned the tables on you! Don't you think it's about time somebody did that?'

Andrea's lips quivered. 'Perhaps. Did – did Janet know what was going on?'

'Not unless you told her yourself. Andrea, I sent you and Janet away on holiday to enjoy yourselves. To meet some decent people for a change. To behave like any other young girls and have a good time. But what happened? You were bored, right from the moment I saw you on to the plane in London, and you thought you could relieve that boredom by making someone squirm. Well, Axel made you squirm, and good luck to him!'

A little of Andrea's spirit reasserted itself. 'You can't deny – he's only a ski-instructor!' Her lips twisted. 'Did it occur to you that he might play you at your own game?'

'What do you mean?'

'He could have done all the things he said he had done. It was quite an opportunity for him, wasn't it?'

Her father shook his head. 'Oh, Andrea, what a cynical mind you have! Don't you know that a man like Axel von Mahlstrom would never stoop to living on his wife's relatives! All right, I agree, he's not a wealthy man – materially wealthy, that is. But he has his pride, and if it's necessary for him to work at teaching the sons and daughters of the *nouveau riche* to ski, then he'll do it. That's the kind of man he is. And I would have hoped that a daughter of mine would have had the intelligence to see that for herself!'

Andrea closed her eyes, pressing her fingertips to her lids. 'I – I've never met anyone like him before,' she protested jerkily.

'That I can believe.'

'I was confused – when the Baroness talked about fishing . . .'

'Sophie von Mahlstrom? You've met Axel's aunt?'

Andrea opened her eyes and saw that her father was frowning. 'Why, yes. She was here when he arrived yesterday.'

'Really? She stayed at the *Schloss*?'

'Why not? Axel brought me here to meet her.'

'I know. But I'm surprised he found it necessary to trouble his aunt. I wouldn't have given you that satisfaction.'

Andrea knew what he meant. She had had no way of

156

knowing whether Axel had been telling her the truth. And in fact, he hadn't – all along. It was humiliating. And worse – devastating. Oh, God, she thought sickly, what has he done to me? Why can't I stop thinking about him? I can't stop wanting him near me! Surely I can't have fallen in love with him? Oh, no, that would be too cruel . . .

'So.' Patrick Connolly got to his feet and walked to the kitchen window. 'Have you made up your mind what you're going to do?'

'Wh – what I'm going to do?' Andrea echoed foolishly. 'I – what do you mean?'

'What are you going to do now? Tim and I are going on to Salzburg. We have to see the von Mahlstrom solicitors there, and there are other matters I need to attend to. Do you want to come with us, or would you rather go back to Grossfeld and finish your holiday there? You've still over a week booked at the Kutzbuhl, you know.'

Andrea couldn't think. 'I – what about Janet?'

'She can join us in Salzburg, if she wants to, if you'd rather come with us. Oh, and by the way, I should tell you that Axel has said he'll keep out of your way until the rest of your holiday is over if you do decide to return to Grossfeld.'

Andrea swallowed with difficulty. There was a lump in her throat and she had the feeling that no amount of crying would shift it. 'I – I don't know what to do. Perhaps you should ask Janet. It is her holiday, too, after all.'

Patrick raised his eyebrows. 'What? You're actually thinking of someone before yourself? My word, this affair must have done you some good!'

'Oh, Daddy!' Andrea could not sustain his amused stare. 'I wasn't so bad, surely?'

'No.' His expression softened. 'I was only joking. Don't tell me you've lost your sense of humour as well as everything else?'

Her sense of humour! Andrea could see no humour in this situation.

'Okay,' her father was saying now. 'When Tim gets back from his explorations, we'll go.'

'Go?'

'Yes, go. You don't expect me to spend a night here, do you?'

'I – I–'

157

'Well, I don't intend to.'

'But it's too late to drive to Grossfeld.'

'I don't intend driving anywhere, except to the railway station. There's a train out of Mahlstrom at four o'clock which will take us to Kufstein. We landed there this morning. Another friend of mine, Klaus Ziller, I don't think you know him, owns a small airfield there. He allows me to use it whenever I choose. Tim and I will fly out tomorrow, with or without you. You can ring Janet from the hotel this evening, and make whatever arrangement suits you both.'

Andrea couldn't take it all in. It had happened too fast. And even after all she had learned, it was incredibly difficult for her to stop thinking about Axel. Where was he at this moment? In Salzburg as her father had said? If she accompanied her father and Tim to Salzburg in the morning, might she see Axel again? It was a tantalizing possibility, but one which she quickly discarded. It was obvious that Axel would not wish to see her again, that was why he had told her father that if she returned to Grossfeld he would keep out of her way. But she found it almost impossible at this moment to face the future if she was never to see him again.

CHAPTER THIRTEEN

THE offices of the Connolly Construction Company occupied the top three floors of a tall block just off Portland Place. The multi-storey building also accommodated a travel agency, an insurance company, and various other smaller organizations, and once Andrea used to amuse herself by integrating all the companies' names into short stories. But today, she was in no mood for that kind of diversion as she rode upward in one of the sleek high-speed lifts.

There was a mirror in the lift, and she examined her reflection with no pleasure in her appearance. She supposed the plain grey suede suit was elegant, its skirt just brushing the tops of the long patent boots she also wore, and the fur jacket around her shoulders, proof against the chill March winds outside, could not be faulted. Mrs. Thomas, her father's housekeeper, had insisted she looked 'very nice', but then she knew Andrea's father had chosen the suit, and she always agreed with him. Andrea's hair, instead of hanging loosely about her shoulders, was confined in a knot on top of her head which added several years to her age, and inwardly she despised herself for allowing her father to dictate to her in this way.

Still, since her return from Austria, she hadn't cared too much what she did, or where she went, or what she wore. Slowly but surely, her father had exercised his authority, gradually turning her, physically at least, into the kind of daughter he had always wanted. Today, for instance, she was joining him and a business colleague for lunch, a common enough occurrence during the past few weeks, but deep inside her Andrea could feel a stirring sense of rebellion. Yet she tried to keep it at bay. She knew that once she allowed herself to think again, and feel – really feel, that was – all the old agony would come back to torment her.

After the shattering revelation of Axel's duplicity, she had felt completely desolated, and it had been almost impossible to hide her distress from her father and Tim Brady. Her father accepted that she was upset, of course, but he fortunately saw it more in the way of a childish tantrum at being thwarted than the emotional upheaval it actually was.

Which was just as well, she knew, although she suspected Tim was not so easily deceived.

Nevertheless, it had not been easy to return to Grossfeld, when Janet baulked at having to cut their holiday short, or a simple thing to behave as though nothing momentous had occurred.

Not that she had to face Axel. He had remained true to his promise to keep out of her way, and it was left to Janet to ponder why he no longer came to the hotel. Perhaps she would have been even more suspicious had Heinrich Reiter not reappeared on the scene and diverted her attention from Andrea's moody disposition.

However, the kind of emotional trauma Andrea had suffered carried its own eventual protection. After a while, a certain numbness had descended upon her, softening the pain and veiling its harshness, so that during the day at least she was able to behave quite rationally. It was only at night that it was really bad, and as the weeks had gone by even the nights had become almost acceptable, with the help of drugs. She knew that the love Axel had so carelessly aroused had turned to hatred, and it was this bitterness which was tearing her apart. But it was only a matter of time before that passed, too, and he would be consigned to some distant memory of an experience too distasteful to remember.

She stepped out of the lift at the penthouse floor and walked along the softly carpeted corridor past offices where typewriters clacked and adding machines discharged their streamers of paper figures. Her father's office was at the end of the corridor, next to the boardroom, and when she entered his secretary's office, the young woman behind the desk smiled politely.

'My father's expecting me, Sarah,' Andrea said, closing the outer door. 'Shall I go in?'

Sarah Holland shook her immaculately groomed head. 'Just a minute, Miss Connolly. I'll check.' She pressed down a button on the inter-communications system. 'Oh, Mr Connolly, your daughter's here. Shall I send her in?'

There was a moment's silence and then Andrea heard her father's voice. 'Yes, that's all right, Sarah. Come on in, Andrea.'

After Sarah had released the button, Andrea frowned. 'Is he alone?'

Sarah shook her head again. 'No. The — er — business

colleague he's invited you to lunch with is with him.'

'Who is it? Don't you know?' Andrea was curious at the restraint in Sarah's voice.

'I – well – do go in, Miss Connolly. Your father's waiting for you.'

It was with a feeling of anxiety that Andrea crossed the floor of Sarah's office. Some instinct warned her that Sarah's discomfort had to do with her in some way, and she had to school her features carefully before entering her father's office.

The office was large and comfortable, two walls made almost completely of glass and shaded by venetian blinds. There was a large leather-topped desk, several leather chairs, two filing cabinets, and an enormous safe.

But Andrea knew the room only too well, and her eyes flickered quickly over her father to rest on the tall, fair man who had risen politely at her entrance and was standing beside her father's desk. Of course, she thought bitterly, she should have known it would be him! That disruptive instinct she had felt in the outer office. Her senses had warned her that he was here.

Her father, tall and distinguished in his pin-striped office suit, was coming across the expanse of plain blue carpeting towards her. 'Andrea,' he said, his eyes appealing to her to react favourably, 'Andrea, as you can see – I have a surprise for you.'

Andrea was tempted to tell him exactly what he could do with his surprise, but the knowledge that to do so would reveal the immaturity of her reaction caused her to remain where she was. But her brain was tormented by Axel's presence, and it was all she could do not to turn and run out of the office. What was he doing here? And why had her father asked her to join them? Surely he must know that Axel was the last person she wanted to see.

But was that strictly true? Didn't her senses leap at the sight of him, lean and attractive in a dark brown suit that accentuated his magnificent tan? Didn't he still arouse the impulse to go to him, be near him, to invite him to put his arms around her and lay that lean sardonic mouth against hers?

She dragged her thoughts back from where th- - her leading. This was madness. This was the n- cheated and betrayed her, who had am-

expense! Was she even thinking of allowing him that kind of opportunity again? No! *No!* Her whole being revolted against it.

She licked lips that had suddenly gone dry. What kind of a reaction was he expecting from her? What kind of reaction could she make to prove to him that he no longer had any power over her? Anger? Contempt? Vituperation? No. Any one of those things he could counter with superb indifference. But indifference was the one thing he would not expect from her.

Drawing a deep steadying breath, she forced a smile to her lips, responding to her father's greeting with an assurance she would not have believed she possessed.

'Good heavens, Axel!' she exclaimed, with just the right amount of surprise and apparent pleasure. 'What are you doing here?'

Patrick Connolly's face was a picture to be seen. Obviously whatever he had expected it had not been this. But as usual Axel remained seemingly unmoved.

'Hello, Andrea,' he said, with that stiff little bow she remembered so well. 'How are you?'

They might have been polite acquaintances meeting again after some time, she thought bitterly, despising the way her hands clung to the strap of her handbag, denying him the right to take her fingers and raise them to his lips as he had done in the past. Her breathing quickened, in spite of herself. How she hated him, she thought fiercely. How she wished she could wipe that smug, supercilious smile from his face. But she couldn't, and as she had started this, she had to go on.

'I'm very well, thank you,' she responded, aware that her voice was a little tighter now. 'And you?'

Axel shrugged. 'I survive.'

'You would,' she retorted, unable to prevent herself. 'You're a survivor.'

Axel's grey eyes sudddenly bored into hers. 'You've lost weight.'

'It's fashionable to do so, didn't you know?'

'You were slim enough.'

'Was I? I shouldn't have expected you to notice.'

She saw with satisfaction that his facial muscles tautened ⁓ implied insult, but his voice was controlled as he said:

Patrick Connolly seemed to think it was time he intervened. 'Will you have a drink, Axel?' he suggested. 'Before we leave for the restaurant. I booked the table for one, so we have plenty of time.'

Axel diverted his attention from Andrea, and inclined his head. 'Thank you. A little Scotch would not come amiss.'

'I'll join you.' Andrea's father breathed a sigh of relief as the tension was somewhat eased. 'How about you, Andrea? I'm afraid sherry is the only alternative to Coke.'

'Nothing for me, Daddy.'

Andrea ignored them both and went to stand by the windows looking down on the panorama of London below. She was fighting desperately to maintain her composure. Axel's comments had disconcerted her as usual, and she couldn't make up her mind whether he was being deliberately personal or merely retaliating to her comment about him. Either way, it was infuriating to know that he could so easily upset her. Somehow she had to show him that she could compete with him at his own game. But how?

While her father and Axel were drinking their Scotch and discussing Patrick's ultimate plans for Schloss Mahlstrom, the telephone rang, and with an apology to his guest, Patrick went to answer it. His monosyllabic responses spoke of his impatience at whatever information was being conveyed, and when he put down the phone his face was grim.

'I'm afraid I've just had some rather upsetting news,' he said, and Andrea turned to look at him. 'There's been a landslide at the site in Hertfordshire. We're extending the Moulton bypass,' he explained for Axel's benefit. 'A man has been killed, and several others are buried. I'll have to leave for the site immediately, so I'm afraid I won't be able to join you for lunch after all.'

'Oh, Daddy!' Andrea took a step forward. 'How awful!'

'I know,' her father nodded tensely. 'It's Harry Page who's been killed, too. God knows how it happened. If there's been negligence . . .'

'Do you want me to come with you?'

For the moment, Andrea was scarcely aware of Axel, but her father shook his head. 'No, there's nothing you can do, love. Nothing I can do either, for that matter, but I must go and find out what's been going on.' He turned to the other man apologetically. 'You understand, don't you, Axel? I can't leave things at a time like this.'

'Of course not,' Axel agreed with him. 'And naturally, if there's anything I can do . . .'

Patrick shook his head again. 'No, no. I'm just sorry I have to upset our arrangements.'

Axel's eyes flickered to Andrea and she was once more made devastatingly aware of his presence. 'If your daughter will permit me, I will take her out to lunch as planned.'

'Oh, no!'

Andrea's cry of protest was almost drowned beneath her father's instant acceptance. 'That's very good of you, Axel,' he was saying with evident relief. 'Particularly in the circumstances . . .' He looked reprovingly at his daughter. 'Of course you'll have lunch with Axel, Andrea. What possible reason can you have to refuse?'

Don't tempt me, oh, don't tempt me, she cried silently, but her mutinous face aroused no sympathy from her father.

'Right. That's settled, then,' he said, picking up his Scotch again. 'Poor Harry! What a tragedy!'

Andrea turned away again. She had known Harry Page, too. But the tears pricking at her eyes were not just at the death of the man who had once allowed her to steer the huge earth-digging machine he had driven.

Patrick Connolly went down with them in the lift, but once outside, he went to get into the chauffeur-driven limousine which was waiting for him, while Andrea and Axel walked the short distance to the restaurant just off Oxford Street where her father had booked a table. The streets were crowded with lunchtime shoppers and Andrea was relieved. It meant that it was impossible to conduct a conversation as they walked, but once inside the select French restaurant with its subdued decor and discreetly lit tables, she knew she was defeated.

While she was making a deliberately prolonged examination of the menu, Axel ordered Martini cocktails, and when they were set before them, he lifted the huge menu out of her hands and laid it to one side, his eyes sparkling dangerously.

'I haven't finished,' she protested sulkily, but he ignored her.

'I'll choose the meal,' he announced coolly. 'Drink your cocktail before someone decides you can't be old enough to enjoy it.'

Andrea sucked in her breath at his insolence, but she would not give him the satisfaction of quelling any retort she might make. Instead, she cupped her chin on her hands and stared moodily round the restaurant.

Axel lit a cheroot, exhaling the fragrant fumes into the air above their heads. Then he said quietly: 'All right, I apologize.'

The unexpectedness of his words brought her eyes back to his with wide disbelief. 'What did you say?'

'I think you heard. No matter that you perhaps deserved what I did, I did not mean to hurt you.'

'You? Hurt me?' Andrea managed to sound outraged. 'I always thought you were the most conceited man I ever met.'

Axel's eyes were narrowed, watching. 'I did not hurt you, then?'

'No.'

'So our relationship meant nothing to you?'

'How could it?' She twisted her lips tauntingly. 'Besides, you forget, I'm a lot younger than you are. I'm always getting involved in something or other.'

'I see.' His tone was flat.

Andrea twisted the watch she was wearing round her wrist. 'You hurt me physically, of course,' she added. 'Those bruises you made on my arm lasted for ages.'

'I am sorry.'

'Are you? Didn't you get a certain sadistic satisfaction out of it?'

'*No!*' His answer was taut. 'I did not intend things to go as far as they did. They got rather out of hand. But you—' He broke off abruptly, and she felt a shiver of remembered emotion at the intense look in his eyes. But then it was gone and she felt cold as he summoned the waiter. 'We will order now.'

Andrea scarcely remembered the meal that followed, only that she ate little of it. Axel ate little, too, and his manner was no longer relaxed or polite. He seemed to have withdrawn into some shell of his own making that brooded no penetration, and although she told herself that she was glad, she knew she was not. This meeting had been a disaster, for both of them, and she was glad when the meal was over and he suggested they should leave.

In Oxford Street, he summoned a cab. 'I will take you home,' he said, but she shook her head.

'I can manage.'

'As you wish.' He ran the palms of his hands down his thighs. 'So – it is not *auf wiedersehen*, but good-bye?'

'Yes.' A cab had stopped near them and Andrea took a step towards it.

'*Andrea!*'

The way he spoke her name weakened her knees, and she stared at him in dismay. For a moment he just looked at her, then one hand curved round her nape, jerking her towards him, and his mouth found the trembling softness of hers. For an instant she felt the intimate pressure increase, and then she was free, and he was striding away into the crowds until she could not see him any more.

'Do you want a cab, lady?'

The cab driver's plaintive comment brought Andrea back to an awareness of her surroundings, and she turned to him almost dazedly.

'I – what – oh, yes, yes. Of course.' She scrambled into the back of the vehicle. 'Hunter's Court, please.'

By the time she reached the apartment she shared with her father, her head was aching abominably, and she was feeling decidedly sick. She couldn't find her key, her head was swimming so badly, and Mrs. Thomas had to let her in.

'Good gracious, miss, whatever is the matter with you—' she was asking, when Andrea fled past her and into her bathroom. Spasm after spasm of retching left the girl weak and trembling and ignoring Mrs. Thomas's adjunct that she should call a doctor, Andrea took off her clothes and crept between the sheets of her bed.

CHAPTER FOURTEEN

ANDREA'S father did not get home that night. Andrea was sitting watching television in her dressing-gown at about nine o'clock when he phoned to say he was spending the night in Moulton. She forced herself to ask all the usual questions, expressing her sympathy with Harry Page's wife, glad all the same that her father was not with her at the moment to see her own distress. After lying sleepless for several hours she had had to get up, but she had refused Mrs. Thomas's offer to get her something to eat, and she looked pale and listless.

By the next morning, make-up was able to hide the worst ravages of grief, and by the time her father arrived at the apartment around midday, she appeared calm and composed.

After he had told her briefly what had been arranged, Patrick poured himself a Scotch and water and said: 'So? And how did your lunch with Axel go?'

Andrea had expected this. 'How do you think it went?' she asked, assuming a light tone. 'The food at the Bohemien is always excellent.'

'I wasn't meaning the food,' retorted her father dryly. 'How did you and Axel get on together? Have you sorted out your differences?'

Andrea's nails dug into her palms. 'I thought you did that, Daddy.'

'Now don't play games with me, Andrea. This business with Axel was of your own making. I'm surprised he still has any patience with you.'

'I didn't ask him to take me to lunch!'

'What else could he do, in the circumstances? Besides, I know he wanted to talk to you. I think he hoped you'd have recovered from your childish tantrums by now.'

'There were not childish tantrums!'

'Very well. Call them what you will. Axel hoped, I think, that you could meet one another on a normal basis.'

'I doubt very much whether Axel even thought about me before he laid eyes on me in your office.'

'You think not?'

'I'm sure of it. He's just as conceited and – and arrogant as ever.'

Her father frowned. 'He's a proud man, I'll grant you that.'

'Thank you.'

'Of course, it's inbred in him. Generations of feudal pride—'

'—and superiority,' put in Andrea tautly. 'Yes, I know.'

'But admirable, just the same. One can't help admiring the man.'

'I can,' said Andrea, turning away, feeling a painful tightness in her chest. 'Excuse me. I have – things to do.'

Her father watched her leave the room with a look of real anxiety on his face, but Andrea was unaware of it.

During the days that followed, Andrea made a determined effort to put the past behind her. She helped Mrs. Thomas spring-clean the flat, she bought new clothes, and she met some of the gang she used to run around with for coffee.

But her heart wasn't really in any of it. Spring-cleaning served the purpose of tiring her physically so that she slept a little better, but buying new clothes wasn't much fun when they hung on her too-slender body. Mrs. Thomas continually berated her for not eating the food that was set before her, but Andrea's appetite was practically non-existent. Meeting the gang again was fun, but she felt somehow out of touch with their activities, and although she refused to admit it they seemed callow and immature after Axel.

Then one afternoon, when she was passing the travel agency in Regent Street where Janet worked, her cousin attracted her attention through the window, gesturing for her to come into the shop. Andrea was reluctant to do so. She had the feeling Janet was going to reminisce about the holiday, and she didn't think she could bear that. But she could hardly walk on and ignore her, so reluctantly she opened the door and entered the agency.

'Hello, Janet,' she said, with a polite smile. 'What's new?'

Janet leaned confidentially on the counter. 'Andrea, you'll never guess what!'

Andrea hid her impatience. 'No. What?'

'Heinrich's in London.'

Andrea's fingers tightened about her handbag. 'Really?'

She thought she managed to sound remarkably casual.

'Yes. He came to see me yesterday. I'm going out with him tonight.'

Andrea lifted her shoulders expressively. 'Lucky you!'

'Yes, aren't I?' Janet sighed ecstatically. 'Oh, Andrea, that was the best holiday I ever had!'

Andrea glanced round the agency. 'You don't appear to be very busy,' she remarked, hoping to change the subject, but Janet was not so easily diverted.

'No. Most people have booked their holidays now,' she replied carelessly. Then: 'I must say, you don't look as if you've had a holiday! You're so thin! What's the matter with you? I heard Uncle Pat telling Daddy he was worried about you.'

Andrea made a dismissing gesture. 'Oh, you know what parents are like, Jan.' She moved away from the counter. 'Well, I'd better be going. I'm picking Mrs. Thomas up from the hairdressers in fifteen minutes and we're going to choose some new curtaining for Daddy's bedroom.'

'Axel was in London, wasn't he?' Janet's comment was low but distinct.

Andrea could feel the colour creeping up her face. 'As a matter of fact, yes.'

'You had lunch with him, didn't you?'

'I – yes.'

Janet nodded, tracing the grain of the counter with her finger. 'I know. Uncle Pat was discussing it with Daddy. What a pity about the *Schloss*, isn't it?'

Andrea had been edging towards the door, but now she stopped abruptly. 'What did you say?'

Janet assumed that annoying attitude she had when she knew something that you didn't. 'I said, it's a pity about the *Schloss*.'

'I heard that,' exclaimed Andrea impatiently. 'What did you mean by it?'

'Don't you know?'

'If I did, I wouldn't be asking, would I?'

'I suppose not. Oh, well, it's no secret, I suppose. Axel has decided not to sell the *Schloss* to the company.'

'What!'

'It's true! I've told you. I heard Daddy and Uncle Pat talking about it. He's decided to let the place rot.'

'Oh, *God*!' Andrea stared at the other girl as if she

169

couldn't believe what she had just heard. 'Why didn't Daddy tell me?'

'I don't know.' Janet shrugged. 'Perhaps he thought you wouldn't be interested. But you are, aren't you?'

Andrea's colour deepened. 'Yes – yes, I'm interested.'

Janet nodded as though she had known it all along. 'Well, now you know. What are you going to do about it?'

Andrea moved her head dazedly from side to side. 'I – I don't know. What can I do about it?'

'Perhaps you should talk to your father,' suggested Janet quietly. 'He knows more about it than I do.'

'Yes, yes, perhaps I should do that.' Andrea felt stunned. 'Er – thanks, Jan.'

Before going into the hairdressers to meet Mrs. Thomas, Andrea went into the nearest tube station and telephoned her father's office. As luck would have it, he was available, but when she heard his voice, her voice broke ignominiously. Struggling to be coherent, she asked him point-blank why he had not told her of the breakdown of his plans.

'Andrea!' Patrick Connolly's concern was evident. 'Andrea, where are you?'

'Oxford Circus.'

'Well, stay there and I'll come and pick you up. We can't talk like this.'

'I can't.' Andrea managed to control herself. 'I – I'm meeting Mrs. Thomas to get that curtaining—'

'To hell with the curtaining! Look, I'll get Sarah to phone the hairdressers and give Mrs. Thomas a message. You stay there. I'll be there in ten minutes.'

Andrea nodded, then realizing her father could not see her, she said: 'Yes. Yes, all right.'

In truth she was only too glad to shift the responsibility on to him. Tears were too close for comfort, and she went into the ladies' room to compose herself before meeting her father. When he came he was in the limousine, but he was driving it himself. He thrust open the nearside door and she got in with haste, feeling an immense relief as the car gathered speed and she could relax.

Patrick glanced at her as he drove through the busy afternoon traffic, but he did not speak. Controlling the vehicle required all his concentration in these conditions. It was not until they had left the main thoroughfares behind that he ventured to comment on her distress.

'You should have told me,' she exclaimed, sniffing. 'Oh, Daddy, what's going on?'

'You tell me.' Patrick shrugged his shoulders. 'All I know is that Axel has decided not to go through with the deal.'

'But why didn't you tell me?'

'If you remember, you seemed singularly loath to discuss anything to do with von Mahlstrom.'

'I know, but – oh, Daddy, you don't understand.'

'What don't I understand?'

Andrea licked her lips, feeling the salty tang of her tears. 'I – I love him,' she murmured unsteadily.

There was silence for some time, and then her father breathed a heavy sigh. 'I see.' He paused. 'Are you sure about this?'

'As sure as I'll ever be.'

'And von Mahlstrom?'

'Oh, no, *no*! He just thinks of me as a child!'

'Does he?'

'What do you mean?'

'I don't know.' Her father raked his hair back with a careless hand. 'I don't know what I mean. Only when he came to London ten days ago he insisted on seeing you.'

'Insisted – on seeing me?' Andrea echoed.

'Yes.' Her father sounded slightly discomfited. 'Look, I might as well tell you. We had a conversation, a peculiar conversation I thought at the time. Now I'm not so sure.'

'How? Why? What was it about?'

Patrick shook his head. 'Well, we were talking about the *Schloss*. I asked him whether he'd never thought of taking it over; you know – we buy it, renovate it, and he moves in as – well, manager, perhaps.'

'What did he say?' Andrea's tears were forgotten in the urgency of the moment.

Her father frowned. 'He got quite angry about it – said he was quite capable of earning a satisfactory living for himself. He wanted no part of my – gratuity. I said – okay. I mean, I didn't see what he had to get so angry about. Now I wonder.'

'What do you wonder?'

Patrick rubbed his nose with a thoughtful finger. 'Well, if I were in his position, perhaps I'd think that someone was trying to take me over.'

'You mean you think he thought you were protecting *my* interests?'

'Well, it's possible—'

'*No!*' Andrea shook her head. 'You're wrong. You must be. Otherwise . . . otherwise . . .'

'Otherwise what?'

'Wouldn't he have said something to me?'

'And didn't he?'

'Oh, Daddy, you know how I felt about that meeting.'

'I didn't know the reason for it then, or I should have had some reservations myself.'

'Why?'

'Andrea, von Mahlstrom is thirty-three! He doesn't have a cent into the bargain. Apart from what he might have made from the sale of the *Schloss*.'

Andrea stared blindly out of the car window. 'Do you think I care?'

'No. No, I don't think you would. I've known you long enough to realize you're no natural sybarite. But you're my daughter – and I'd care.'

'So what would you have me do?' She turned to look at him.

'Well, you are only eighteen, Andrea. Young enough to find someone else—'

'Don't say that!'

'Well then, there's university.'

'No, I can't go to university now. Daddy, I know what I want from life. I always did. Long before you sent me to Grossfeld, I was bored with the life I was leading. Janet should have been your daughter. She'd have lapped up what you could do for her.'

Her father's lips tightened. 'I'm a fool to listen to you.'

'So why do you?'

'Because for the past few weeks I've been worried to death about you. I've seen you change from a vivacious, sometimes irritating teenager, into a brittle lacklustre shadow of your former self. You don't eat, you need pills to make you sleep! Do you think I haven't noticed what's been happening to you? My God, the times I've wished I'd never sent you to Grossfeld!'

'But you did.'

'I know it.'

Andrea shifted in her seat. 'If only you'd told me that Axel wanted to see me. Not just – sprung it on me like that.'

'That was his doing, not mine. Look, Andrea, if you want my honest opinion, I think he cares about you. But probably too much to do anything about it.'

'What's that supposed to mean?'

'As I've told you, he's a proud man. He wants no handouts from me. So what could he possibly offer a girl like you?'

'Himself,' said Andrea simply, closing her eyes for a moment. 'Daddy, I'm going to Grossfeld.'

'What?'

'I'm going to Grossfeld. I'm going to see Axel, and ask him why he changed his mind about the *Schloss*.'

'You'd do that?'

Andrea looked up. 'Well, let's put it this way – I have to know. One way or the other. You do understand that, don't you?'

Her father's face was grim. 'I suppose so. But don't expect too much, Andrea, then you won't be disappointed.'

She frowned. 'What are you saying?'

'I'm saying that Axel may – want you, but not want to marry you.'

Andrea flushed. 'Oh!' She swallowed. 'Well, that's all right by me.'

'Well, it's not all right by me, damn you,' thundered her father, bringing the car to an abrupt halt at the side of the road and turning to face her. 'All right Andrea, go to Grossfeld. See your Baron. But if things go wrong, they go wrong. There'll be no half measures. Or, by God, I'll come out there and thrash the pair of you! Do you understand?'

Andrea's lips trembled. 'Oh, Daddy, you're quite Victorian at heart, aren't you?'

'You'll find out,' her father warned grimly. 'Say one more word and I'll send Tim with you.'

'You wouldn't!' Andrea was alarmed.

'Try me. Just try me.'

Spring was coming late to this region of the Tyrol, but although there was still ice in the air the sun was warm and the flowers were beginning to flourish. When Andrea left the hotel to walk along the main street of Grossfeld, she found she could unbutton her suede coat and allow the sun to penetrate the sweater beneath. Grossfeld itself looked reassuringly the same, and she forced herself to look about her as the other tourists were doing, and not walk too quickly up the road to Axel's chalet. She had thought of hiring a car, or even one of the horse-drawn sleighs, but she did not want to advertise her arrival, so she had decided to walk. All the same, her legs were aching by the time she reached the chalet, and she stopped a few moments to recover her breath before opening the gate.

She half expected the shepherd to start barking when the gate swung back on its hinges, but there was no sound from within, so either Axel had seen her and quieted the dog, or they were both out.

Hoping it was the former, she knocked at the door and waited. No one came to answer, and she knocked again, more loudly this time. But again there was no answer and she thrust her hands impatiently into her jacket pockets. It had taken some courage to come here at all and now, finding him out, she felt somehow enervated.

Stamping her feet, she looked round the back of the chalet. There was no sign of life and as she stood there she noticed that the whole place had a derelict air. She frowned and walked round the back of the building. Shutters had been closed over the windows here, and it was obvious from the thin layer of snow which lay over the step that no one had stepped out here for some time.

An awful feeling of helplessness sweeping over her she walked out of the gate again and closed it behind her. Then she looked about her. There were no other houses or chalets within calling distance, no one from whom she could inquire his whereabouts. Then she remembered Nicolas Leiber at the hotel. Of course, why hadn't she thought of him before? He might know where Axel had gone.

But Nicolas Leiber was little help.

'I am afraid Axel did not confide in me, *Fräulein*,' he told her apologetically. 'One day he was here, the next he was not. I do not know where he has gone, unless it is perhaps to his aunt in Salzburg.'

The Baroness!

Andrea had almost forgotten her. But that sounded reasonable. Perhaps Axel had gone there. It was worth a try.

'Er – is the Baroness on the telephone?' she asked.

Nicolas frowned. 'I think she might be. It is an easy matter to check. One moment, *Fräulein*, I will find out.'

When he came back he was nodding. 'Yes, the Baroness

does have a telephone, *Fraülein*. You wish we should get the number for you?'

'I – yes. Yes, please.' Andrea hesitated. 'I'll take it in my room.'

'Very well. It will only take a moment. Thank you, *Fraülein*.'

'Oh – thank you.'

But when Andrea got through to the Baroness, Axel was not there either.

'Why do you wish to contact my nephew, my dear?' she asked, with aristocratic authority. 'I understand your father is no longer interested in renovating the *Schloss*.'

'Oh, but that's not true! It's – it's Axel who has withdrawn. My father is just as interested as he ever was.'

'Is that so?' The Baroness sounded surprised. 'Is this what you have to tell my nephew?'

'Well, yes. Yes, I suppose so. But he already knows it. I mean – he altered the situation, not my father.'

'So you say.'

'It's the truth, believe me!'

The Baroness sighed. 'Have you tried Mahlstrom?'

'The *Schloss*? No, why?'

'I think perhaps you should.' The Baroness sounded anxious now. 'If Axel is there, he's alone. Carl left Mahlstrom several days ago to spend two weeks with his sister in Vienna.'

After Andrea had put down the phone, she sat for several minutes just staring at it. Then she got determinedly to her feet and went downstairs. Nicolas Leiber was in his office.

'How can I get to Mahlstrom?' she asked.

It was eventually twenty-four hours before Andrea arrived at the small railway station which served the tiny hamlet of Mahlstrom. Fretting about the amount of time she was wasting, Andrea herself was taut and nervous by the time the train deposited her on the platform, and the news that there was no cab to take her out to the *Schloss* distracted her still more. At last, the stationmaster himself was prevailed upon to drive her up the valley, and it was from the windows of his old Volkswagen that she saw the chimneys of Schloss Mahlstrom again.

He dropped her at the gates and she walked the short distance up to the house, looking for signs of habitation. But there were none, and she wished she had told him to come back for her in an hour instead of the two hours she had stipulated.

The front of the building was as derelict as usual, and she marched determinedly round the side, following the covered passageway to the kitchen quarters. Her fingers trembled as she knocked at the door, but although she knocked heavily there was no reply.

Nervously she reached for the handle of the door and turned it. She never expected it to give, and when it did and the door swung inwards, she uttered a stifled gasp. Surely Carl wouldn't go away and leave the building open like this. And if he hadn't . . .

She stopped cautiously inside. The remains of a fire spluttered in the hearth, and her spirits rose. Someone was living here, she was sure of that now. And surely the *Schloss* was too remote to attract squatters.

'Axel?' she called, aware that her voice was swallowed up in the vastness of the place. 'Axel, where are you?'

She closed the outer door and crossed the kitchen to the inner one. The passageway with its shabby carpet stretched away before her as before, and she had to steel herself to go on.

'Axel?' she called again, less confidently this time. 'Axel, can you hear me?'

Again there was no response and she pressed her lips together uncertainly. What should she do? Examine every room in the wing until she found him? Keep on calling until he answered? Or go back to the kitchen and wait until hunger, or the other demands of his body, brought him to her.

Her nerves were stretched to such a pitch that the idea of waiting patiently in the kitchen until he chose to appear did not bear thinking about. And what if she was wrong? What if the Baroness was wrong? Axel might not be here. It could be someone else, some friend of Carl's who was looking after the place until his return.

She sighed frustratedly, walking slowly along the hall. She saw the door which had led to the rooms she and the Baroness had occupied when they were here. On impulse, she opened the door and stood staring up the stairs. Axel might not even be in the building, she realized. He could be out walking, or down by the river. Did he fish? Had the

Baroness said it was one of his pleasures? She couldn't remember.

A sound from up the stairs suddenly froze her blood. It was a groan, a definite groan, and her throat went dry with fear. What was it Axel had said about ghosts in the *Schloss*? She couldn't remember that either. But the sound was sufficient to send cold shivers of fear up her spine.

Her fingers gripping the door handle trembled, and she stood panic-stricken for a moment, not knowing what to do, not able to move. Then the sound came again, this time accompanied by a low curse, echoing hollowly down the empty stairwell, and her heart leapt into her throat. That was Axel's voice, she was sure of it, and with a fast beating heart she began to ascend the stairs.

She stopped on the first landing, sure it must have come from there, but another sound, this time of someone moving about, came from the second floor. Gripping the rail tightly, she went on up, halting on the landing when she saw the door to the room she had occupied was open.

Stepping carefully, she approached the room and looked inside. But what she saw brought a gasp of dismay from her lips. Axel was there, lying on his back on her bed, an empty glass on the table beside him. He was dressed in pants and a roll-necked sweater, but his face was pale, his brow beaded with sweat. He had not heard her approach, nor her instinctive exclamation, and the sounds she had heard must have been him shifting his position on the bed.

'Axel!' she murmured tentatively. 'Axel – are you all right?'

For several seconds he made no movement or sound, it was almost as though he had suspended breathing, and then he turned his head and stared at her in stunned disbelief. His jawline was darkened by a night's growth of beard, and his hair was rumpled and untidy. But for an instant she glimpsed a look in his eyes which sent the blood pounding through her veins. Then it was gone, and he was swinging his legs to the floor, getting unsteadily to his feet.

'You are trespassing,' he enunciated slowly. 'This is private property. Please – get out of here!'

Andrea clenched her fists by her sides. 'I – I came to find you, Axel. I – what is it? Are you ill? You look – terrible.'

'I am perfectly all right,' he assured her harshly. 'Now,

please go. You have no right here. The deal for the *Schloss* is off.'

'I – I know that. I wanted to talk to you about—' she began, but he cut her short.

'Ah, I see. You come on your father's behalf. Well, I regret I have nothing more to say.'

'I did not come on my father's behalf.' Andrea spoke vehemently. 'Axel, I wanted to see you—'

'There is nothing to be said!' he said grimly, glancing down with distaste at his crumpled appearance. He ran a questing hand over the beard on his chin. 'As you can see, I am in no fit state to entertain visitors.'

'Oh, Axel!' Andrea felt a rising sense of frustration. 'Axel, what's been happening?'

'Happening?' His eyes were cold. 'I do not understand. What could have been happening?' He swayed a little and grasped the bedpost for support. 'Andrea, who told you I was here? Why have you come? I wanted to be alone, that was all. Your being here – offends me.'

Andrea caught her breath. 'That's a rotten thing to say! Axel, why did you decide not to sell the *Schloss*?'

'Ah, we come to the purpose of your visit again—'

'It is not the purpose of my visit. At least, only indirectly. Axel, I only want to know why you changed your mind. Stop looking at me like that – as if – as if you hated me.'

'I am sorry.' He straightened, squaring his shoulders, and then doubled up as a spasm of pain seemed to strike him. She took an involuntary step forward, but he gestured her away, staggering as he managed to right himself again. 'A little – indigestion,' he told her reluctantly. 'Look, I cannot discuss anything with you. You are wasting your time, and you will please express my apologies to your father for wasting his so-valuable time also.'

'Axel, stop it! Stop it! What's wrong with you? You must tell me.'

On impulse, she brushed past him, moving further into the bedroom to lift the empty glass from the bedside table. She intended to sniff it to see what it was he had been taking, when a horrible sour smell assailed her nostrils. With an exclamation, she evaded Axel's would-be detaining hand and went round the other side of the bed. A bucket was standing on the floor beside the bed, and she didn't need to go any further to know he had been violently sick.

'Oh, Axel!' she exclaimed, turning back to him, and he raked a weary hand through his unkempt hair.

'Leave me alone, Andrea,' he appealed, sinking down on to the side of the bed and resting his head in his hands. 'Just leave me alone!'

Andrea hesitated, sniffing at the glass. It had contained brandy, she thought, realizing he must have been taking the spirit to relieve his pain. Setting the glass down again, she came to where he was sitting and sank down on the bed beside him.

'Tell me,' she insisted softly.

'*Gott*, what is there to tell? I have poisoned myself, I think. There was no fresh food when I came to Mahlstrom, so I ate what there was. I did not care much one way or the other. Now I am suffering for my foolishness.'

Andrea looked at his bent head, then lifted her hand and rested it coolly on the nape of his neck. He flinched at her touch, but he did not drag himself away and she gained confidence.

'Why didn't you care, Axel?' she murmured, laying her cheek against his shoulder, and he uttered a protesting groan.

'Go away, Andrea, please – go away!'

'I can't do that, Axel,' she breathed, turning her lips against his sleeve. 'Not yet anyway.' She slid her fingers over his thigh, feeling the hardening muscles beneath her hand. 'Not until you send me away – really send me away, I mean.'

He lifted his head to look at her, his face pale and drawn. 'You don't know what you're saying,' he muttered hoarsely, covering her hand with his, his grip so tight it was a pain.

'I do.'

'How did you get here? Who is with you?'

'No one. I came alone, by train from Grossfeld. I went to the chalet first, you see.'

'You are crazy, do you know that?'

'Why?'

'Well, because – because we are alone here. And right now I—' He broke off, looking down at his hand covering hers. 'What are you trying to do to me?'

Andrea's fingers slid up his neck into his hair, and she leant towards him, caressing his rough cheek with her lips. She could feel his quickened breathing, smell the brandy on his breath, the way his body started to tremble when she pressed closer. 'You kissed me in London,' she whispered. 'Can I kiss you now?'

Axel's shuddering groan of protest died beneath the urgency of her mouth. One hand slid behind her neck, holding her against him, and when she sank back amongst the rumpled bedcovers, he went with her, crushing her beneath him. He kissed her many times, leaving her in no doubt as to the extent of his desire for her, but when she would have had him take off his sweater, he held her back, his hands tangled in her hair.

'We shouldn't be doing this,' he protested. 'Not here. I – I need a shave, a change of clothes . . .'

'I'll help you change,' she breathed teasingly. 'And I've never shaved anyone, but I'm always willing to try. I'm sure I'd make a good maidservant.'

She saw the sudden clouding expression that invaded his eyes, and with a stifled curse he dragged himself away from her, getting to his feet and straightening his clothes with grim determination. 'Get up, Andrea,' he told her harshly. 'It's no use. I can't go through with it.'

'What are you talking about?' Andrea got reluctantly off the bed, compelled by the look in his eyes. 'Axel, what's wrong now?'

He drew a deep breath. 'Go downstairs, Andrea. Give me time to make myself presentable. Then I'll join you.'

'Give you time to build up your defences against me, you mean!' she declared tremulously. She went to him, sliding her arms around his waist. 'Axel, Axel, I love you. There, I've said it! Does it give you a feeling of satisfaction?'

Axel lifted his hands to tear hers from around him, but they refused to obey him, lingering on her shoulders, inevitably making him hold her nearer. 'Oh, *Gott*! Andrea, this is madness!'

'Why? Why is it madness? You want me, don't you?'

'Of course I want you! I would be a fool to try and deny it. But – loving someone does not automatically solve the problems it has created.'

'I think it does,' exclaimed Andrea eagerly, but now Axel thrust her away from him.

'No. No, it does not.' He walked rather unsteadily to the door. 'Go – go downstairs. I will join you presently.'

He was so adamant, Andrea had no choice but to obey

him. But she looked at him as she passed him, and saw that he averted his eyes from the pleading in hers.

By the time he joined her in the kitchen, Andrea had boiled the kettle and made some coffee. She had had to do something to occupy herself, and she was sitting nervously at the wooden table when he came in. Shaved and changed into cream suede pants and a matching knitted shirt, he looked pale but composed, and although her senses cried out to her to throw herself on his mercy, she remained where she was.

'Do you want some coffee?' she asked, but he shook his head, disguising a shudder.

'No. Thank you.' He walked to the fire and threw another log on the embers, settling it with his booted foot, and then he turned to face her. 'Tell me,' he asked, 'did your father tell you why I came to London?'

Andrea frowned. 'Yes. He said you came to discuss the sale of the *Schloss*.'

'That is so. I did. But did he tell you what I had intended doing with the money?'

'Did he know?' Andrea shrugged confusedly. 'No, he said nothing to me.'

Axel nodded. 'I thought not.'

'What should he have said? What did you intend doing with the money?' Andrea's lips trembled.

Axel shook his head. 'It's not important—'

'Oh, don't be silly!' Andrea was frustrated. 'Of course it's important. Everything to do with you is important to me, you should know that! Are you trying to tell me that Daddy has kept something from me? Something you had told him?'

'No. No, that's not what I'm saying at all.'

He raked both hands through his hair and it was all Andrea could do just to remain where she was. 'Axel, please,' she pleaded. 'Stop tormenting me like this!'

'Me? Tormenting you?' Axel's laugh was bitter. 'Oh, Andrea, don't you think you're tormenting me, coming here like this, making me go through it all again, knowing that ultimately the result will be the same.'

'What result? Axel, you're confusing me.'

'All right.' He took a deep breath. 'All right, I'll tell you.' He paused. 'The ski school at Grossfeld is for sale. It was offered to me. I told your father that I was considering using the money I got from the sale of the *Schloss* to buy it.'

'Oh, Axel!' Andrea's eyes were bright. 'What did he say?'

Axel bent his head, scuffing his toe against a leg of the table. 'He suggested that I considered taking over the hotel he intended making of the *Schloss*.'

'Oh, yes, he – he told me that.'

'Did he? Did he also tell you what I said?'

Andrea nodded slowly. 'I think so. He said – he couldn't understand why you got so angry about it.'

'He – couldn't – understand?' Axel clenched his fists. 'Oh, no. That I will not take. He knew perfectly well why I was angry. Andrea, your father and I have been stalking round one another for weeks, like adversaries waiting for the other to make the first move.'

'But – but why?'

'This business with you – it backfired. Your father knew this.'

Andrea could feel the butterflies of excitement in her stomach, but she refused to allow any feeling of euphoria to envelop her. 'It – backfired?'

'Yes, yes. *Gott*, were you not aware of it, also? That night we spent here together?'

'I – I thought perhaps you didn't want to leave me . . .'

'Leave you? If Tante Sophie had not interrupted us . . .' He shrugged expressively. 'But of course, I was afraid of that. That was why I prevailed upon Tante Sophie to join us.'

'Did – did she know?'

'How I felt? I think perhaps she suspected it. I am not in the habit of invading young women's bedrooms and making love to them.' His lips twisted.

'Daddy wondered why you asked the Baroness to come to Mahlstrom,' murmured Andrea wonderingly.

'He would.' Axel's tone was harsh. 'He did not possess all the facts then. They came later.'

'When? How?'

'Oh, Andrea, your father and I have had many conversations.' He sighed, pressing a hand to the nape of his neck. 'How can I explain to you my position?' He paused. 'As I told you on the tape, your father and I have known one another for some time, and his reasons for asking me to keep an eye on you were reasonable enough. It was only when I became too clever for my own good that things began to go wrong.'

'Why?'

'Andrea, I did not take into account the kind of reaction I would have to you. I was quite clear about the kind of reaction you would have to me, but I stupidly thought I could remain immune. It was impossible. Within a few days I knew it couldn't go on. That was why I kept out of your way. Because I didn't trust myself.'

'But you did such horrible things!'

'Like ignoring you, I know. I was a swine – I admit it. But I had no idea you would—' He broke off, turning away, shaking his head. 'Andrea, your father suspected something was wrong when I called it off. I told him the truth.'

'What?'

'Oh, yes, I told him. I had no expectations of it going any further, but I am not a liar, and it was impossible for me to give him any other explanation that would satisfy him. Your father is an astute man, Andrea. It was easier to tell the truth.'

'But afterwards . . .'

'Afterwards I came to London. I saw you – oh, not that day we had lunch together but before that. I saw you, but you didn't see me. I thought, if I can just see her one more time, assure myself that she's happy. But you didn't look happy. You looked pale – and miserable. That was when I decided to go and see your father and tell him I wanted to speak to you.'

'But why didn't you speak to me?' she cried.

Axel turned to stare at her. 'That is not how things are done in my family. And now you know what your father said – he suggested this idea about the *Schloss*.'

'Oh, Axel!'

He shook his head. 'He knew how I would react to that. But even so, I still insisted upon seeing you. And you know what happened when I did.'

Andrea could sit still no longer. With a little sob, she flung herself across the room and into his arms, and this time he did not try to stop her. 'Axel, Axel, I love you,' she breathed, pressing her face against his chest. 'If only you'd told me how you felt instead of torturing us both like this!'

Axel's hands slid across her back to her shoulders, caressing her almost despairingly. 'Andrea, the situation hasn't changed. And the torment will come when I have to let you go.'

'Let me go?' she echoed blankly.

'Yes. Let you go,' he said flatly. 'It's no good, Andrea. I can't marry you, even if you'd have me. Your father was right.'

Andrea lifted her head and stared disbelievingly at him. 'You can't mean that!'

He nodded. 'I'm afraid I do.'

Andrea shook her head. After all she had gone through, after believing it was going to be all right. He couldn't do this to her!

With a sob, she dragged herself out of his arms, turning away, hiding the agony she knew must be in her face. She somehow made her way across the room, but before leaving she turned, her face twisted with emotion.

'Don't bother to say any more,' she exclaimed tremulously. 'It's obvious. You're too proud and arrogant to consider marrying someone with more money than breeding.'

'Breeding has nothing to do with it,' he ejaculated.

'Hasn't it? So what's stopping you?'

'I won't be the kind of parasite you once accused me of being. And I won't prostitute my principles by managing some hotel manufactured by your father for your benefit!'

'I didn't say you should.'

'It would have come. Andrea, all your life you've got what you wanted . . .'

'So?'

'So don't pretend you could share my kind of existence.'

'Some opinion you have of me, haven't you?' she got out unsteadily.

'A realistic one!' he asserted.

'How do you know that?'

'Andrea, I'm older than you are, as you once pointed out. Nor am I the kind of man to take my marriage vows lightly. Once married to me there would be no going back – no changing your mind because there are no servants to do your bidding, no allowances from your father to soften the bed you'd chosen to lie on—'

'You're too blinded by prejudice to see!' she retorted, feeling sick. Her whole world was tumbling about her ears and she knew she couldn't take much more without breaking down completely. 'Oh, let me get out of here!'

She stumbled to the door, grappling with the latch which refused to obey her, sobbing to herself in frustration. And then she felt him right behind her, his breath fanning her neck, and his arms slid round her, hauling her back against him.

'Oh, Andrea, Andrea!' he groaned violently. 'I cannot let you go like this. *Gott* help me! What am I going to do with you?'

'Marry me,' she answered jerkily, horrified at her own temerity, when she realized what she had said.

'I won't live on your father's money,' he declared, his mouth burning the nape of her neck.

'Did – did I ask you to?' she questioned, finding it incredibly difficult even to breathe with his hands roaming freely over her body, pressing her intimately against him.

'No,' he conceded, shuddering when she slid her hands down the sides of his legs. 'All right. I will sell the *Schloss* and buy the ski school as I intended to do. But we will be independent.'

'All right, all right. Anything you say,' agreed Andrea, twisting round in his arms and burrowing beneath his sweater next to his smooth flesh. 'Hmm, you smell so nice and male! Oh, Axel, haven't we wasted enough time? The stationmaster is coming back for me soon, and I so want you to make love to me . . .'

Almost a year later, Andrea entered the master bedroom of the Schloss Mahlstrom to find her husband stretched out on their bed, studying a heavy, leather-bound Bible. Andrea went towards him curiously, flushed and sweetly smelling from her bath, her semi-transparent robe of palest turquoise chiffon drifting softly about her.

'What are you doing?' she asked, looking down at him.

Axel rolled on to his back. They had given a small dinner party that evening, and he was still wearing the frilled shirt and dark trousers of his evening suit, although he had shed his jacket and tie, and opened the shirt almost to his waist.

'I was considering where we should enter our son's birth when that time comes,' he told her lazily, stretching out a hand and pulling her down beside him. 'Mmm, you look enchanting. Come here.'

For several minutes there was silence in the massive apartment, and then Axel reluctantly stirred. 'I need a shower. Don't go away.'

'Axel!' Andrea caught his hands as he would have drawn away. 'Axel, you are pleased about the baby, aren't you?'

Axel's lips twisted humorously. '*Liebchen*, you drive me to distraction. What did you expect? I can't leave you alone.' He raised her fingers to his lips.

'I know, but—'

'But nothing. Why? Are you sorry?' His eyes darkened.

'Me?' Andrea shifted luxuriously. 'Oh, Axel, I wanted your baby – so much.'

'And I wanted to plant my seed inside you. There does that satisfy you?' he teased.

Andrea nodded, stretching her legs contentedly. 'And – and the *Schloss*? You're not angry any more?'

Axel uttered an amused sound. 'My darling, I am furious about the *Schloss*. Your father has tricked me yet again. But how could I object to so magnificent a first wedding anniversary gift? Besides,' he was serious now, 'I am sufficiently proud of my ancestry to feel a certain satisfaction in the knowledge that our son will own this place. And such a place!' He shook his head, half smiling again. 'But it is good to see it restored to its former glory, even though we may find it impossible to maintain. One way or another, your father is determined that I shall be an hotel proprietor.'

'You wouldn't—'

'No. It shall be as he wishes – our home.' He bent his head to kiss her once more. 'Mmm, *Liebling*, let me go and shower. Then we will go to bed.'

Andrea let him go reluctantly, and he began to take off his shirt under her watchful eyes. Then he went to take his shower, and Andrea closed the heavy Bible and placed it on the bedside table. Then she followed her husband into the bathroom.

'I think Tante Sophie is delighted, don't you?' she murmured, watching him as he took his shower. 'I've never seen her so animated as she was this evening.'

'I think your father is responsible for that,' commented Axel, stepping out of the cubicle to wrap himself in a huge blue bath sheet. 'I did not realize he could be so charming.'

Andrea chuckled. 'It was a nice party, wasn't it? Our first in the *Schloss*.' He nodded, and she probed her stomach with her fingers. 'Do I look fat? Will you still care about me when the autumn comes and I'm enormous?'

Axel finished drying himself and came towards her, picking her up effortlessly in his strong arms. 'What do you think?' he asked, burying his face in the hollow of her neck. 'Come on, it's time all pregnant parents were in bed!'

Harlequin Presents...

By popular demand...

36 original novels from this series—by 3 of the world's greatest romance authors.

These back issues by Anne Hampson, Anne Mather and Violet Winspear have been out of print for some time. So don't miss out; order your copies now!

All the above titles are available at 95¢ each. Please use the attached order form to indicate your requirements.
Offer expires May 31, 1977.

Harlequin Reader Service
ORDER FORM

Mail coupon to:
Harlequin Reader Service,
M.P.O. Box 707,
Niagara Falls, New York 14302

Canadian Residents send to:
Harlequin Reader Service,
Stratford, Ont. N5A 6W4

Please send me by return mail the books that I have checked.
I am enclosing 95¢ for each book ordered.

Please check volumes requested:

☐ 1	☐ 11	☐ 20	☐ 29
☐ 2	☐ 12	☐ 21	☐ 30
☐ 3	☐ 13	☐ 22	☐ 31
☐ 4	☐ 14	☐ 23	☐ 32
☐ 5	☐ 15	☐ 24	☐ 33
☐ 7	☐ 16	☐ 25	☐ 34
☐ 8	☐ 17	☐ 26	☐ 35
☐ 9	☐ 18	☐ 27	☐ 36
☐ 10	☐ 19	☐ 28	☐ 37

Number of books ordered_____ @ 95¢ each = $_____

Postage and handling = $_____.25

TOTAL = $_____

NAME _____
(please print)

ADDRESS _____

CITY _____

STATE/PROV. _____ ZIP/POSTAL CODE _____

OFFER EXPIRES MAY 31, 1977   PRS 173

YOU'LL L♥VE
Harlequin Magazine

for women who enjoy reading fascinating stories of exciting romance in exotic places

SUBSCRIBE NOW!

This is a colorful magazine especially designed and published for the readers of Harlequin novels.

Now you can receive your very own copy delivered right to your home every month throughout the year for only 75¢ an issue.

This colorful magazine is available only through Harlequin Reader Service, so enter your subscription now!

In every issue...

ere's what you'll find:

♥ a complete, full-length romantic novel...illustrated in color.

♥ exotic travel feature...an adventurous visit to a romantic faraway corner of the world.

♥ delightful recipes from around the world...to bring delectable new ideas to your table.

♥ reader's page...your chance to exchange news and views with other Harlequin readers.

♥ other features on a wide variety of interesting subjects.

tart enjoying your own copies of Harlequin magazine mmediately by completing the subscription reservation form.

Not sold in stores!